THE CARE TAKERS

THE CARETAKERS

Copyright © 2025 by Marie Butler.

All rights reserved.

ISBN (paperback) 978-0-9831463-1-5
ISBN (e-book) 978-0-9831463-2-2
Library of Congress Control Number: 2024918488

Published by Fitch Mountain Press Healdsburg, California, USA

Cover and interior design by We Got You Covered Book Design

THE CARE TAKERS

A Sonoma County Mystery

MARIE BUTLER

ACKNOWLEDGMENTS

Thank you to my patient beta readers and editors: Rosanne Polidora, Kate MacMurray, Bill Hanson, Jan Downing, Nancy Buchanan, and Candy Smith. To Tanya Hosner for her technical help.

To Corey and Mitsuyo Butler

I am grateful to the experts who provided valuable technical and medical information: Kirstin Jorgenson, DVM, Janice Garner, RN, Tom Whitemore (Healdsburg Police Department - Retired), and Holly Hoods, Executive Director and Curator, Healdsburg Museum. Any errors made are mine.

To my "Old Pal" and lifelong partner in crime,
Geraldine McGrath, with whom I began this mystery.

And to **DEDICATED CARETAKERS** everywhere.

MILLER'S CREEK

Somewhere in Sonoma County, California

Welcome to Miller's Creek

MILLER'S CREEK WAS NOT ONE of the better-known Sonoma County wine country towns. Which was just fine with its 3,908 residents. It was established shortly after 1849 by the aptly-named farmer C. Miller. Failing at the gold mines, Mr. Miller built a grist mill on the productive creek (and in the emerging town) that came to bear his name.

The tall water wheel, built from coast redwoods and Douglas firs, became a central meeting spot early on. Now, Main Street shops, commerce, and parks radiated out from this historic source of town pride. The creek itself was birthed in the nearby, low Sandstone Mountain range.

On the south, the town was cradled by the Coho River, named after the once abundant salmon that had made the waterway their home and spawning grounds. Gathered more to the north-east were those vineyards and wineries that regularly drew visitors searching for the perfect pinot and charming ambiance. To the west, old summer cabins perched on hillsides thick with redwood trees and ferns. Apple orchards, farms, and ranches, where grazing sheep could be observed, meandered toward the rocky coast — 18 miles away, as the squawking native crow flies. The fog that inched in at night was a welcome relief during hot summers.

"Natural air conditioning," the locals called it.

So all in all, most of the residents were quite pleased to have found themselves, by birth or good luck, to be living in Miller's Creek. **And nobody would have ever expected a murder. Or two.**

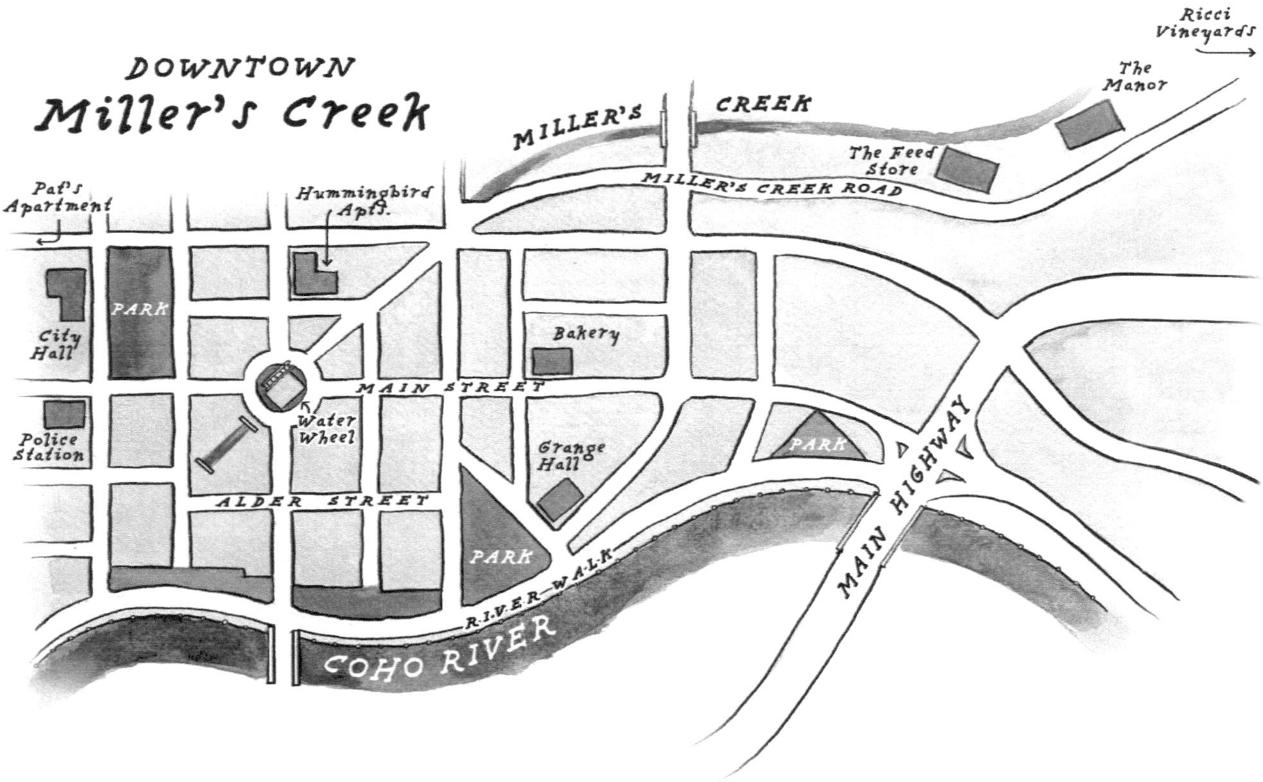
DOWNTOWN
Miller's Creek
Ricci Vineyards
The Manor
MILLER'S
CREEK
The Feed Store
MILLER'S CREEK ROAD
Pat's Apartment
Hummingbird Apts.
PARK
City Hall
Bakery
MAIN STREET
Police Station
Water Wheel
Grange Hall
PARK
MAIN HIGHWAY
ALDER STREET
PARK
RIVER WALK
COHO RIVER

PROLOGUE

Javier

ELEVEN-YEAR-OLD JAVIER WAS on a mission. He had spent the summer photographing insects to be used toward his Scout Insect Study Merit Badge. Other kids may have thought that was "nerdy." But as much as he enjoyed this summer, and hanging out with his older brother, Javier was secretly happy to be going back to school. He missed his friends and Scout buddies. And science classes.

He had studied the bees and hives behind the high school's Ag department. The teacher was his dad's friend and helped him find the queen and figure out how much honey was in the hive. He had spent late spring and summer photographing various species of insects in their habitats. Now, he had 18 of the 20 necessary photos of insects for that portion of the requirement: western honeybee, milkweed bug, seven-spotted ladybug, yellow garden spider, a praying mantis … and more. He had carefully listed each by both its scientific and common name in his scrapbook.

Javier was looking, though, for those two elusive last insects.

Maybe he'd come across something special. Unique. Something to wow the Scoutmaster and other kids. Javier had heard that in the old days, people had collected the actual bugs, pinning them onto boards for observation. *Gross.* He shook his head at the thought. He loved photographing the insects, their many colors, and shapes. It was another little world-within-a-world that most people ignored.

He wandered along the near-dry creek bed, kicking up dust, and poking at the prickly shrubs. Finding nothing to his liking, he crossed the road to the area behind the low, grey building that was the *Miller's Creek Manor - Senior Living and Rehab* facility (*aka* "The Manor"), and its high, fenced gardens. His great-grandma had lived there, so he knew that's what it was. His dad and he had visited her. But that was when he was little, and he didn't remember much about the place. Just that it was hot inside and smelled like mashed potatoes. His abuelita smelled like lavender, though.

Not finding anything new among the plants there, he turned to head home. But a glint of gold and vibrant emerald green stopped him. *Is that a piece of broken glass?*

He leaned down to look. And what Javier saw was the most beautiful beetle he could have conjured up in his imagination. A creature so shiny, it looked like metal and glowed in the late afternoon sun. It was oblong, with a blue, green, gold, and red body, and a dark head and antennae. Small, though, probably not even a half-inch long.

Javier pulled a phone from his jeans pocket and took as many pictures as he could before the insect disappeared into the base of the plant. As he was turning to go, he saw another bug: one that looked almost like the first, only an iridescent blue. He gasped. *Two?* How lucky to find his final two insects in one place. He took another ten photos before that bug disappeared, too.

He had no idea what these were. But he was looking forward to finding out.

ONE

Lou Makes a Discovery

LOUISE "LOU" CURTIS OPENED THE glass door to Hill's Homestyle Bakery and could almost feel the cinnamon and Ethiopian coffee wrap around her, pulling her inside. She greeted the "Dots" domino club members sitting in the corner. A light game looked to be in progress. The morning's coastal fog was lifting, and a bit of sunlight glinted off their white coffee mugs.

"Hey, guys," she called to the four players.

"Morning, Lou." The oldest gentleman at the table responded, looking up briefly from the game. "Where's Steve?"

"Oh, he's waiting outside. I won't be a minute. Just getting my blueberry muffin fix for the day."

Lou walked across the café area to the wooden counter and placed her order with the young cashier. *Another college student,* Lou guessed. The girl looked like … maybe one of the Hanson kids? Lou couldn't keep track of this latest generation.

"One vegan blueberry muffin. And one cheese doggie cookie, please," Lou said, putting three dollar bills on the counter. The cookie was free, she knew.

As she was leaving, with the little white bag in hand, she poked her head into the adjacent room. Once a separate storefront, the owners had annexed it a while back to serve as an informal meeting room, or for an overflow breakfast crowd.

She caught the eye of the retired police chief, Yvonne Rousseau, who was sitting with the current fire chief, and the mayor. Lou liked Yvonne, her neighbor of almost twenty years, from down the street. Slim, but of sturdy build, attractive, with short, curly brown hair, and brown eyes, the ex-chief looked ten years younger than 62. People only underestimated her once.

Yvonne smiled and waved.

Wonder what they're concocting, Lou pondered.

Lou returned the wave and headed outside. "Steve," she said. "Look what I've got for you!"

A multi-colored, multi-breed dog had been lounging by the green bench in front of the bakery, his leash wrapped loosely around the arm. *A Super-Mutt,* Lou always called him, proudly. About forty pounds of dog stood up and sniffed the cookie Lou had handed him. Steve gently took it and crunched until it was gone.

Lou liked to joke with new acquaintances that she and Steve just loved to cuddle at night. At their raised eyebrows, she would reveal that Steve was a dog.

"But more company than my last husband," she'd add.

Taking his leash, Lou walked the two blocks home to Alder Street, near the park by the river.

Lou's compact, wood frame home was once a vibrant turquoise

blue, which befitted the artist and potter she was. Now, it had faded to the color of the nearby Pacific Ocean on a cloudy day. The driveway separating the house and detached garage/studio was lined with art: sculpted urns, disembodied Buddha heads, and male torsos (the latter to the disapproval of the neighbor across the street). The backyard held a collection of metal art that Lou had dabbled in when she lived in San Francisco in the 1960s and '70s. Her legal grow of six marijuana plants resided next to a large blue and purple tin peacock.

Lou sold her creations at the weekly Farmers' Market and held pop-up sales at her studio once or twice a year. In fact, she was preparing to do her annual fall sale, right before the Harvest Festival. So, after eating her muffin with chai tea, and feeding Steve, Lou went to work in her studio. She wrapped her greying hair back into a bun and settled down. She needed a few more pieces for her show, so was intent on finishing that last batch of mugs. They always sold well.

Steve had been snoring next to her work table. He nudged her foot around two o'clock for his lunch and a potty break. Lou took care of him, grabbed some fruit, and kept working. It was close to five-thirty when she realized the light was fading quickly in the studio.

"Okay, Steve," she said, standing, and rolling her shoulders. "That's it for today. We better go for our walk before it gets too dark." Sunset was coming earlier and earlier, even with daylight saving time.

It was getting chillier, too, unseasonably so, and Lou could feel the evening dampness in her bones. She wore a heavy wool sweater over her work jeans and flannel shirt in acknowledgment of that change from summer to autumn. October was only days away.

Because of the temperature and time, Lou decided it would be a short walk today, to the mini children's park and playground one block away. It would be even cooler, there, she thought, since the park abutted the river walkway.

Two steps onto the sidewalk, past a Buddha head, Lou shivered. *Maybe I should have worn gloves.*

"Hurry," she urged Steve, who didn't seem to mind the cold and was taking an interest in one particular shrub. "Hurry up."

They had just rounded the far edge of the park, past the culvert and the back fence covered with ivy. Redwoods guarded the western side. The deciduous maples were already dropping their leaves, covering the ground with a crunchy, burnt orange carpet.

"Okay, let's go home, boy." They were in the last lap. Lou tugged the leash a little impatiently as she turned toward their house. The park was deserted, and the sun was drifting down behind the trees. "Come on."

Steve, usually the most agreeable of dogs, stopped suddenly. He turned, pulling sharply in the opposite direction, nearly upending Lou.

She lost the leash in the process, as Steve ran to the farthest corner of the playground, past the redwood trees and bare maples, to the fence and culvert.

Lou gasped. "Steve!" she called, half-running after him. "Where are you going?"

Steve stopped as abruptly as he started. Then he began

barking. Loudly. At each bark, his front paws lifted a little off the ground. He was fixated on an object only barely visible in the twilight shadows.

"What? What is it?" Lou said to him, starting to reach for the leash. *Maybe he cornered a skunk. Oh, Lord, please don't let it be a skunk!* She wanted to leave even more quickly now, back to her warm house and fireplace.

Steve quit barking but didn't budge. As Lou bent to pick up the leash, she saw it too. Something white, and something dark. But much too big for a skunk. She pushed her glasses up on her nose and leaned in. Took two steps, and then another two.

And screamed. It was the body of a woman with long, dark hair *(in what looked like nursing scrubs, Lou would relate later)*. A few maple leaves lay on top of the inert form, like ghoulish fall decorations.

Backing up, and running now, with Steve beside her, Lou yelled out into the empty park. "Help! Help me." But no one was there.

TWO

Robin and Lucia

IT WOULD BE ANOTHER HOUR before the town would learn of the gruesome discovery.

Lou was just reaching the park's edge when Lucia Morales Ricci pulled up to her best friend's home. A long day was about to get even longer.

And Lucia was already bone-tired. All she wanted to do was lie in a deep tub of hot water and soothe her aching 50-plus-year-old body. The hectic crush was over, and it had been a relatively normal and early wine harvest this year (*whatever normal was in the wine industry*), with a slightly lighter yield. No lingering heatwaves, fire, or chilling frost waylaid the crops, thank God. Farming was farming, no matter what was growing. The main issue now at her family's business, Ricci Redwood Grove Vineyards & Winery, was her father and brother's ongoing argument about dry-farming the lower block.

Her oldest brother, Salvador, was insisting it was the way of the future. Climate change would demand it. While her dad, Roberto, was old-school in his approach toward the vineyards and "his" precious grapes. She let them argue. Things were more peaceful in the tasting room, which she managed.

But instead of a rewarding bubble bath, she was sitting at the round, oak kitchen table across from Robin Hill O'Connor, her best friend since high school, and uncorking a second bottle of Sauvignon Blanc to top off Robin's glass.

Lucia loved having her friend back home in Miller's Creek, but not the circumstances of the move. Who could be happy that Robin's sweet husband, Patrick, had been murdered? It had taken barely a year after Patrick was shot and killed for Robin to find living in San Francisco intolerable. Reminders of him were everywhere. She got a shockingly good price for their flat and moved back to nearby Sonoma County and into her small, childhood Craftsman house.

In theory, they were at Robin's to work on plans for the upcoming October Harvest Festival at the Grange Hall. It was part trade show, and part town self-celebration and awards. Lucia would be pouring wine from her family's winery at one booth. Robin would be serving treats from Hill's Bakery at another; she had taken over the business from her widowed, ailing mother, who now lived at *The Manor*, recovering from a nasty fall, broken hip, and subsequent surgery.

Robin wanted to showcase a new pastry at the festival, so she kept bringing her neighbors and Lucia different creations to sample. Tonight it was a savory chive and gruyere cheese scone. Last weekend it was the cheddar-bacon bread twist. The goat cheese tart had been two weeks ago. Her shop's young baker, Thad, was on a creative roll, and delighted in making something other than muffins and cookies.

"Lucia, thanks for listening." Robin raised her glass, filled now with crisp, bright wine. She took a sip and put it down. Robin sighed, and broke off a corner of the scone, but didn't eat any, crumbling it instead onto a coral-colored napkin. She ran a hand through her thick auburn hair, with its signature white streak in the front. Some crumbs stuck in the strands.

"I know I'm obsessing. It's just that with the second anniversary of Patrick's death coming up, I can't concentrate. Luce, what if it wasn't random? What if someone purposely killed him that night in the bodega? I'm … was … a reporter. A good one in the city. Wouldn't I have found something, if it was … ?" Robin stopped short of saying the word "murder."

Lucia nodded. "I know, I know. What could you do? The police said it was a robbery gone wrong. Nothing to do with his job at the DOJ."

"But the police never caught them," Robin cried for probably the thousandth time. "They never found who killed my husband, Lucia."

"Yeah. That's not fair to Patrick. Or you."

Lucia wished, again, that she could ease her friend's pain. But nothing would, she knew. *I can serve up wine and sympathy tonight, though.*

"Do you want to wallow?" she asked. "Or do you want to talk about the Festival — a distraction? I'm okay with either one. And I happen to like this scone the best if you want to know my honest opinion on what to serve that night."

"God, I keep going round and round and getting nowhere. It doesn't bring Patrick back, right? We've got the committee meeting tomorrow. Let's work on that. We still need to finalize the layout for the booths, and the parking logistics. Thanks, Lucia."

"Of course." Lucia moved her wine glass to one side and opened a file folder. "Well, to start, the animal shelter is bringing puppies."

Their phones buzzed at the same time. It was a text from their mutual pal, Yvonne.

Call me. Now.

THREE

The Harvest Festival

MILLER'S CREEK HARVEST FESTIVAL WAS usually the second most popular event in town, running only behind the Fourth of July parade. Oh, the townspeople loved the parade, where school children rode on hand-decorated floats, the junior high marching band valiantly performed "Classical Gas," and local candidates running for office handed out campaign buttons and threw hard candy into the crowd. Horses, bicycles, pets, old cars — the parade had it all. The third most popular gathering was the fire department's annual all-you-can-eat pancake breakfast in April. They served real maple syrup.

But by the end of the year, when the grapes were harvested, summer crops were done, and the fall sun kissed the pumpkins, people were ready to relax a bit. It was time to drink good wine and cider, sample cheeses, chili, Gravenstein apple desserts, and dance a little to the local band, "Hops 'n Vibes."

This year, however, the Harvest Festival was *THE* most popular event. Attendance was way up, according to those taking tickets at the front door. Everyone wanted to gather and talk about the murder, the first one since, well, you had to go way back. The old-timers said that the other one (and the last murder they could remember) had involved a brawl on the edge of town at a honky-tonk, now long closed. And does that really count, when it wasn't even within the city limits?

So the Festival was the perfect opportunity for people to eat, drink, and gab. The rumor mill had been spinning as swiftly as the town's water wheel — discarding some theories, acquiring others.

The murder had made the local and area newspapers, too, above the fold. The current police chief was quoted reassuring the populace, and saying the department was "thoroughly investigating and following all leads" (of which there were few). Even the eleven o'clock news hour had a brief mention.

Lucia had been pouring wine at her family's booth for two hours and was ready for a breather. She was grateful that this was the last big hurrah of the year for her.

"Sal, I need a break." She called to her brother who was preaching the virtues of their Petite Syrah to a cluster of senior citizens, and their entourage. The seniors had taken the shuttle bus to the Grange from The Manor, and they were enjoying the free happy hour wines and tasty food samples. The group had acquired a temporary celebrity status too, since the murder victim had worked as a Certified Nursing Assistant at the facility.

"Sandy Foster was her name," one senior informed the other

attendees who had gathered around them.

"She was so sweet and always watched out for us," another lamented.

"I can't believe she's gone," still another said.

"Murdered," an older man whispered low.

"Sal!" Lucia called to him again. He nodded, excused himself, and walked behind the long folding table outfitted with a burgundy cloth.

"Jeez, Okay, okay. I'm here."

"I won't be long," Lucia told him, as she slipped quickly out the other side. She hurried to the opposite end of the Grange, where Robin had set up the bakery's booth. Lucia was dressed in her customary jeans, boots, and peasant shirt (soon the shirts would switch to warm turtleneck sweaters). The combination of Latin and Italian genes looked good on her, contributing to her shoulder-length brunette hair (only lightly touched up), and surprising dark blue eyes inherited from a northern Italian grandmother.

She wove past crowds of people munching and chatting, and by the award-winning displays by the Boy Scouts that lined the walls. The band had taken a break; their stage was on the side farthest from the vendors.

Lucia ignored the admiring looks from some of the men, most of whom she had known all of her life. She had been single ever since her teenage marriage was annulled by her shocked family. For Lucia, a B.S. in Viticulture and Enology, and a series of long-term boyfriends had followed, but no other wedding. Both of her grandmothers had despaired at her unmarried state and regularly lit candles at St. Isidore's

Catholic Church. Lucia didn't care. At the moment, she was casually dating Tom Kikugawa, a generally regarded "nice guy" who owned an apple orchard nearby.

She finally reached Robin. "Hey, can you get a minute? I need some air."

"Sure." Robin motioned to her baker, Thad, and their part-time helper, Jen Hanson. She held up her hand, waving five fingers. *Five minutes*, she mouthed. The chive and gruyere scones were a hit, and she was raffling a pumpkin pie, as well. It was brisk business at the bakery booth. She couldn't be gone long.

They took a shortcut through the utilitarian kitchen to behind the building. The kitchen door was open, and they stepped out onto the large concrete pad. Others had the same idea. The cool river breeze felt refreshing on this fall afternoon.

They spotted the retired police chief and called to her.

"Yvonne!"

The woman broke away from the people she had been speaking with to join them.

"God, it's crazy in there. And out here," Yvonne nodded toward the knots of residents standing around. "All anyone wants to talk about is the murder of that poor woman."

"Tell me," Robin replied. "Everyone coming into the bakery is preoccupied with it. *Everyone* is an expert sleuth. But nobody seemed to actually know her. Sandy. I guess she was only in town for a few months. Mom said she worked there at The Manor and was always kind to her and the other residents there."

"Well, the rumors I heard were either that she was hit over

the head, stabbed, or choked. Or all three." Lucia shivered.

Yvonne lowered her voice. "The county coroner is at a conference in Vancouver, and his assistant is on maternity leave. So some new guy was brought in to handle the case." She rolled her eyes. "I haven't heard stellar things about him."

"How is Lou?" Lucia asked. "I heard you spent the night at her place after she found the body."

"Oh, you know Lou. She was pretty shaken that night, but she's tough. Didn't you see her earlier, dancing in front of the band? And she's got Steve, thankfully."

"No suspects?" Robin wondered.

Yvonne shook her head 'no.' "That group," she indicated a clutch of folks nearby, "is saying it was a transient from down the river. Or a crazy local. Just what we need with Halloween coming up."

"I overheard the customers at the bakery talking about getting porch cameras, and double-locking their doors. They're pulling out their hunting rifles," Robin told them. "I think they're going to storm the city council meeting next week, demanding answers."

"Well, the talk in the tasting room and at the bar is just as bad," Lucia added.

"I've got to get back in and hold that raffle. Keep us posted?" Robin asked Yvonne.

"I will." Yvonne paused. "Listen, I'm not saying you need to worry, but be careful."

Robin and Lucia walked back into the hot, noisy hall. Before parting, Lucia remarked, "I thought I'd see your mom tonight. I miss Charlotte. She was the face of the bakery, and all."

"I tried to get her to come," Robin answered. "But this murder really upset her. And she's having some sort of new heart issue now. Having someone who she liked killed is bringing up Patrick's death again."

"For you, too, dear friend. For you, too." Lucia patted Robin's arm. "Catch up with you later."

FOUR

Robin Ponders

IT HAD BEEN A LONG day. A long couple of days, Robin admitted. *Weeks?* Getting ready for the Festival was like juggling plates: running the bakery, managing the staff, planning, packing, and unpacking for the event. In her mid-fifties, she acknowledged that while she tried to keep in shape with tennis and exercise, she didn't have the energy she had at thirty. She laughed to herself. At least the premature, natural white streak in her auburn hair wasn't from old age. It had appeared in her early twenties, a genetic inheritance from a grandmother.

Rupert, her mother's Ragamuffin cat, was waiting for her as she came in from the Festival. Remembering Yvonne's mild warning, she double-locked the old wooden front door, giving it a little shove with her shoulder to make sure it took. She debated leaving the porch light on but thought that was too much. She'd never been afraid in her hometown before. And she didn't like that feeling. She had left fear behind in San Francisco, she thought.

"Man, do I deserve a glass of wine," she told Rupert. "After I feed you."

Feeding Rupert was a production. He had been spoiled by her parents, especially so after her dad had died, and her mom was alone. That cat could eat. He was company for her, though.

Feeling like she had done her duty to "Rupert - Who Must Be Served," Robin threw on her pajamas and lit a fire in the tiled fireplace. She had chosen an earthy Chardonnay to drink tonight. She needed something substantial.

If she acknowledged the truth, she *was* a little nervous about that woman's murder. Of Sandy Foster's murder, she reminded herself. A real person. She said a quick prayer. *May perpetual light shine upon her.*

And sitting there, ruminating about it all brought back Patrick's death, just like Lucia had said it might.

Lucia, and everyone, had been so fond of Patrick. They all were devastated when he died. The good-looking, boyish Patrick was Robin's heart-mate, and he adored her. With his role as a U.S. Attorney in the DOJ's San Francisco office and Robin's job as an investigative reporter for the *San Francisco Tribune and Times*, they were a power couple in their circles. They were photographed attending charity fundraisers, but working at their church's food pantry, and quietly supporting causes dear to them were where they thrived.

One fateful Wednesday evening in October, almost two years ago, Patrick stopped by the neighborhood bodega to buy a lottery ticket, as was his habit. An only child, he had inherited his family's estate when they passed; he and Robin had no children, so they donated generously instead.

"If I win big," Patrick always joked, "the seniors at the center are going to be eating filet mignon!"

He had just walked in and greeted the clerk he knew well. As Patrick pulled out his wallet, there was a commotion at the door. He turned, and before he could utter a word, he was shot four times in the chest. *Four deadly times.* The robbers took his wallet, and emptied the cash register, but left the shaking clerk unharmed. The broken security cameras were of no help.

Our Lady of Grace Church was packed for the funeral. Even the mayor made an appearance.

"What a tragedy," everyone said, and they bemoaned the recent proliferation of grocery and liquor store robberies in the city. At the reception later in the hall, though, a small group of Patrick's co-workers from the DOJ huddled by the charcuterie table, and muttered low about how the DA had mishandled this and maybe it really was a hit job. Patrick had worked on some sensitive racketeering cases over the years. Who knows? They shook their heads. It stunk; this was a cover-up. Maybe.

They glanced over at the stricken widow. It was a shame, they all agreed. And they ate the food and drank the whiskey and fine wines, and drifted off to their lives. Only Brian, his best friend, would quietly dig further. He found nothing.

She had buried Patrick in the local Miller's Creek cemetery, alongside the weeping angel monuments, and crypts.

Moving back home was for the best. Robin had no stomach

for investigative reporting now. For much of anything, really. Her dad, John, had died of a stroke shortly after Patrick. Her mom, Charlotte, continued to run the family bakery. But failing health soon put Charlotte into The Manor – at her own insistence. The stress of John and Patrick's passing had taken its toll on Charlotte. She had become more distracted and forgetful. Then, a fall, and a shattered hip. Robin hoped to bring her mother back home eventually and had talked about preparing a downstairs bedroom for easy walker access. It hadn't happened.

Once back in Miller's Creek, Robin had agreed to take over the bakery, a place she had almost lived in as a child. It was easy to get lost in the day-to-day demands there: ordering flour, sugar, and almonds, and reviewing spreadsheets, bills, and payroll. Serving coffee or tea to locals who knew her all of her life, and cared about her. Robin had even started thinking about adding a happy hour (serving Lucia's wines, naturally). She had brought her small, portable pizza oven along with her; it would be perfect for mini pizzas to go with the wine. Thad was eager to start on that new project. Small-town demands and politics could be intense, but this was home. And locals protected their own.

When she moved from the flat in the city, she'd kept their art, kitchen gadgets, and personal mementos, but sold most of the furniture. The Craftsman house was too small to hold two sets of sofas, tables, and desks. She had saved Patrick's clothes, boxed up now in the garage. All except his favorite sweatshirt. That hung in her closet.

Really, it was full circle, Robin thought. *Maybe meant to*

be. As she grew up, her parents always thought her creativity and love of baking would make her a natural successor to the business, started by her grandparents. But writing was also a love. So after college, she moved to San Francisco to pursue a career in journalism.

She met Patrick at a street fair in the Marina district, shortly thereafter. Her streaked auburn-red hair and hazel eyes made her unforgettable to the tall, ruddy Patrick O'Connor. They married at the Catholic Church in Miller's Creek within the year. And now, 30 years later, she was a widow.

It was late. She was exhausted. Robin checked the front door again, just in case, and went to bed, with Rupert following behind her.

FIVE

Just Call Me Pat

PATRICIA ANN ("*CALL ME PAT*") Breward sat at her computer desk and smiled. The numbers she saw on the screen would make her investors happy, she knew. Nice, neat columns of numbers that represented a very positive cash flow. *What a relief!* Things had been so much better these last two quarters.

Outside her office and closed door, the late morning activities at The Manor were muted. She could hear the occasional call of "Bingo!" and a clatter of porcelain as the cart carrying breakfast dishes and silverware rolled past. Mostly, though, it was quiet. Peaceful. As she liked it.

When Pat had taken ownership of the town's beloved Miller's Creek Manor - Senior Living and Rehab over a year ago, the 48-bed, genteel-shabby building had needed some work. Face it, a lot of work. Pat had pitched the sale to a few investors with money to burn, and they had "bought into" the altruistic nature of the purchase. Fixing up a place for granny to spend her last days looked good on their portfolios, and for the philanthropic boards they sat on.

Pat also presented her own resume and skill set. As a former administrator of nursing homes in Mexico and the U.S., she brought her 40 years of experience, a certificate from community college, an R.N., a B.S. in Biology, a B.S. in Health Administration, and licenses to the job. She was ready to be the boss this time, too, not just report to fickle corporations.

Pat's friendly, grandmotherly demeanor helped. Her bobbed grey hair matched her grey eyes. She wore reading glasses that hung from a beaded neck chain, and she stuffed her somewhat ample, short figure into her signature cotton, polyester-blend pantsuits. It all invited trust.

So when the prior owners retired, Pat was ready with a check and assurances that she would bring The Manor back to its past … well, not grandeur, because it was never grand, but perhaps to its maintained respectability. The setting itself had always been perfect, with rolling meadows and the creek nearby, but the small structure and low resident quotas needed a little help.

Now that the numbers had improved, Pat was going to get bids on painting the exterior. That would be costly. It was a project for spring, perhaps, after she had pumped up that maintenance account. Everything helped to that end. There was a rent increase, naturally, given a new owner. And look at all of the added amenities residents could purchase: chapel services, a beautician, a massage therapist, wine tasting, excursions! *Almost* all the beds were filled in the independent living wing, and in the rehab center; it was *almost* at capacity. Almost.

She glanced at her email. The local hospital confirmed they

were transferring a new patient within a day to The Manor for rehab: a Ms. Maisie Burnett. Broken clavicle. *Good.*

A knock on the door interrupted her. Pat closed the laptop screen and snapped the cover shut. She unwrapped a butterscotch candy and popped it into her mouth.

"Come in," she called, stretching out the "in."

"So sorry to bother you, Miss Pat. I have the menu for next week for you to review."

"Oh, Ricardo, it's never a bother to see you. Sit down." She gestured to a floral-print pseudo-Queen Anne chair, left over from a previous resident.

Pat congratulated herself once again on bringing Ricardo along with her. The chef had followed Pat from place to place over her last few employments. She had met him at a resort-like facility in Mexico 11 years ago.

"Your talents are wasted here," she told him. "Come work for me in Nevada. There are lots of retired people there. I'll make it worth your while." So he went.

"Let's see what tidbits you have planned for our guests." Pat scanned the menu. "Good, good, yes, let's use pumpkin. And zucchini before it's gone. Maybe more soups? It's the right season, don't you think?"

Ricardo nodded, always happy to oblige his generous boss. He laughed silently — he knew what side his bread was buttered on. *That's a good chef joke*, he thought.

"I'll take care of it, Miss Pat. Any special menu requests this week?"

"Mmmm, not this week. Thank you." As he turned to leave, she said, "Oh, and you can leave the door open now."

Walking out behind him, she passed by the front desk. A memorial photo of the facility's late CNA, Sandy Foster, was on display, with a white silk rose resting beside it. Pat didn't notice.

She passed a resident. "Going for a constitutional, Mr. Hanson? Have a nice time outside, dear." She didn't wait for a reply, or to see Jack Hanson's grimace.

Pat walked through the lobby and turned left into the office of Dr. Denton Tracy. *How lucky these residents are to have their own personal physician.* A rarity, she knew. They contracted out for their rehab physical therapy services, but to have a doctor on site was a coup. Pat and the doctor first became acquainted at the facility in Nevada, the one close to the strip in Reno. The doctor was not much younger than some of the residents at The Manor, and he looked a little uncomfortably cadaverous to some eyes: thin face and body, mostly bald, and becoming more stooped with age.

Pat didn't knock. She strode in, closing the door behind her. "So, how are things going, Denton?"

SIX

Maisie Burnett

MAISIE BURNETT HAD FALLEN ASLEEP in her recliner. She stirred and awoke chilled. The television in the corner of her small living room was the only illumination. Late-night news anchors were discussing dire world events.

Maisie picked up the remote and clicked the "off" button. The room darkened considerably.

"Time for bed," she muttered, annoyed that she had dropped off to sleep during her favorite game show. She pushed on the arms of the recliner and lifted herself off the polyester tweed chair.

One step, two. A little dizzy, and not quite awake, Maisie pitched headfirst. She instinctively reached out an arm, but it crumpled like a chicken wing as she hit the thin, blue hooked rug, and hard floor beneath. The sharp pain in her bony shoulder made Maisie swear.

"Damn," she cried out to the empty room. "Well, damn, now I've done it."

Victoria Hernandez had been Maisie's neighbor at the

Hummingbird Senior Villas (or "The Bird," as locals called it) for five years. It was a pleasant complex, painted in bright colors, with window boxes filled with seasonal flowers.

Vicky was one of those cheerful people who hung floral wreaths on her front door in spring and piled pumpkins on her walkway in fall. It was Saturday afternoon, and she had gotten off the bus, after her weekly shopping trip to George's Market and Hill's Bakery. She passed the first apartment in the row, waving to the man leaning forward in his lawn chair.

"Hey, Buddy," she called loudly.

Buddy nodded in acknowledgement. Next was Maisie's place. The curtains there were drawn when Vicky had left early that morning. It was now after two o'clock, and they were still closed. Should she check on her neighbor? Maisie was notoriously private, but still, what if something was wrong?

Vicky decided to investigate. Walking up the short path, she called out, "Maisie?" Nothing. She knocked. No answer. "Maisie, hello?"

There was a noise inside, a thump. Then a voice. Maisie's. "Hold on."

Vicky waited. When the door opened a little, Vicky was treated to a sight. Maisie was in a summer shift, with a grey sweater draped over one shoulder, and dangling off the other. A red, winter muffler was wrapped around her right arm and over her neck, like a sling. The side of her face was a bluish-purple.

Vicky gasped, and blurted, "Good God, Maisie, what happened?"

Maisie reluctantly opened the door all the way. "Oh, I don't know. Too damn old, I guess. I tripped or something getting up from my chair last night. Hit the floor kind of hard. Banged up my shoulder, that's all." Maisie hesitated. "Maybe hit my head, too. I took a couple aspirins. I'll be okay," she said, swaying a little.

Vicky knew for Maisie to take one aspirin, let alone a couple rated up there as an emergency.

"Maisie, you need to go to Urgent Care. Buddy can drive us."

"No!" Maisie went to wave her arms and winced. She managed to yell "no" one more time before she fainted.

And that ... was that.

Now, Maisie shifted uncomfortably in the narrow hospital bed. Her roommate was snoring lightly, the shared, unwatched television playing a 1970s detective show. At least the volume was on low. The woman in *Bed A* seemed to be asleep most of the time.

Or else she's drugged.

Maisie hadn't shared a room since she was a kid. And that was a long time ago. She had been on her own since she was eighteen, and the confines and intrusions of the hospital setting were chafing.

Her one-bedroom apartment at The Bird may be simple, but it was all hers, darn it. She was antsy to return. Her doctor had other plans. The physician had swung by before lunch and reported Maisie's surgery was successful. He was pleased but cautioned her not to overdo it or reinjure herself.

"It's harder to bounce back as you age," he noted.

Furthermore, she would still need rehab and physical therapy.

"Is there someone at home who can help you?" he asked.

"No. I take care of myself."

After some stern warnings, he convinced her that since she lived alone, a short stay at a facility called The Manor would be to her long-term benefit. Medicare insurance would undoubtedly cover it.

So Maisie signed all the necessary paperwork that afternoon and spoke to social services and the Ombudsman. They took care of everything.

Next stop was rehab at that place near town. The Manor.

Yeah, I just bet it's a "manor."

Vicky stopped by right before dinner. Knocking lightly at the half-open door, Vicky entered and pulled a blue plastic chair closer to the bed.

She leaned in. "You gave us quite a scare, Maisie. How are you doing?"

Maisie sighed and then related the details and prognosis, finishing with the news about The Manor.

"I said I'd be fine at home, but they," she pointed to the hallway, "seem to think I'm an invalid. Or an idiot. So I'm going to be doing rehab at *The Manor*." The last two words were punctuated by Maisie flourishing her good arm. "Pfft."

"Oh, Maisie. I'm sure it's for the best. I can help you sometimes, but babysitting my grandson means I'm not always available."

"I know, I know," Maisie muttered. "It's just that I saw my mother and sister fade away and die in those nursing homes. That's not going to be me!"

"Of course not. And I'll come and visit. You'll be back in no time."

"Hmmph."

Dinner arrived shortly after Vicky left. Maisie poked at it, with little interest. Finally, she pushed the red button for the nurse. Her dinner table was stuck and hovering over her, with the uneaten beige food sitting on the equally beige tray.

The nurse entered the room, moved the obstinate table to the side, and turned off the lights and television. "Big day tomorrow, Ms. Burnett," she commented.

Maisie grunted a response.

SEVEN

Happy Hour at the Bakery

"COMING THROUGH!" ROBIN CALLED OUT loudly. She was balancing a hot pizza tray in one hand, and three mismatched wine glasses in the other.

She angled past a group of three guests laughing uproariously about the recent antics of a state senator, dodged Noreen's two grandchildren who ran by, and almost tripped over Yvonne's old, chocolate lab, Madison, sprawled by the doorway.

"Her hip is bothering her, with this weather," Yvonne said. "So I didn't want to leave her alone at home, or in the truck." She added, "You know Madison. She won't be any trouble."

Robin spotted Lou in the crowd, so Steve would likely be close by, too. It all felt like controlled chaos.

Why, oh why, did I think a Friday happy hour would be a good idea? She asked herself for the hundredth time that night. Finally making it to the bakery's "front room" without a mishap, Robin placed the mushroom-herb pizza, bubbling with extra cheese, in front of the domino members. She gave three latecomers - the newspaper's editor, the mayor, and his wife - their wine glasses.

"Lucia has the wine over there," Robin said, pointing to a far table. "She'll help you." She remembered to smile.

The soft opening of the bakery's new happy hour was a huge success. Robin had invited what she thought would be a small group of regulars and a couple of people from church to test-drive the new idea. Everyone who was asked (and a few more) showed up.

And no wonder. From the outside, the bakery looked inviting and hospitable on that cold autumn night. The lights were on, and cream-colored votive candles sparkled on the tables. The chatter and laughter leaked out through the front door. On the dark street, the wind whistled a counter-tune, and oak leaves whirled like dervishes.

Inside, the aroma of tomato, basil, and fresh rye bread had replaced the usual sugary scents. Thad had loved the pizza oven and convinced Robin to buy two more. Tonight, they had decided to try a pretty basic pizza. In addition, Robin was serving the bakery's signature sourdough rye baguettes, with three cheeses from local farms: one goat cheese (caprino-style), an organic American blue, and a tangy cheddar. Lucia was pouring the Ricci wines; they would always hold favored status.

Thad was singing in the back kitchen. *Well, I'm glad he's happy.* Her mother had snapped him up right after he graduated from the junior college's culinary program. Maybe keeping him involved in something new was good.

When most everyone was served, eating, and drinking, Robin walked over to where Charlotte sat with Bev, a friend from

The Manor. Charlotte had been holding court that evening, visiting with the bakery customers who had missed seeing her.

Robin signaled to Lucia and waved her over. The wine portion of the night was wrapping up, and carafes of water were now on the tables.

Robin sat by her mother on the padded bench and scooted over for Lucia. They scrunched in. Lucia had brought over two glasses of white wine and placed one on the table in front of Robin. The glasses were different in shape, and sported logos from wine events long ago. Nobody that night minded using the old stemware that Robin had found in the storage unit.

"Colorful," they had claimed, and, "Yeah, I remember 1987."

"How are you doing, Mom?"

"Oh, I'm having such fun tonight, honey. Really. Don't worry about me. I'm glad you talked me into coming out." Charlotte was beaming. She was in her element, surrounded by friends. Dressed in shades of deep green, her outfit complemented her fair coloring. Her hair, once strawberry-blonde, was now faded more to grey. Robin had her hazel eyes.

"Well, I love seeing you here, Charlotte," Lucia lifted her glass. "Alla nostra salute," she toasted in Italian.

"Thank you. Cheers to you, too. This is the best I've felt for weeks," Charlotte took a sip from her own wine, the glass still a third full. "Isn't that right, Bev?"

Bev nodded. "Yes. This is such a nice distraction from, you know, all that ugly business about poor Sandy. I still can't believe it. So, so sad. And scary."

Sitting at the next table over was a clutch of people which

included Yvonne, her cousin Father Arthur Walter Reardon, Mayor Joaquin Martin and his wife Angelica, and the Fire Chief, Tim Miller. Yvonne had overheard the toast.

"And santé," she said, calling to Charlotte.

Father Art reached across her to add, "Sláinte."

"Show-off," Yvonne told him. "He can speak French *and* Gaelic," she said to Bev, "which makes him insufferable at times."

"Don't forget Latin." Art smiled.

Mayor Martin chimed into the conversation.

"This has been a wonderful evening, Robin and Charlotte. Congratulations to Thad, too. It's nice to have something so enjoyable to do on a Friday night."

The mayor had a great smile, photogenic and perfect for campaign posters. An athletic man in his mid-forties, he had been elected to make exciting things happen in their small town while also keeping it just the same. An impossible challenge he seemed to warmly accept. His wife Angelica, an attorney, had jumped into civic causes, as well.

The fire chief, Tim Miller, a descendent of the original C. Miller, was a more taciturn sort. He nodded and listened but didn't join in. They were all gym buddies of Yvonne's.

While Bev, Charlotte, and the group chatted about the merits of various pizzas, Yvonne scooted her chair over and leaned in to talk to Lucia and Robin.

"Listen, off the record, I heard something about the victim."

"Off the record?" Robin repeated quickly. Old reporting habits die hard.

"Yeah. That assistant to the assistant coroner filed his report.

It will be out in a day or so. Blunt force trauma to her head."

"No stab wounds? She wasn't strangled?" Lucia asked.

"No, not according to him. I wish our usual guy was around. But." Yvonne let that sentence drop.

"Still no suspect?" Robin asked next.

"None."

"Damn," said Lucia, voicing all of their thoughts. She fingered the silver cross she was wearing.

"Hey, there. Excuse me, ladies."

Their conversation was interrupted by a deep voice directly above them. It belonged to the six-foot-plus, sandy-haired Scott Phillips. Fairly new to the area, and already a frequent bakery patron, Scott had bought the feed and garden supply store on Miller's Creek Road. His marital status (single) and age (almost fifty) were discussed at the bakery, beauty salon, and riding stables soon after he arrived.

"Hey," he repeated. "Sorry to interrupt. Thank you again for inviting me, Robin. I really enjoy a good pizza with a great red wine. And Lucia, your family makes the best Syrah." He smiled at them.

"Uh, so, Yvonne. Right?" he spoke directly now to her. "I'm Scott. We have a mutual acquaintance. You know Carl, the Animal Control guy, right?"

Yvonne nodded yes.

"Well, he and I have been talking. We're seeing something … I don't know … weird, behind my store and by the creek, with some of the rabbits and feral cats dying." He shook his head. "It may be nothing. But Carl said you were the chief of police here for a long time. He told me to talk to you and see if I could pick your brain. Check if you've ever seen anything like this before. Carl hasn't. If it would work out, I was wondering if you could swing by the store next week. I can explain more then."

"Yeah. I guess I could do that. Maybe Tuesday afternoon?"

"That would be good. I'll be in the store all day. Well, thanks again." He raised his hand in a half-wave and walked out.

"Yvonne Jeannette," Father Art said to his cousin. "Is there something you want to tell me?" He winked.

"Oh, for God's sake … no offense, Art. I don't even know him. I have no idea what that's about."

"Well, maybe you can find out," Charlotte quipped. "And let us know. I live vicariously, now."

"Who was that?" Bev asked.

At the explanation, Angelica added, "Every single woman in town between eighteen and eighty seems to think he's like a hunk."

"Don't dismiss the over-eighty crowd," Bev responded.

Lucia volunteered to drive Charlotte and Bev back to The Manor, so Robin finished packing the cleaned glassware and made certain everything was ready for the next morning. Saturdays were busy. She might have to rethink having a happy hour on Friday evenings. And maybe give Thad a raise.

She turned off the bakery's lights, set the alarm, and locked the door. Her car was right across the street, and she hurried to it. *No suspect. Yet.*

"Damn," she said out loud, repeating Lucia.

EIGHT

Yvonne and Scott at the Feed Store

YVONNE'S BRAIN WAS FULL. SHE was finishing a quick lunch with the mayor and the current police chief at the taqueria. The topic of conversation was the murder, of course.

They were having their usual Tuesday get-together, in the more private, corner booth. She watched as the chief added more hot sauce to his fish tacos.

"Man, I probably shouldn't do this," the chief said, shaking the crimson juice liberally, and turning the fish from white to red.

"Angelo," Yvonne said to him, "I don't want Rosalie calling and blaming me tonight if your ulcer flares up."

"My ulcer is already flared up," Angelo replied. He reluctantly put the bottle down on the table.

"You're also insulting the chef," Joaquin told him. "You don't see me drowning *my* lunch." The mayor was having his usual Camarones al Mojo de Ajo. He loved his garlic shrimp just the way they came out of the kitchen.

Yvonne had opted for the vegetarian burrito with black

beans today. She skipped the extra guacamole.

They had waited to discuss the murder until everyone had ordered, and been served. Now, they got down to business and to the meal at the same time.

"So," Yvonne began, "anything new that you can tell us? Did Lou recall anything else? Any tips?"

Angelo shook his head, swallowed, and replied, "Not a thing. I've got residents calling and coming by the station. Our official line is that an investigation is underway and we are exhausting all leads."

"Yes, that message works *so* well," Joacquin said sarcastically. "They are pounding down the door at city hall, too. And calling me at all hours. Not that I blame them."

"People are scared," Yvonne noted. "And that makes them skittish and angry. I don't envy you now. I heard the newspaper is doing a second follow-up story."

"Yeah, you retired in time. Well, it didn't help that idiot assistant coroner put out his own press release before we could. No cooperation with our department!" Angelo was working up a head of steam. "An idiot," he repeated.

Joaquin put down his fork. "The truth is, Yvonne, we're stuck. The Chief and I have been over and over this. It could have been a mugging — an inopportune meeting. Or not. I don't know. Angelo says the sheriff hasn't seen any similar cases in the county."

"Initial reports are that the victim didn't have any known enemies, and she hadn't been here very long. Wasn't rich or wore flashy jewelry," Angelo added. "My sergeant did interviews at The Manor, and it sounds as if she was well-liked at her job. There was nothing found at the crime scene that could be used as evidence. That part of the park isn't in range of any cameras. No sign of a struggle. No murder weapon, either. In fact, it's weird that there wasn't more blood."

Yvonne was on alert. "Do you think she was killed elsewhere and brought there? But if so, why?"

"I'm not going on the record yet, but no, I don't think she was killed in the park," Angelo replied. "That complicates things. As to the who, why, or where?" He shrugged.

"If she was moved from elsewhere, that makes it more personal, not random," Yvonne mused. "And yes, more complicated."

After a bit more discussion, and wrangling for the bill, Yvonne said, "I've got to run. The new guy at the feed store, Scott, asked me to come by to 'pick my brain' about some dead feral cats or rabbits that have turned up over there. I don't know what that's about. Guess he thought you would be too busy, Chief," she told Angelo.

"Oh, that's great, a dead body and now dead bunnies. The newspaper is going to have a field day. And my head!"

———

Yvonne was uncharacteristically distracted on the drive and almost missed the turnoff. Given her line of work, as a detective and eventually police chief of Miller's Creek, of course, she had seen the dead. But it had been mostly accident victims or death from natural causes; a few overdoses. She felt pity for poor Sandy Foster, and anger that a murderer had tainted her town.

It was around one-thirty when she pulled her SUV into the barely paved parking lot at the feed store. No other cars were there, only a weathered pickup truck way in the back. The barn-like structure was located off of Miller's Creek Road and was close to The Manor, and the Ricci Redwood Grove Vineyards. Yvonne planned to pick up some wine on her way home. Maybe she'd catch Lucia there, and see if she'd heard anything about the murder through the local grapevine.

Yvonne stepped out of her SUV and brushed off her navy-blue sweater, tan shirt, and slacks, making sure no tortilla chip crumbs had dropped onto them. Her sassy grown children kidded her that her clothing style was Sonoma County meets Ralph Lauren. She thought that it was more Eddie Bauer-like. They also joked that the SUV she bought when she retired was sturdier than any squad car she had driven. That might be true, but she liked the safety of the larger vehicle, with its four-wheel drive. It was good for country living.

Her ex-husband probably thought her look was "uptight," like everything else he felt about her.

She cracked the car windows open, hit the lock and alarm, and left the snoring Maddie in the back seat's large, plaid dog bed. It had been a huge extravagance — a designer dog bed. The old Labrador was worth it, though. Yvonne's revolver was in the car's hidden safety lockbox, accessible only by her fingerprint.

She had learned long ago how to compartmentalize problems. Collecting herself now, she walked in through the open, double barn doors. The store smelled the same as it had with the previous owner, and with the owner before that: hay, rabbit pellets, chicken feed, salt licks, chunky dog kibble, and dust. A pyramid of pumpkins sat by the entrance, next to a couple flats of yellow chrysanthemums. The mercantile section was by the long, front counter, and held a few western-wear shirts and hats on a wooden rack. Belts with large brass buckles hung from a hook.

It took a second for her eyes to adjust to the darker store. Rays of autumn afternoon light, littered with dust motes, cut through in spots.

"Hello," she called out. "Scott? Anyone here?"

"Be right there," a deep voice answered from the back corner. And then Scott appeared.

It's like he was made for this place. Central casting, Yvonne silently observed. He was tall and angular but not skinny. He was wearing jeans (definitely not designer ones), work boots, and a flannel shirt. Yup, Yvonne could see where some local women might swoon.

"Hey, Scott. You asked me to stop by?"

"Yeah, thanks for coming. Sorry to bother you." He walked past the counter and motioned to some hay bales. Closer up, she noticed a little grey in his blond hair. "Want to sit down?"

She sat. He talked.

"Carl said to contact you, that you'd be a good resource. This may be a wasted trip, though," Scott shrugged. "He and I came across some strange stuff around back. I called him a few weeks ago about a couple of dead rabbits I found near the creek. There weren't any signs of them having been attacked. I could have just buried them. But then I thought Carl or someone from Animal Control might want to take a look."

"Okay," Yvonne said, wondering how she fit into this.

"So, by the time he came out, I had found two dead cats, too. Feral cats. But just the same." Scott looked down. "I keep a few barn cats around here for the rats and mice. I'd hate for them to die like that."

"What do you, or Carl, think happened?"

"Well, Carl thinks they were deliberately poisoned or got into some poison. It seems like that to me, too. They had the signs of it. One of the cats looked like it had been vomiting. I was raised on a ranch in the Sierras, and I've seen my share of sick animals." He paused and gestured around the store. "I keep all of my weed killers — organic, by the way — and ant poison locked up. I checked, and nothing is missing. No boxes were gnawed, or anything like that. The poison wasn't from my stock."

Yvonne still wasn't sure what he wanted. So she just asked. "What is it you think I can do?"

"You still have connections in the police department here. With the chief, and the deputies, right? Carl is bogged down with calls, and there's too much bureaucracy at his office. We believe that someone has poisoned these wild animals on purpose. Some sick bastard. And if that's true, then what's to stop them from killing domestic pets? Cats, dogs. There are a lot of ranches and farms out here. People would be hurting to see their sheepdog die a painful death, like that. And it's not only these animals. If an owl picked up a poisoned rabbit for dinner, he'd likely die, too. So can you investigate? Get this on record, or get someone to pay attention? You know this place better than I do."

"You really believe this was deliberate?"

Scott nodded. "Probably. Yeah, we both do. I wouldn't bother you, otherwise. I take poisoning an animal seriously."

"Well, all right. I'm not sure who I can get to listen right now. The department is up to its eyeballs with this recent murder."

"We're just asking that you try. Thank you. Yeah, that was an ugly thing to happen to that woman. Guess they didn't catch anyone yet?"

"No. Not yet."

"Well, I always keep my handgun out here. I bet you're prepared, too."

Yvonne thought of her revolver in the car. "Yes. Old habits from being on the force."

They both stood up. The feed store was getting chilly.

"Thanks, again. You don't know me well, so I appreciate it." Scott extended his hand. "Maybe I can check back with you in a week, or so. Meet at the bakery? And see what you've learned. I'll keep watching here. I've already warned my customers to be careful."

Yvonne shook his hand. Strong. "Sure. I can't promise anything, but I'll try. I have a dog, myself, so, I understand. I don't want that kind of sicko around, either."

One brief goodbye and she walked out to her car. Maddie was still snoring and barely moved when Yvonne started the motor. *Another worry for us. Angelo was right.* Yvonne turned the SUV to the left and took the road to the winery. Hopefully, Lucia would be there.

NINE

Lucia Finds Flossie

WALKING THE PROPERTY LINE ALWAYS gave Lucia joy. It would be impossible to count how many miles she had logged there since childhood. First, running and playing with her brothers on their ranch adjoining the winery acreage. Then, as a teenager, she had spent hours wandering along the roads and daydreaming under the trees. And every year she was always harvesting the full, ripe grapes with her family and crew.

Lucia loved how, in summer, the vines seemed to reach out and connect to each other like a row of chorus girls, adorned in purple and green. In fall, their golden leaves mimicked the surrounding maple trees. In wintertime, they rested, bare and brooding.

As she got older, Lucia liked taking time to inspect the vines and fencing and felt comfort in being a good steward of the land.

Sometimes, though, like today, it was good to just take a brisk walk with her dog, Annie. Annie was the unofficial ambassador and greeter at the winery. As a Red Heeler and

McNab mix, Annie believed it was her duty to herd the visitors up to the tasting room bar, and watch for any strays. She took her job seriously. Like all good winery dogs, she usually wore a colorful bandana scarf as her accessory. The tasting room was on the property, in a refurbished barn not far from the creek. The exterior was a natural wood color, not the traditional red. But "barn" was too casual a term. Picnic tables with flowered oilcloth coverings, and sturdy benches dotted the grounds. The hay bales outside were for atmosphere. Red-wine-stained American oak barrels (which cost hundreds of dollars each) stood on end as high-top tables. The rustic bar top itself had been handcrafted by a local artisan from an old-growth redwood plank. Music, usually light jazz, was piped in using the best sound equipment. And the wagon wheel chandeliers cost a mint. Still, the overall effect was charming, and the floors were covered with genuine Sonoma County dirt.

On this, her day off, Lucia had chosen to sleep in at her comfortable farmhouse, down the road a few miles from the winery property, and closer to town. Yes, her house was owned by the family, but it was not located *within* the family compound. That made the difference, as far as she was concerned. Sal, the oldest brother and winemaker, and his wife and kids were living cheek-to-jowl next door to her parents, Roberto and Carmen. Too close for comfort, for Lucia. The next brother, Ray, and his fiancée lived in town; he managed the wine sales. The youngest, Eduardo, or "Little Eddy," still lived in her parents' guest suite above the garage. He was the vineyard manager and justified his living arrangements by stating, often loudly, that he needed to be close to the vines.

And close to Mama's cooking, Lucia thought.

After lounging in bed and sipping two cups of coffee, Lucia showered, dressed, and took Annie for a late morning walk. No Pilates class today. She drove her truck over to the ranch and parked in front of her parents' two-story house. She waved to her mother, who was gesturing "come in," from the kitchen window.

"I'll come after my walk," Lucia shouted and gestured back.

She wished she had worn a warmer jacket. It was cold and damp, with dreary grey clouds on the western horizon. *No long hike today.* She had hoped to clear her head. This ... murder ... was on everyone's minds and tongues. People were on edge. The *official* theory from the coroner was that Sandy had been mugged as she went for an evening stroll near the park; wrong place and wrong time. That's what Yvonne had reported in a text. And if so, who was the killer? *Someone still in town? God, someone they might even know?* Lucia absently patted the cross she wore. With a murderer loose, she knew her mother would be pushing to have her move back in with them. Lucia would argue that she wasn't a child and that Annie would protect her. And since she was raised on a ranch, she knew how to use a shotgun.

Annie ran ahead, knowing the way as well as Lucia. They headed toward the small pastureland in the corner where the family still kept a few sheep as pets. Years ago, as children, they had all been active in 4-H, and these were the progeny of the original couple of lambs. A favorite, Flossie 4.0, was the great-granddaughter of the first Flossie.

It didn't hurt the winery's bucolic image to have some farm animals on site either.

Lucia let the dog through the two gates and stepped back out. The sheep were used to Annie and took her gentle herding as a matter of course. While Annie did her thing, Lucia placed a booted foot on the fence railing and leaned over.

"Hi, girls," she called to them. The earthy animal smells seemed stronger in the damp air.

She counted the black noses of the hefty Suffolk ewes. "One, two … six, seven." *Seven?* One was missing. There were supposed to be eight sheep. Lucia looked more closely and recounted. Seven again. *Oh, oh.*

She went through the first fence, closed that heavy wooden gate, and opened the next slatted, metal entry. Annie sensed something was happening.

"Hold!" Lucia called to Annie, using the command for the dog to keep the sheep where they were, in the corner.

The grazing area was open, and she could see all around except behind the shelter. Walking through the mud, she turned past the sheep and Annie. There, on the back side of the large, three-sided shed, she saw the missing ewe. Lying on the ground was Flossie.

The sheep was breathing heavily and trembling. She was drooling and her pupils were noticeably dilated.

"Merda," Lucia swore in Italian. "Damn, damn. Flossie!" She knelt in the muck, leaned over, and petted the ailing animal. "It's okay. It will be okay," she crooned to her.

Lucia was no veterinarian, but she had seen signs of animal

poisoning before. She got up quickly, called Annie, and rushed through the two gates, pausing only to lock them.

They started to run back to the house. Pulling her phone from her jacket pocket, Lucia called her mother.

"Mama, call the vet. Call Doc Lopez," she said, her words coming in staccato puffs in the cold air. "Get Daddy over to the paddock. Flossie is down. Looks like poison."

All thoughts of a killer were forgotten.

TEN

Stormy Weather

"TO THE BONEYARD!" BOTH GROANS and cheers erupted from the domino players sitting by the window. The Dots members were deeply engrossed in their game, and on their second cups of coffee. Empty plates that had once held rich chocolate croissants and plump blueberry muffins were stacked precariously on the table's edge.

Robin looked up from the bakery's front counter and shook her head. *Who knew that dominoes could be so cutthroat?*

The morning drizzle had deterred a few weekday customers. Lou and Steve had been waiting at the door when Robin opened at early o'clock, though. Lou ordered her usual vegan muffin — to go, this morning — and Steve munched on his free cookie; they trundled away before the rain began.

She does seem to have bounced back. No lingering stress or effects from finding the body, thankfully, Robin mused. Everyone in town was quietly keeping an eye on Lou, Robin included.

Except for the raucous Dots, it was evolving into a slow day.

And that was just fine, Robin thought. She was training a new employee. The young man, Mateo, was eager to learn and had some background in hospitality. *Okay, maybe it was a little background.* His references had been positive, though.

Robin wanted someone else working front-of-store full-time. Jen, and the other part-time college student workers, were great, but the bakery needed more consistency. She couldn't ask Thad or his assistants to pitch in; they were busy enough in the back. And, God help her, creating even more new pastries and menu ideas for a happy hour.

Robin had to admit that Mateo caught on quickly. He had mastered their point-of-sale system after two tries. She decided to send him into the fray and pointed to the noisy table.

"How about you check in with the Dots, and see if anyone wants a refill? And would you please clear those plates, while you're at it?" Robin feared the small round dishes were creeping toward a disastrous, crashing end.

"Yes, ma'am!" Mateo responded. Grabbing a towel and coffeepot, off he went.

Ma'am? Ooof. The moniker made Robin feel ancient. She'd remind him later that it was okay to call her Robin. She knew that the white streak in her hair threw off the younger employees. They couldn't pinpoint her age. She had used that genetic characteristic to her advantage back when she was a rookie reporter in the city. It had made her seem more mature then. Even "witchy" to some superstitious sources. *But this morning, maybe I could use with a little less, um, stature.*

She hoped Mateo would work out. She wanted to spend less time at the bakery for a few reasons, although she enjoyed the customers and the pace. Her mother was worrying her lately – a heart issue? There wasn't any family history of cardiac problems, so that was odd. Robin also noticed that Charlotte was back to relying much more on the walker, instead of her cane.

And to be honest, Robin needed time for herself, too. The anniversary of Patrick's death had come and gone. She lit a tall candle at St. Isidore's for him and spent the rest of the evening quietly at home. Mentally, she closed the file on finding his killers. For now. Two years; it was two years since Patrick was gone. She took off her wedding rings that night, kissed them, and placed them in her jewel box. No other rings replaced them.

The chill, damp air poured into the bakery, as the front door opened. Seeing it was Yvonne, she came around from the counter.

"Hi! I didn't expect you in today. What can I get you?"

"I just left the gym, so I better stick with coffee. Well, maybe a bear claw for later. And a dog cookie for Maddie." Yvonne unzipped her quilted navy jacket. Her short brown hair was damp and curling from the gym and the weather.

"Where *is* Madison?" Robin peered through the window to Yvonne's SUV parked outside.

"At home, still in her soft bed. It was too cold for her bones this morning." Yvonne absently rubbed her left shoulder. It ached from an old work injury that had brought about her early retirement. "I empathize."

"I'll take a break and sit with you."

Robin filled two mugs and dropped the pastry and three dog cookies into a white bag.

"Mateo, I'll be in the other room if you need me," she called.

He nodded. She noted that he was adeptly balancing the rescued plates in one hand, and coffeepot in the other. *Yes, he'll work out fine.*

One of the pleasant parts of having good friends is knowing exactly how they take their coffee, whether they love or hate raisins, and when little twitches or tics mean they are concerned. Yvonne was twitching.

They moved into the adjacent, almost empty room and sat down. The drizzle outside was threatening to spit out a cold rain. *November is coming,* it seemed to say. *Get ready.*

"Okay, what's up?"

Yvonne laughed. "Is that how you interviewed people? Subtle."

"Right. I'll let you enjoy your coffee first." Robin took a sip from her mug.

"Should I be asking *you* if everything is all right? Not to pry, but I see you aren't wearing your rings."

"Good eye, Chief. No, I'm doing better. It was time. You know?"

Yvonne nodded. They sat in companionable silence for a minute.

Then Yvonne spoke, "I saw Lucia at the gym. She had finished her Pilates class and was going to the winery. Said to say hi if I saw you."

"Thanks, I'll call her later. I should probably join the gym again, too. I know I keep saying that. You all seem to like it there. And with winter almost on us, I'm not going to get much tennis in."

"Yeah, give it another try. Oh, and Lucia told me that Flossie has fully recovered. I'm glad. I guess she ate something she shouldn't have. Lucia said the vet was pretty aggressive with the treatment. He gave Flossie activated charcoal, atropine, *and* IVs."

"I'm glad, too. Yes, for a sheep, Flossie has always been a little piggy. One reason we all love her." Robin added, "Luce found her just in time."

"So speaking of that."

"Okay, and now are we getting into what's bothering you?"

"Uh-huh. Remember how at the happy hour Scott asked me to go to his feed store and take a look at something 'weird' — his words — going on?"

"Sure."

"Well, I did. And he's right. There is something weird. Or maybe it's coincidental." Yvonne proceeded to tell her Scott and Carl's findings and their suspicion that animals had been purposely poisoned.

"That's terrible! Is that what you think, too?"

"Well, here's the thing. I'm not sure. If it is true, then we may be dealing with another sick perpetrator in the area, besides a murderer. Whether it's on purpose or not, someone, like Animal Control, or a veterinarian, needs to determine what's killing them. And Carl's agency is too busy."

"Could a vet do a necropsy and find out for sure? I mean,

find out if it's a poison?"

"Maybe. I don't know if any of the local docs could do it or if they would need to send it somewhere bigger, like U.C. Davis. Maybe I can speak with Lucia's vet first, the one they used for Flossie."

"Flossie? You think she was poisoned on purpose?" Robin was shocked. *Who would want to hurt that sweet, old sheep? A gentle pet?*

"I talked to Lucia more about it today. She said that her dad and the crew cleaned up all the area around the paddock. Mowed everything down to the ground. The vet told them Flossie got into something, all right. But there wasn't a trace of anything toxic in her feed. The other sheep were fine. They didn't find any plants nearby that were lethal. So if she *did* eat something bad that was growing by the fence, she chomped it all."

"Whew." Robin sat back. "Wait. The winery isn't that far from the feed store."

"Bingo."

"Well. What next?"

"Good question. I called Angelo and asked if he'd mind if I did some more snooping. Professional courtesy and all that. I don't want to step on any toes there."

"I'd bet the police department would be thrilled to have you handle this."

"So it appears. He said, 'Go for it.' To tell him if I learned anything. And he'd make a note for the files. I can call around to other county departments, and see if they've had incidents like this. Maybe there's some pattern. I'll follow up with Scott, too, and let him know about Flossie. See if we can make any connections."

"I'd love to help, if you need it. I'm good at research, you know." From habit, she was already mentally making notes.

"Thanks. I may call on you. Wait until I talk to a few more people."

Robin's coffee was now lukewarm. Yvonne's cup was still half-full.

"Let me get you a refill. This is cold." Robin gestured to the mugs and started to get up.

"No, that's okay. I'd better get back home to Madison." She peeked into the bakery bag. "Wow, three cookies? Lucky girl. What do I owe you?"

"On the house. Hey, be careful, Yvonne."

"I always am."

Robin watched Yvonne drive off. She then walked slowly to the main part of the bakery, weighing their conversation. The overhead lights seemed to sparkle even more brightly against the dreary day. Mateo had moved to behind the counter and was restocking a tray with warm, gingersnap cookies. The Dots had finished their game and were bundling up in jackets and coats.

"Looks like a storm is coming," one of them said to Robin.

"Be careful," she responded again automatically.

ELEVEN

Mass and the Manor

"**LET US GO FORTH IN** peace, and with a happy heart." Father Art blessed his parishioners at the end of Sunday Mass.

The town's modest church was almost full. *We're small but mighty,* he thought. *But part of the reason for the crowd lately is that poor woman's murder.* People were uneasy, he knew. Praying together was some comfort. Sandy Foster hadn't been a member of their church; the priest had quietly said a rosary for the repose of her soul, anyway.

"Amen." Lucia and Robin crossed themselves and slid to the end of the wooden pew. The organist and choir had decided to go with "Be Not Afraid" as their closing hymn.

The friends passed Noreen in the second pew. She was trying unsuccessfully to corral her two grandchildren, who had kept their fidgeting to a minimum for the last hour, and were now bounding out to play in the vacant field adjacent to St. Isidore's.

"Hey, Noreen. The kids were so good during church," Robin told her. "Stop by the bakery later, and tell Jen I said they could each have a treat on the house."

"Hi, Robin. Lucia. Thanks so much. I was going to drop by there anyway and pick up a loaf of bread for dinner. You aren't going to be at the bakery today?" She asked of Robin.

"No, Luce and I are going to visit Mom. They should be having lunch about now." Robin glanced at her watch: 11:32, it flashed.

"Oh, well, tell her hi for me." Noreen had given up on catching the children. "I sure do miss seeing Charlotte. Do you think she's going to make it back home anytime soon? Is her hip all healed? Gee, it was such a bad break."

"It's better," Robin acknowledged. "And I still want to bring her home. But she's developed some weird heart thing. It recently popped up."

The three of them were moving as a group toward the double doors, caught up in the flow of congregants leaving for home, football games, chores, and Sunday brunch. The last chords of the hymn reverberated around them.

"Well, sorry to hear that." They walked outside, to crisp October air that smelled like wet earth, leaves, and smoke from edge-of-town potbelly stoves. Noreen was glancing away from them, looking for her grandkids.

"Gotta run. You ladies take care." And she was off.

Father Art stood on the steps, chatting with parishioners who wanted to complain about his sermon, invite him to dinner, or ask for prayers. Maybe all three.

Robin and Lucia stood aside, as he was in an earnest conversation with an elderly woman who was recently widowed. The priest helped her down the few steps and turned to the two friends.

"Good morning! A wonderful morning, unless you're going to critique my homily from today." He laughed. "One parishioner timed it and said it was three minutes longer than last week. That one was already too long, according to him."

"No, no." Lucia took the lead. "Robin and I were wondering if you wanted to go over to see Charlotte with us. We'll take you to a late lunch for tacos afterward at El Sol."

"Ah, sounds good. But I have to meet with a family at one o'clock about a quinceanera. I'll take a rain check."

"Deal," Robin said.

They bid their goodbyes and had made it a couple of paces onto the sidewalk and almost past the church when Father called out. "Oh, Lucia, bring your friend Tom to Mass someday!"

Lucia waved and gave a tight smile.

"Oh?" Robin nudged her arm. "Does Father Art know something your best friend doesn't?"

Lucia rolled her eyes. "Oh, my mother or grandmothers must have ordered another novena for me," she sighed. "Isn't there anything private in this town? And yes, that was a rhetorical question."

"Oh come on, you know the saying, *'The nice thing about living in a small town is that when you don't know what you're doing, someone else does.'*"

"Yeah, yeah," Lucia muttered.

Lunch was wrapping up by the time Lucia and Robin arrived. The dining room was decorated for the season. Mini pumpkins and rust-colored silk leaves were on the tables, and a cornucopia arrangement was on the sideboard next to the coffeepots. Soothing, non-descript music hummed from invisible speakers.

They walked over to where Charlotte was seated with her friends, Bev and Jack, along with a woman whom Robin didn't recognize.

They greeted Charlotte and her tablemates.

"Hi, Mom." Robin bent to kiss her mother's cheek. "Hello, Bev. Hi, Jack."

"Oh, don't you girls look nice!" Charlotte exclaimed before even saying hello. "Bring some chairs. Sit down. Get settled."

They scooted two padded dining chairs over from a nearby empty table. Lucia's chair gave a little squeak when she sat, and Robin's had a slight wobble.

Ever the hostess, Charlotte addressed them. "I'm sorry I can't offer you some lunch." She gave a small shrug. "Help yourselves to coffee, though."

"Well, you didn't miss much at lunch." The new woman at the table spoke up. "That soup had an odd spice in it if you ask me."

"I'm sorry. Where are my manners? Let me introduce you all." Charlotte gestured. "Maisie, this is my daughter, Robin, and her best friend — and my second daughter — Lucia Ricci. Girls, this is Maisie Burnett, a rehab resident. She's hoping to go home soon."

After "nice to meet you" greetings were exchanged with Maisie, Jack interjected about the meal.

"I don't mind the seasonings. Although, they're kind of bland for my taste. What I hate, is that in summer it seemed like all they ever gave us were salads and sandwiches. Now it's soup. We need some real food!"

Jack Hanson was an imposing six-foot-plus man, a retired Professor of Botany who had stayed on at The Manor in an independent living apartment after his wife died. The Hanson family was huge, and Jack's youngest granddaughter, Jen, worked at the bakery. She claimed she was his favorite grandchild, and brought him pastries all the time.

Croissants and muffins may be delicious, but alas, not enough of a consolation. Obviously, soup and salads were not working for Jack.

He ticked off a few alternatives that used to be served under the old owners. "Beef stew, turkey and fixings, chicken cacciatore, salmon! Now those are meals," he grumbled. "Salmon," he repeated.

"Have you asked for improvements?" Robin ventured a toe into the conversation. She hadn't heard her mother complain about the food.

Charlotte gave her daughter a cautionary glance. "Well, Jack has put menu ideas into the suggestion box in the foyer, but he says they drop straight into Hades."

Maisie snorted.

"Damn right," Jack said. "I've tried to meet with Pat but she either agrees and does nothing, or is too busy to talk with me. That chef, Ricardo, is just as evasive. Says it's up to the administration."

"I told Jack we need to talk to an Ombudsman," Maisie added. "Shake things up."

"I'm afraid it's an ongoing issue," Charlotte said. She pushed her chair away from the table and reached for her walker. "Let's go outside and get some fresh air."

They picked up a light jacket from Charlotte's room, walked the short hall, and passed the photo of the deceased Sandy at the front desk. Charlotte shook her head as they walked out the glass doors.

"I wish they'd find whoever did that to the poor girl. She was so sweet. Have you heard anything more in town, or from Yvonne?" Charlotte frowned.

"No, Mom. But I do know the police and sheriff are both working on it. I'm sure you're safe here. It was just a very sad, isolated incident," Robin said, soothingly.

"There are alarms here, and the doors are locked at night, right?" Lucia added, sharing a look with Robin. "Hey, call me anytime. Annie and I will come over and keep you company if you want. I'll bring the wine. And Annie loves you!"

"That's because I keep a jar of her favorite dog biscuits on my counter," Charlotte replied. "Anyway, aren't your evenings busy with that handsome rancher, Tom Kikugawa?"

"You, too? Did my mother call you?" Lucia exclaimed, causing them all to laugh.

They wound their way to the rear gardens and Charlotte breathed deeply. "I love the autumn air. Don't you?"

Agreeing, Robin added. "Just don't get too tired out, Mom." She didn't want to discuss any recent heart issues and ruin the afternoon. Charlotte always dismissed her health concerns and Robin suspected her mother was purposely lingering at The Manor. In Charlotte's mind, she was easing any perceived burden on her daughter that way. The truth was, though, that Robin could easily afford to pay for any necessary caretakers.

And she missed her mother. But Charlotte could be strong and stubborn, in a genteel, polite way; so she stayed put. For now.

They strolled past a blue, metal sculpture of a heron, tucked into a garden bed of yellow marigolds and crimson mums. The summer's ornamental grasses had faded.

"When did that hothouse go in?" Lucia asked, pointing to the right. "Frank didn't mention anything about that at the family dinner last month." Her cousin, one of many, had been the maintenance manager at The Manor for years.

"It's been there for a while. Shortly after Pat took over." Charlotte responded.

"Hmmm. Fancy. Guess that's where your rent money is going, instead of for salmon," Lucia commented. "And all new fencing, too." Lucia stopped and eyed the tall redwood posts and slats on the creek side of the property. "Now, I know *that's* expensive. As kids, we used to be able to cut through to the bank from that path over there. Remember?" She gestured. "It looks all blocked off now."

"For safety?" Robin hazarded a guess. *To keep intruders out or residents in?*

"Probably," Charlotte said. "Well, we should turn back soon. I guess it's chillier out here than I realized."

TWELVE

Jack Hanson

MAYBE A WALK IS A *good idea.* Jack ruminated on the thought, planted by Charlotte's comment earlier at lunch. *Stretch my legs and all that.*

He made his way down the short corridor to his room, to get his hat. He wrinkled his nose at the faint, unpleasant odor of a generic sanitizer in the hallway.

Years of fieldwork as a tenured professor of botany and plant sciences ("Plant Biology") at the University of California, Berkley had given Jack an episode or two of skin cancer. His doctor had been adamant about him wearing sunscreen and a hat ever since.

"Probably too little, too late," Jack had told him. He complied, though, mostly because his late wife, Marge, insisted upon it. She had even bought him a selection of jaunty hats and caps for all seasons. He felt a bit foppish in them but would do ... still did ... anything for Marge.

Jack selected a blue plaid tam-o-shanter from the rack by the door. The pom-pom on top was long gone. He reached for a windbreaker from the small closet in his two-bedroom apartment and paused, to look at the framed photo of his wife on the mahogany dresser by the bed.

"It was soup again for lunch, Margie," he said aloud. Jack shook his head. "I was going to say it was 'slop' but it wasn't that bad. I'm turning into a crotchety curmudgeon without you, my dear." He blew a kiss to the picture.

Jack had always loved that particular photo of her on the rocky beach. In it, she was a healthy and laughing brunette, posing against a boulder, a bright red scarf around her neck. It was before her Parkinson's diagnosis had changed everything.

They had just retired to Miller's Creek, downsizing from their home in the Bay Area and moving to the wine country where they had cousins, children, and grandchildren nearby. Their first move was to a townhouse in a retirement community. When Marge's Parkinson's demanded more care, they decided upon The Manor, rejecting their daughter's appeal to move in with her and that large branch of the family. Independence had always been important to the couple.

Now, Jack could barely even drive. His eyesight was failing at ninety-two, but he still had his license. He started the Volvo up every week, to keep the battery going. He wasn't fond of taking the local shuttle bus into town, and the only Uber driver in the area was a retired plumber who was not particularly reliable; the Uber was often found parked outside the town's watering hole. Jack's family made sure he had what he needed, though, and they checked in all the time. *Maybe too much.*

At least his long legs were still strong. So he mostly ambled around the property and nearby paths for exercise and diversion. He enjoyed seeing the seasonal changes in the gardens and in the wild plants along the roadside. The recent fencing along the creek's edge had put a damper on his wanderings down there, though. Once more, he lamented how the old owners had moved to Oregon and sold the place to Pat. When his physician had also retired, Jack was left stuck with the on-site Dr. Denton Tracy. "Unctuous man," he had commented to Charlotte and Bev, his tablemates. It was a small consolation that Marge had passed away before Dr. Tracy came on board.

Sighing, Jack zipped up the jacket and walked out of the apartment and toward an exterior side door, one for residents' access only. He pushed on the brass handle and stepped outside; it locked behind him. The path from there led to the gardens, and eventually, the main road to town.

He grudgingly admitted that he was glad he wore the hat. The wind was picking up from the coast, and threatening to send grey clouds tumbling over by that evening. He decided it would be a short outing, and headed in the direction of the hothouse for a quick look.

The week prior, Jack and the maintenance manager, Frank, had one of their many discussions about the structure. Good buddies, they had bonded over their shared love and knowledge of obscure plants and native trees. Frank was naturally observant and self-taught; Jack was the more esoteric professor. They matched wits well.

"What do you think Pat's growing in there, Frank?" Jack asked for the hundredth time. "Pot?"

Frank shrugged. "I don't think so. Our water and electric

usage would be sky-high, if so." He laughed at his joke. "Get it, 'sky-high'?"

Jack chuckled. "She tells the residents she's growing 'orchids' in there. That it's her passion. *It was true that there were a lot of flowering plants inside the lobby and dining room.* "A true hobbyist would know the difference between a Dendrobium and a Phalaenopsis. And the plants sitting in the lobby are Phalaenopsis Schilleriana. Not just any 'orchids.' And why not grow something native, like Calypso Bulbosa?" He shook his head, and pointing his finger at the locked hothouse, he added, "No, Frank, Pat's not growing only 'orchids' in there."

Frank nodded in agreement. "Well, only Pat has the password to the keypad, Jack. So I guess we may never know."

"Won't stop us from trying, though, right?"

THIRTEEN

RIP Edith

EDITH SMYTHE WAS DEAD AT the respectable age of 99 and three-quarters-years-old, and nobody mourned her passing more than Pat.

Damn. Pat cursed silently. "Oh, dear, not our poor Edith," was what she responded to the CNA who reluctantly gave her the bad news early that Wednesday morning. Pat sent Dr. Denton Tracy to make sure, of course, before she called the family or mortuary.

Another empty bed. The second in two weeks. Things had been going so well! And she had such plans for Edith's upcoming birthday, too. Such grand, promotional plans.

Despite her advanced age, Edith was quite spry and everyone had fully expected she would make it to her centennial year. Pat, in fact, had counted on it. She had already contacted the local newspaper and arranged a photo shoot for that day.

"Darlene, you're a doll!" she said when she called the paper. "It will make things so special for Edith to have you here. She'll love the attention!"

On her calendar, Pat had listed the items needed for the festivities: pink balloons, a bouquet of roses for Edith, and a small, colorful (but tasteful) banner. Ricardo and the staff were to serve punch and a chocolate cake with vanilla buttercream — Edith's favorite. Fondant posies were to lavishly adorn the cake top. Pat was prepared to go all out.

Now, she was left with … ashes. That's what it felt like. No color spread in the newspaper, no photos for the website or social media. Edith had lived at The Manor for ten years, and Pat had the copy already written in her mind: *Imagine, 100 years old! It must be due to the wonderful care Edith has received here for these last ten years.* (Although, Edith's genes might have argued with that premise.)

Maybe worse, Pat had an inside lead on a small, failing nursing home in the ritzier next county over. The current owners were poorly suited for this type of business and wanted out. Now. It had been up-scale once but was now declining into Miss Havisham territory. She was preparing to pitch the purchase to two wealthy, tech investors (and to potential residents) as a glamorous, country club-style retirement home. Pat knew she could add more activities like a bridge club, and popular and inexpensive amenities such as a coffee and biscotti bar, and a happy hour. She would paint the exterior, and throw six-foot artificial ficus trees in the lobby. The locale would allow her to charge so much more than at The Manor. It was, she had thought, the next step in her business strategy. Edith's 100th birthday celebration and the attendant media hoopla had been part of her presentation.

And now, Edith had gone and died.

The second loss. Pat bit her lip and absently reached for a butterscotch from the ceramic bowl on her desk. She crunched the hard candy like it was an ice cube. Mr. Murray's impending departure was not due to death, though. After Ralph Murray's mini-stroke a month earlier, his son had talked about moving him to Washington to be closer to family. As the resident physician, Denton had expressed sincere professional concern about moving Mr. Murray right now; the son was not deterred. Ralph was leaving tomorrow. *Although,* she thought, *on the bright side, he had been living in one of the rare two-bedroom apartments.* Now, she could raise the rates for the next residents. Like hotels, "heads in beds" was the motto to success in her industry, as well. She just had to keep them here.

Something needed to be done. Now, with Edith and Ralph gone, Pat would probably have to make the dreaded circuit again, speaking to Rotary and Kiwanis. She would bring the latest brochures and photos of happy residents at Bingo or flower arranging and tout the advantages of staying local. The last time she had to do this, she had better luck with the Garden Club. More women than men were members, and the ladies were usually either caretakers of elderly mothers and mothers-in-law, or inching their own way to a comfortable retirement themselves. One broken hip and their loved one would need rehab. Pat would reassure them: *The Manor was close by, familiar, and, look: Bingo, flower arranging!*

Yes, indeed, something must be done quickly before any more damage was done, or someone else moved. Or died.

FOURTEEN

Halloween Plans

IT WAS LOOKING TO BE a glum Halloween. For the children's sake, parents may have hung silky ghosts from the porch railings and placed carved jack-o-lanterns with crooked grins on the front stoops. And true, bags of chocolate candy and fruity suckers were tucked into pantries. But the mood was dark. How could it not be, with an unsolved murder in their small town?

In late October, the city council members and local merchants assembled one evening and made a decision. A kiddie parade was hastily arranged for Halloween afternoon, after school. The parade would circle the old mill in the center of the town once, and then children could disperse to the nearby shops to collect candy, stickers, cookies, or whatever loot they could cajole. Parents were somewhat mollified; they had no intention of sending the little ones into the night to trick-or-treat this year. There was no joy in the traditional costumes and parties (or pilfered candy after the children went to bed).

Even the high schoolers' usual bravado was faltering; the October sale of eggs and toilet paper was down at George's Market, further evidence of waning mischief afoot. The school's annual, "covert" senior gathering at the cemetery (well-known and monitored by the police) was vetoed by most, although a few of the kids would surely bring beer and lie behind the mossy headstones and crypts anyway, in wait for ghosts — or murderers — to appear.

A rumored séance was to be canceled, as well (if anything like that was going to be held at all). Nobody seemed to be quite sure the where, or what — or whom — of it, though. Except that now it wasn't even going to take place. So they heard.

Robin had participated in the meeting at city hall. She was fine with providing pumpkin and bat-shaped sugar cookies to trick-or-treaters. The bakery had been offering them already in the display cases. Thad and an assistant would just bake extra. She had checked and there were plenty of individual cellophane bags in storage, and black ribbon to tie them closed. Each child would receive one, colorful cookie, bright with orange or purple sugar sprinkles. Jen had said she'd work that afternoon and help Robin pass them out at the door.

"I have some witches' hats we can wear!" Jen was oh-so-enthusiastic about their attire for the event. "Or other hats. I mean, if you don't want to be a witch. Maybe you want to be a pirate? Or, have bunny ears?"

"A witch hat will be fine, thanks, Jen," Robin responded.

Combined with her white-streaked hair, she thought she'd look quite authentic to the children. Halloween wasn't her thing, although she made sure the bakery was properly decorated for that and all the holidays. No, Halloween was more her mother's celebration. If she didn't know better, she'd have said that Charlotte and Lou were capable of hosting that (rumored) clandestine séance for their friends.

Robin had other plans for later that night. Lucia had texted Yvonne and her to come for dinner.

Hi. Come for Halloween. I'll fix something delicious in my cauldron – LOL! Robin, bring a dessert. Yvonne, bring gossip. See you around 6:30 pm. xo

She had texted back her "yes" before Yvonne responded. When she *did* answer, Yvonne's text was intriguing.

Thanks. Will be there. Went to Davis with Scott. Will fill you in — treats or tricks?

FIFTEEN

A Trip to Davis

YVONNE HOLSTERED HER REVOLVER AND tossed her paper score sheet in the trash basket by the clubhouse door as she left. She was in a pissy mood and it reflected in her day's poor shooting. *Pissy.* She had left Madison home and gone early to the Leather Oak Shooting Range, a members-only club in the boonies, miles away from Miller's Creek. Calling it a clubhouse was using that term kindly. It was a rustic structure, with some furnishings, and a kitchen.

Usually, she saw a few friends there: former and current law enforcement officers and personnel, firefighters, EMTs, and local ranchers. But it was quiet this October morning. Nobody was training or doing an active shooter drill.

Good! Yvonne wasn't in the mood for camaraderie or banter. Flossie's poisoning, and the sick, dead animals near Scott's store — in Yvonne's mind, this was no coincidence. Town residents were already on edge from the murder. When they got wind of poisoned animals too, well, that wouldn't be pretty. So far, no ranchers or veterinarians she had checked in with had reported anything unusual. Only Flossie had been sickened. *Was she targeted?* That was a sobering and grim thought.

When Yvonne had called her contacts in the sheriff's office and in outlying towns, the responses were the same: "No," "Nope," And, "Do you count roadkill?" Whatever was going on seemed centered only around Miller's Creek. *Great.* She had told Angelo she'd check things out, and she had nothing.

Cell coverage was spotty at the shooting range, and it wasn't until she had driven a mile down the mountain that her phone pinged a few times. She glanced at the readout. "Scott Phillips." *Now what?*

When she reached the one-lane road at the bottom, she pulled over into a farm's dusty driveway and hit the phone's green re-call button.

"Feed Store."

"Hey, Scott. It's Yvonne. You called?"

"Yeah, thanks for getting back to me. I found one more dead rabbit this morning. Have you heard anything? Any other outbreaks or weird animal deaths in the county?"

"Nothing."

"Okay." He paused. "Well, then. I have the body in cold storage and bringing it to Davis today. No local vets seem to be able, or want, to do a necropsy quickly. I thought you might like to go along since I got you involved."

"U.C. Davis? As in the school of veterinary medicine there?"

"Yeah. I sort of have a contact in the Department of Pathology."

"A contact?"

"An uncle. Dr. Richard Collier. Uncle Rick. He usually deals with large animals, but said he'd take a look. I have to get the body to him today. He said, 'Time is of the essence.' So do you want to come? We can make it in about two hours, I think."

"I'll drive. Pick you up in twenty minutes." Yvonne turned the SUV toward town. *This could be interesting.*

Yvonne pulled into the feed store driveway and parked. Scott was already waiting outside, sitting on a beat-up, mustard-yellow, metal cooler. He stood up, and she popped open the back of the car. He slid the cooler in and positioned it against the blankets and emergency bag she always carried there.

Scott turned and waved to an older man in overalls, who was standing in the doorway of the store. "See you later, Pedro. Thanks."

Opening the passenger door, Scott climbed in. His long legs hinged like a clothespin, with knees almost grazing his chin.

"Oh, push the seat back. I pull it up for Madison."

"No problem." Scott adjusted the lever, and it — and he — sprang back.

"Ready?" Yvonne asked. "My GPS says we'll be there in two hours and seventeen minutes if we drive straight through."

"That's fine. Hit it. We're on a mission. Like in *The Blues Brothers.*

Yvonne burst out laughing. "My God. How do you know that movie?"

"What can I say? It's a classic."

"Well, aren't you full of surprises."

After a moment, Scott asked, "Where's Madison today?"

"She didn't feel like getting out of bed. I called my neighbor, Lou, and she'll check on her. Maddie loves Lou, and will be spoiled by the time I get home."

"I know who Lou is. Must have been tough on her. Finding that woman's body."

"Yeah, well." Yvonne pushed some buttons on the dashboard. "Some R&B okay?"

"Great. Driver gets to choose, right?"

Traffic was light on a weekday morning. They drove in silence until a few miles onto the freeway. Marvin Gaye, Aretha Franklin, and Smokey Robinson made good traveling companions.

Yvonne lowered the volume in between songs. Looking straight ahead, she asked, "You have an uncle, a vet, at the University of California, Davis, *the* number one veterinary school in the country, and that wasn't your Plan A?"

Scott smiled. "I was wondering when you'd get around to asking."

"And here I thought I was being patient."

He stretched a little. "It's complicated. My family is complicated."

Yvonne glanced over. "Well, we have another two hours before Davis. And Collier? It's been a long time since I was in the Davis area. Why does that name sound familiar?"

"You probably recall seeing it on billboards, if you were in a 100-mile radius: 'Collier Sonora Beef Company,' 'Collier Inn and Restaurant.' 'Collier Sonora Dude Ranch.' " He winced a little at the last.

"Yes! That's your uncle?"

"That's my family. Mom was a Collier."

"Wow. How did you land in Miller's Creek, and not in the family business? Sorry, does it feel like I'm interrogating you? Comes with being a cop."

"Understood. You could say that I chose a different path. Got my B.S. Degree from Sacramento State in Environmental Studies. I was going for my Masters in Marine Science but got a job offer at a non-profit in Southern California, so I took it."

"Southern California is pretty far from Sonora."

"That was the point."

Yvonne let that one alone. The Etta James song ended, and she repeated. "So, still. Why Miller's Creek?"

"I had been through there a few times, driving around the area on my way to Mendocino County and the coast. It seemed friendly. I had left the original non-profit, and been the director at two others. I got burned out. Too much politics, too many boards of directors. Schmoozing for funds, scrimping to pay my staff and bills." He sighed. "Life in a small town, and being my own boss seemed right."

"How on earth did you hear about the feed store being for sale?"

"Oh, I left my name with a local realtor on one trip. You must know Tania. She clued me in. And to answer your next, inevitable, but maybe unasked question, how could I, a non-profit guy, afford it? I can thank Grandma Collier for that. God bless her. I had a modest inheritance."

He looked over at Yvonne. "Anything else?"

"Nope. That about does it. For now."

"Okay, then." Scott pushed his seat back further and closed his eyes.

The rest of the trip was low in conversation, except for comments on the music. The long, grey building housing the School of Veterinary Medicine was easy to find. Scott knew where his uncle's office was, so he led the way, with only one missed hallway detour. He was carrying the cooler, but nobody glanced at them. The passing students and vets had seen much stranger things. A faint odor of formaldehyde wafted through the cool corridors.

Dr. Collier ("Uncle Rick") was cordial in his greetings and introductions, but not effusive. The vet was shorter and stockier than Scott; Yvonne could still see the family resemblance, though. Scott placed the cooler next to a desk overflowing with manila file folders. There was an assortment of boxes adjacent to it.

Scott had evidently filled his uncle in before they arrived, so there was no need for chit-chat. Dr. Collier didn't ask his visitors to sit down. But really, there weren't too many available spots.

"Can I assume you collected and packaged the carcass correctly? It's chilled?" he addressed Scott.

"Of course," Scott responded.

"Good boy, then." Dr. Collier tapped the cooler with his foot. "You know it will take a few days to get the results back, don't you?" The older man looked at his nephew. "The gross necropsy could be available within one to four days. The ancillary testing may take longer. We're swamped right now." He waved a hand around his office.

"I understand. Thanks for doing this favor, Uncle Rick. I appreciate it. We appreciate it." Scott pointed to Yvonne.

"We do," Yvonne replied, prompted to answer (the few words she spoke).

"Well, I know you must want to get back on the road. Long drive for one day." The vet started walking them out. He stopped at the door. "Are you going to make it home for Thanksgiving this year, Scott?"

"We'll see."

"Don't break your mother's heart. Just come."

He then looked directly at Yvonne. "I hope there isn't some S.O.B. poisoning your animals. The necropsy, biopsy, and ancillary tests will be helpful and tell us what is involved. You'll have to take care of the rest."

Scott and Yvonne silently made their way back to the car and buckled in. Yvonne hadn't pushed the ignition yet.

"Well, that was fun," Scott breathed out.

"How about a quick lunch?" Yvonne suggested. "We can grab a sandwich at that place we passed off campus?"

"Yeah. Sure. My treat since you've paid for the gas here."

"It's a deal. How do you feel about NPR?" Yvonne asked.

"I enjoy it."

Yvonne turned the car on and pointed it back toward Miller's Creek. National Public Radio kept them company on the way home.

SIXTEEN

Halloween Evening at Lucia's – Part One

RICH, RED BUBBLES OF SAUCE burst like tiny volcanoes on the surface of the stew. Lucia turned down the flame under the stockpot. Reaching into a nearby drawer, she took out a soup spoon and scooped a bit of the almost-done mixture into the ladle. Tapping her foot, she blew on the sauce and waited for it to cool to a temperature fit for human consumption.

A sip. *Oh, yeah!* The autumn fish stew was coming together perfectly. Onions, garlic, parsley, herbs — all of the aromatics were singing. The wine and stock danced together. Once she added the fish, it would be a full sea shanty! And ready when her friends arrived.

—————

Lucia had skipped out of work at noon. When Halloween fell on a weekday, the tasting room was quiet; her assistants could handle it. Before leaving, she snagged one nice, serviceable bottle of Sauvignon Blanc for the stew and two award-winning ones for dinner. She made the winding 18-mile trip to the coast and found fresh cod at her favorite fish market. The fog grew heavy as she got closer to the Pacific Ocean, the air salty and calling to her like a siren. Lucia loved the beach. She lingered at the market's tiny restaurant to have a bowl of milky clam chowder. How could she resist?

On the way back, she stopped by her parents' house, up the road from hers. They weren't home, but she had a key and went into their pantry. There, Lucia liberated a mason jar of Roma tomatoes which her mother had canned that summer. The rest of the stew ingredients Lucia had picked up the day before from George's Market.

Once home, she put the fish and wine in the refrigerator, next to some artisan cheeses and salad. Tying on an apron, she started the stew and set the table with colorful Portuguese pottery and a hurricane candle.

Lucia's small farmhouse was quite clean enough. Her friends wouldn't care if there was a dust bunny here and there. She swept often, but Annie shed fur just as quickly behind the broom. The mini powder room, once a hall closet, was presentable, and Lucia added fresh towels. Done.

Robin was the first to arrive, promptly at six-thirty. Annie had let out a bark before Lucia even heard the car pull in next to her truck.

"Hi. Come in — Happy Halloween! How was the trick-or-treating downtown?"

Robin handed Lucia a bakery box and a loaf of sourdough bread. "Good. Fewer kids than we expected. You'll find some pumpkin and bat cookies in there along with an apple pie."

"Yum! Thanks for the bread, too. I forgot to ask if you could bring some. You must have read my mind."

"Something smells good." Robin walked into the kitchen and hung up her jacket. She petted Annie, giving her proper acknowledgment. After washing her hands at the farmhouse sink (an original), Robin took three wine glasses from a shelf and opened the fridge.

"Ummm, the good stuff," she commented, taking out the chilled wine.

"*Our* treat tonight," Lucia responded.

She brought the assembled cheese tray from the counter and placed it on a trunk in the adjacent living room. The heirloom trunk served as a table and sat in front of the paisley-print loveseat and two chairs. The fireplace stove, the only heat in that part of the house, was chugging along nicely. Annie followed from the kitchen, to be closer to them, the fire, and the cheese.

"Cheers!" They clinked glasses.

"So what do you think Yvonne was up to in Davis?" Lucia asked first.

"No idea. What was she doing there with Scott, is another question."

When Yvonne pulled into the gravel driveway fifteen minutes later, Annie barked but didn't move from her comfy spot.

"Well, I guess we'll know soon," Lucia said.

SEVENTEEN

Halloween Evening at Lucia's – Part Two

LUCIA GOT TO THE KITCHEN'S back door at the same time that Yvonne did.

"Trick or treat!" Yvonne shook a small white bag, with a gold and maroon emblem. "I picked up some gourmet candy from that new chocolate shop off Main Street."

"Ooh, perfect. Robin brought a Gravenstein apple pie and sugar cookies, so we'll feast like little kids tonight." Lucia opened the door wide and peered down. "Why, hello, Madison."

The old lab wagged her tail at Lucia's greeting.

"I hope it's okay that she comes tonight. I didn't want to leave her alone at the house, in case any stray trick-or-treaters come by and startle her. Although, she might not even hear them, anymore." Yvonne patted the dog's head.

"Oh, my God, of course. Annie loves her buddy. Don't you, Annie?" Lucia ushered them in.

Robin and Annie had stepped into the cozy kitchen now, as well. The two dogs wiggled and sniffed each other briefly.

Annie gave a bark, and Madison followed her into the next room where heat, soft beds, and snacks awaited them.

"I'll get you a glass of wine," Robin offered.

"Yes, settle in." Lucia pointed to the living room. "Take your jacket off. Catch your breath. Then we want to hear why you and Scott were in Davis."

Yvonne took a sip of the Sauvignon Blanc, and a couple bites of a Camembert di Pecora. A tiny bit (or two) made its way to Annie and Madison, and not so surreptitiously, either.

"Are you giving that good Carletta cheese to the dogs?" Robin asked. She petted Annie as the dog brushed by on her second trip around the trunk toward Yvonne.

"Me?" Yvonne dangled her arm over the chair and dropped two crackers.

"Spoiled doggies!" Lucia said. "But spoiled sweet, right?"

Madison sat by Lucia, earning an ear rub, and hoping for extra treats, as a favored canine guest. Lucia crumbled a piece of Irish cheddar for Madison and leaned forward.

"Okay, dinner can be ready in minutes. Start your story, and we can continue talking over the stew."

Yvonne began by describing her meeting with Scott at the feed store, which occurred a few days after the bakery's happy hour. She briefly explained to the others about the animals that Scott and Carl had found and their suspicions that animals were being poisoned. On purpose.

"I told Angelo about the potential poisonings. He wasn't

happy, as you can imagine." Lucia and Robin nodded. They knew the current police chief and his colorful personality. "I volunteered to ask around to other county agencies. See if anything else like this was happening in their communities. He gave me the go-ahead. Our department is overloaded right now with the murder, so he's preoccupied." She turned the stem of her half-empty glass. "By the way, they've interviewed all the neighbors around the park to see if they saw anything or anyone suspicious that day, or the night before. Any prowlers or vandals. Anything out of the ordinary."

"And?" Robin asked.

"Nothing," Yvonne responded. "The sheriff's department was brought in, too. This is not for public consumption yet, although that news seems to be known around town, *and* at the bakery and gym."

"Yeah, it's a gossip mill there. Sorry," Lucia shrugged to Robin.

"Anyway," Yvonne continued, "there was nothing to be found on my end either, about other animals. It ... whatever it is ... seems to be centered in Miller's Creek."

Lucia put her glass on the wooden trunk with a 'thunk.' The dogs jumped. "Flossie! Was Flossie purposely poisoned by someone? We thought she just got into something she shouldn't have."

"Lucia, I don't know. I hope not." Yvonne looked her way.

"The other animals were fine. My dad's dogs never got sick." Lucia paused. She circled a finger downwards on the trunk as if pointing to an imaginary map. "The winery, my folks' house, and the sheep compound aren't far from the feed store." Lucia continued, "The Manor is sitting between the store and them. Frank hasn't mentioned anything weird there. But I haven't seen my cousin for a few weeks."

They were silent for a heartbeat or two.

"How does Davis fit into this?" Robin asked, changing course.

"Scott wanted to find out more if he could. He had discovered another dead rabbit. He has an uncle who's a veterinarian at U.C. Davis, contacted him, and we brought the rabbit there for a necropsy. Scott asked me to go along since I had been 'investigating' this, at his initial request."

"Scott has an uncle who's a vet? At Davis?" Robin asked.

"Yes. My first thoughts, exactly. We drove there. I mean I drove. Met his uncle. He said the full necropsy will take time. Hopefully, we'll discover what toxins, if any, are in the animal's system, even if we don't know the 'who did it.' "

"I have to get my brain around this," Lucia said, standing up. "I think I should talk to Cousin Frank, and ask if he's seen anything unusual. Ladies, I'm going to get our dinner ready. We can continue this at the table. And I do want to know more about Scott."

EIGHTEEN

Halloween Night at The Manor

THE PINGING ALARM AWAKENED FRANK from a wonderful dream. He was fishing in Montana, wading into the waters. He could hear the sound of a hawk overhead. Again and again. Only it wasn't a hawk. *It's that damn alarm!*

He quickly picked up his phone from the nightstand and turned the volume off.

"ALERT – HIGH USAGE. ALERT – HIGH USAGE!" The notice flickered on the screen.

Frank looked over at his wife. Gabrielle sighed and turned on her side, away from the noise, but didn't open her eyes. *Good! No reason we both should be bothered.*

Wide awake now, Frank knew exactly what the alarm was. It was that stupid app that Pat had insisted he put on his phone to monitor the water usage and any leaks at The Manor's gardens and apartments.

"We need it to make sure that we don't waste *any* water! This system and app will be a great help, Frank. So ecological, too," Pat had told him, extolling the virtues of this marvelous device.

"We" meant Frank. As maintenance manager, it fell to him. He couldn't wait until the new guy came on board to help. *And guess who would be getting the midnight calls, then?* Not Frank. He would be dreaming of Montana.

He checked his phone again. The readout flashed 11:05 p.m. *Okay, so it wasn't quite midnight.* Frank grumbled silently.

He moved off the bed as quietly as possible and walked into the bathroom and closet that adjoined their bedroom. He pulled some work jeans, a plaid shirt, and socks from the dirty clothes hamper. His boots were by the front door, and he padded across the short hallway, weaving around their old cat who was always begging for food.

"No, Bella. Shhhh! You aren't getting any chicken. You have to stay here." Frank sat on a nearby chair and pulled on his boots. His heavy jacket was on the coat rack, still hanging there from earlier. He edged out the door, keeping Bella at bay. Gabrielle and Frank were especially careful to keep her in on Halloween. A black cat could get into trouble on that night, even an old one with a grey muzzle, like Bella.

Frank didn't expect Halloween problems, exactly, but he made sure to lock the door behind him. He looked up and down the block before he got into his RAM truck. Frank let out the brake, coasted down the driveway, and then started it up.

The last day of October was spitting out a fine mist in the dark night. Frank switched on the windshield wipers a few times to clear his sightline. The Manor wasn't far from his house. He knew exactly which drip system and valve were the problems.

In anticipation of the season's first substantial rain predicted for the following week, Frank had already turned off almost all the watering systems. *Except.* Except for the one in the corner of the gardens that had watered the late fall vegetables. Pat wanted that portion running until the very last of the onions and grotesque overgrown zucchini were harvested.

"Fall veggies are wonderful for our residents. They love them on the menu," she exuded.

Frank had jerry-rigged that one faulty system to last for another week. But it blew tonight. Well, he'd turn off the water, and deal with it tomorrow in the light. Maybe, he'd tell Pat that a brand new, expensive system was needed, just to see her sputter. *Naw, that wouldn't be very kind. It sure would be a little bit of compensation for this middle-of-the-night interruption, though.*

He parked his truck at the far end of the lot, where the troublesome drip and shut-off valve were located. No visible lights were on in the main building, except for one dim lamp in the reception area. No lamps or televisions flickered in the residents' rooms. No ghosts, no ghouls roamed around and rattled chains, either, he half chuckled. It was only a hiss of spraying water, a slick pavement, and saturated earth. Still, he took the time to look around before he switched the valve to 'off.'

The spurting water fell with a sigh. Frank wiped his hands on a handkerchief and reached for the truck's door. He stopped abruptly, hand on the handle. A noise — an animal? Faint, but a rhythmic pattern to it. Not an animal. *Footsteps.* Oh, how he wished he had hold of that baseball bat he always kept behind the driver's seat. Could he get the door open quietly? It tended to creak like a rusty gate. He stooped over, one hand still on the night-chilled handle.

Before he could decide to risk it and open the door, he saw a glint. A flashlight's beam moved in coordination with the steps. And he could make out a shape: short, round, and familiar. Someone was walking down a path forty feet away from Frank. And they were oblivious to him there in the shadows. *Pat!*

What in the hell is she doing out at this hour? Frank knew she wasn't on that alarm notification. So he crouched down a little further and watched. He should have called out to her, but that thought crossed his mind, and ran. *Why? Why engage her?* Better to see what she was up to.

Pat walked directly to the hothouse, a woman on a midnight mission. She aimed the flashlight at the keypad lock and pushed some buttons. The door opened, and Frank saw a light go on in the small building. Pat closed the door behind her.

Frank was getting cramped, and the night air was dank. *My knees and back will pay for this tomorrow. Should I get up and leave?*

About five minutes later, Pat emerged, none too soon for Frank. She was carrying something tall and large in one arm. Before she turned out the light and locked the door, he caught a glimpse of it. An orchid plant!

She was out here on Halloween night for a darn orchid? Well, if that doesn't beat all. Wait until he talked to Jack tomorrow and regaled him about this strange night. And that, despite their theories, it looked like Pat really did have orchids growing in the hothouse. Frank shook his head. *Crazy.*

He waited until he saw Pat enter the side door of the facility. The flashlight beam wobbled for a second or two and disappeared, presumably around a corner. He stood, rubbed his knees, and carefully, slowly opened the door. He kept the creak to a minimum. For the second time that night, he released the brake and eased the truck down the path. At the last minute, he turned on the ignition and headed home.

What a weird night. An orchid!

NINETEEN

Lucia Speaks with Frank

IT WAS GNAWING AT HER. Lucia couldn't get last night's conversation with Yvonne and Robin out of her head. *Dead animals. Flossie so sick! What is going on?*

As she unloaded the dishwasher, she made up her mind. She'd talk to Frank today. Check if he'd seen anything odd. She could report what he said to Yvonne.

Lucia didn't have to be at the winery until noon. There was plenty of time to drop Annie off at her folks' place to run with her dad's dogs, go to church for All Saint's Day Mass, and see Frank on her way back from town. *Yes, and I can visit Charlotte while I'm there.*

Lucia pulled a chunky turquoise sweater from her dresser drawer. It contrasted well with the black jeans and boots that she was wearing. The weather was definitely changing; the house was chilled when she got up that morning.

She tied a matching blue scarf around Annie's neck.

"You look so cute, Annie!"

The dog did a twirl and then sat, watching Lucia's every

move. Expectantly. "Action Annie," her dad called Lucia's dog. Yup, that was her. Lucia hoped a day of running in the fields and vineyards would wear off some of that shepherd energy.

"You were very patient with sweet, old Madison last night. Thank you." Annie wriggled in response.

They left right away. Lucia emptied a restless Annie from the truck and said a quick 'hi and bye' to her dad and brother, Eddy. Should she wait until later to mention what Yvonne and Scott were investigating? *Yes. Let's see what Frank says first.*

Mass at St. Isidore's was over quickly, with the pews mostly vacant on an overcast weekday morning. Before she left the church, Lucia lit one candle for Patrick and one for her family members who had passed. Now, on to The Manor.

She texted Robin before she got into her truck.

Had fun last night! Going to talk to Frank on my way to the winery. I'll check on your mom while there. Catch up later?

The country roads leading back to The Manor were gloomy this first day of November. There was a heavy, damp fog, not the kind mariners sing about, or which weaves its way through moody moors. No, this was a deep grey murkiness that weighed on a person's spirit.

Lucia pulled into the driveway and parked away from the main entrance. She decided to look for Frank in the back garden area first. If he wasn't there, she'd hunt for him in his office. She could say hello to Charlotte afterward.

The pathway had been mostly cleared of leaves, with a few strays littering the concrete walkway. A leaf blower and rake were propped by the facility's wall. Lucia spotted Frank in a corner, by the vegetable garden. Or the remains of it. Dry stalks of corn lay on the dirt. Yellowed vines clung together nearby.

"Hey, Frank!" she called to him.

"Baby Cousin! Hi — what are you doing out here? Come to see Charlotte?"

Lucia shook her head at the old nickname. "I came to see you. *And* Charlotte."

"Me? What's up? Everything okay with the family?" He put the wrench he was holding into a toolbox at his feet, and walked closer.

"Everything is fine with them. Don't worry. It's just, I learned last night about something kind of weird going on. Out in this part of Miller's Creek Road. And I wanted to ask you a question." Lucia lowered her voice at this last part.

"Weird? You want to talk about weird?" Frank crossed himself quickly. "There are strange things going on around this place, I can tell you!" He lowered his voice to match hers.

"What? What strange things?" she asked.

"You first," he told her.

"Well, I can't exactly say where I heard this," Lucia put up her hand as Frank opened his mouth. "But there have been some dead animals showing up behind the feed store, and maybe elsewhere. Wild rabbits, feral cats. There's a chance they were poisoned intentionally. And you heard about Flossie, right?"

Frank crossed himself again. "Poisoned? You think Flossie was poisoned? By who?"

"I don't know if she was, on purpose. But our property is pretty close to the feed store, and this is in the middle. Have you seen dead gophers, cats, or anything around the grounds? Or by the creek?" Lucia pointed to the fence that blocked the facility from the Coho River tributary on the other side.

Frank shook his head. "No. Nothing here. I mean nothing unusual."

Lucia was surprised at her own reaction. She felt … what … at his response? *Disappointment?* She was almost certain her cousin would have found something, too.

"I don't know about the creek side. I don't go past that fence," he added. "There's no easy access anymore."

"Why did they put the fence up, anyway? I've been meaning to ask you."

"Who knows! It was Pat's idea. One day, she had a fence company come, and – boom – it was up. She made some noise about it being for safety. And that is one high fence."

"Redwood. Cost a bundle, I bet." Lucia eyed the long stretch of boards.

"Yeah, and she's cheap. The residents used to like to walk along the banks. I mean the paths were wide and safe. The county kept them in good shape. Remember that Aquatic Walk project a few years back? There were benches, too." He sighed. "Wish I could help about the poisonings, Luce. I'll keep an eye out, and let you know."

"Thanks. It may be nothing. Don't say anything yet. There's a necropsy being done on one animal and someone is checking it all out."

Frank nodded.

"Okay," Lucia said. "So what are *you* talking about? What's weird around this place?"

"I'm telling you, cousin, that Pat is one strange bird." Frank regaled her with his Halloween tale, adding a hooting owl and bats to the scenario for effect.

"Well, I get that it was an odd time of night, but why is it a problem that she was carrying an orchid?" Lucia wasn't exactly a fan of Pat's either. The woman rubbed her the wrong way the few times she met her at functions and at The Manor.

"It's everything!" Frank tried to explain. "A hothouse that has a keypad. Who does that? Who locks their maintenance man out of a hothouse? For orchids? Where *are* all of these plants, if so? And why did she need one at midnight? They're not even that exotic." Frank was waving his arms. "Add in that fence. And she brought Dr. Tracy here, and he seems half-dead most of the time. Jack and I think she's up to something. I'm going to tell him what I saw last night, too."

"Well, don't get into trouble, or get yourself fired, Frank. You're too close to retirement."

"Yeah, I know."

"Listen, I'm going to say hi to Charlotte, and then I need to get to work. Give my love to Gabrielle. See you at Thanksgiving, okay?" Lucia gave Frank a quick kiss on his cheek. "Call me if you see anything suspicious. About *animals*."

Frank continued the weeding for another hour. The growing pile of dried plants was ready to be mulched. He had capped the problematic valve and drip that morning and planned to talk to Pat at lunchtime.

Poisoned, he thought, reverting to his conversation with Lucia. He thought of his Bella and was glad once more that the cat stayed indoors. *That's a hell of a thing. I wonder who told Lucia about it.* Robin was his first thought. Then, *I bet it was Yvonne.* An ex-police chief was the more logical guess.

He checked his phone. Noon. Frank left the gardens and went into his "office." The room was in a low building several steps from the main facility. The office held a third-hand desk, green leather office chair, and shelves for tools and files. It had been his domain for years.

Across a short breezeway from that was another building that housed the main laundry, a storage area, and a small bathroom. Frank went over and washed his hands and face in the restroom. He crossed a path and walked through the main reception lobby and straight to Pat's office. The door was closed. He knocked.

No answer. He was ready to knock again, when he heard, "Yes, come in."

Frank entered. "Hello, Pat."

Pat looked at her wristwatch. "Almost lunchtime, Frank. What is it?" She smiled but didn't ask him to sit down.

"Well, I want to let you know the last drip system we had going for the vegetables just blew. It's totally shot."

"Gone?" Pat's smile faded to a pinched line. "Can't it be repaired?"

"Nope. It will have to be pulled out and replaced with a new line, new valves, the works."

"I see. You're sure?"

Frank nodded. "I've shut everything off, and capped it."

"I guess it's a good thing that we won't need it, with winter coming. That will save on the water bills, too." She tapped a pen on her desk. "Leave it alone until spring. We'll deal with it then, Frank."

"Sure, if that's what you want."

"Yes, it is. Don't order any parts, or make plans. Nothing for now. Is there anything else?"

"No, that's it," Frank said.

"Fine. Please close the door on your way out. Remember, just leave it."

Frank left without another word and shut the door. He walked toward the dining room, hoping to find Jack. Maybe they could talk after lunch.

TWENTY

Maisie Makes a Move

MAISIE WOKE UP FEELING PUNK. Her broken clavicle had healed nicely, she thought. Sure she was still sore, especially after a day of physical therapy, but that wasn't it.

It's those damn heart pills, the ones that Doc Tracy gave me. Maisie sat up in the narrow twin bed and looked around the clean, stark room. *I never had heart ailments before I came here,* she reflected again. *This place will be the death of me if I stay. I'm going home. I'll talk to the doctor and sign myself out today.*

Feeling satisfied now that she had a plan, Maisie washed her face, did a quick sponge bath, and dressed. Her blue slip-on shoes were thick-soled, comfortable, and quiet as she walked along the vinyl corridor leading from her room to Dr. Denton Tracy's office.

She had skipped breakfast but could smell the remains of scrambled eggs and slightly burnt coffee in the hallway. The doctor's office door was ajar, and she was ready to knock when she heard voices inside. Hand raised, she hesitated and then leaned in to listen.

She recognized the voices. *Thank God my hearing is still sharp*, she thought proudly. It was Ricardo speaking with the doctor.

"We have another special menu request, today, Doctor." Ricardo addressed the physician. "Lois Rogers, Room 15. And there's a rehab transfer from the hospital arriving in a week." Maisie heard a rustling of paper. "The new admit has two broken legs. So she'll be here a while. You got all that?"

"Yes, yes. Pat will be happy," Denton replied.

"That's the goal, right?"

Ricardo nearly bumped into Maisie as he walked out of the office. "Ms. Burnett! I could have knocked you over." He frowned and turned back to glance at Denton, standing beside his beige Formica desk. "Do you need something?"

"Yes. I'm here to talk to the doc," she pointed. "But why is Lois getting special treatment and *special food* while we get gruel? What is she getting that we don't? Filet mignon? Lois has dentures!"

Ricardo shifted the folders he was holding. His mouth was tight and he looked down at Maisie. "You must have misunderstood what you heard, Ms. Burnett. Anyway, I'm not allowed to discuss other residents. Or their dietary needs. Excuse me." He hurried off down the hall.

"Can I help you, Maisie?" Dr. Tracy motioned her inside. "Are you feeling unwell?"

I feel better than you look, Maisie thought, walking into the tiny office. "I'm leaving, doc. Checking myself out. Today."

Dr. Tracy coughed. "I don't recommend that. No, not at all. You could become dizzy from your medications or have a heart episode. What if you fall when you are alone? You could break more than a clavicle." He shook his head. "It is much safer for you to be here where we can monitor you. Much safer," he repeated.

"I'll take that chance, doc."

"I urge you to reconsider. I can't authorize it."

Maisie squinted at him, a look that had caused stronger men than Denton to shudder. "Can't or won't?"

Denton glanced down at the papers on his desk. "Well, let me review the notes from the physical therapist. I suppose if she gave you the okay, then … ."

"Fine. I'll come by after lunch to sign any papers you people need me to autograph before I'm sprung." Maisie turned and left, feeling lighter than when she had awakened.

She walked toward the common area, a combination lounge, card, and television room. As Maisie drew closer, she saw Charlotte talking with someone. *I'll miss her and Jack. But I can take the bus back here and visit them. Or meet them at the bakery!* Yes, Maisie was really perking up, now.

"Maisie, come sit down. You remember Lucia? Robin's friend?" Charlotte smiled.

"Yes, hello." Maisie nodded quickly at Lucia, then blurted, "Charlotte, I'm leaving today. I'm going home."

"Home?" Charlotte answered in surprise. "Are you well enough?"

"Yup."

"Well, that's good news. We'll miss you, Maisie."

"That's wonderful," Lucia added.

"Where is Maisie going?" Jack had rounded the corner and

come up from behind them.

"Jack, she's going home," Charlotte explained.

"Today," added Maisie.

"Wow. Good for you, Maisie." Jack smiled.

"Thanks." Maisie sat down on a burnt orange velveteen chair, hunched over, and motioned for them to gather around. They folded themselves over a low, pine coffee table.

Half-whispering, Maisie said, "And listen, I overheard Ricardo saying something to the doctor about 'special menus.' They've been holding out on us. Some people are getting preferential treatment around here."

"A special menu?" Lucia said. "Different foods, you mean?"

"Yeah. *Better* foods, I bet. Somebody is getting salmon around here, but it isn't us, Jack!"

"Well, that's not right! Robin and I will look into it." Lucia patted Charlotte's hand. "We'll get to the bottom of this. Thank you, Maisie, for letting us know." Lucia stood up. "I have to get to work now. But I promise I'll call Robin tonight and fill her in." She kissed Charlotte. "Best of luck to you, Maisie."

After Lucia had left, Maisie moved and sat in the chair next to Charlotte.

"You should go home, too, Charlotte. Your daughter would take care of you."

"Oh, no. I'm not ready. She's had a lot on her mind, and the last thing she needs to worry about is her mother there."

"I doubt she would think that," Jack answered.

"Well, maybe when I get this heart thing under control. Maybe then," Charlotte nodded. "I'm really going to miss you, Maisie."

—————————

Denton, Ricardo, and Pat huddled in her office. The door was firmly closed. And locked.

"Well, we have to let her go, now," Pat said. She was sitting behind her desk, tapping a pencil, while the men stood. "The sooner the better. Sign off on any paperwork. Immediately, Denton."

The men glanced at each other.

"Fortunately for *all* of us, we have that rehab transfer coming in. I have a lead on another transfer for next week, too." Pat sat back in her chair. "Good thing I have cultivated contacts at the hospitals. I do *my* job well."

The two men shifted their feet.

"And you're taking good care of Lois, correct?"

They nodded in the affirmative.

"Denton, do *your* job. You know how to be creative, don't you?"

The doctor sighed. "Yes."

"Ricardo, write up some new menus for November. Something … exciting, tastier than originally planned, to quell any rumors. No soup these next two weeks. And post the new menus on the bulletin board outside the dining room by this afternoon."

Ricardo was taking notes. "Anything else?" he asked.

"Add extra garnish."

TWENTY-ONE

Pat Visits Lois

THE BUILDING WAS STIFLING. ALL *nursing homes and assisted facilities were*, Pat reflected. *Cold bones needed more heat.* The monthly utility bills created one of the biggest expenses for The Manor. The beastly, gaping furnace was Pat's constant nemesis.

The walls of her office seemed too close that day and almost vibrated with the excessive heat. The small oscillating fan on the oak file cabinet was not helping.

I'll take a walk outside, and get some fresh air. It's not raining. Maybe Lois will join me. Nurturing that idea, Pat closed her computer and the accounting books she had been reviewing, locked the desk drawers, and left her office. She made certain that door was locked, as well. Lunch was over, and afternoon activities had not yet begun. The heavy air encouraged naps.

Denton had sent a message that Maisie Burnett had, indeed, left. *Good riddance! That woman was trouble. Snooping at Denton's door, and quizzing Ricardo. No, it's much better that Maisie was gone before anything happened.* It did leave one less resident, and less Medicare and rehab funding, though.

Pat was annoyed and felt uneasy in her skin. *It's this artificial heat.* She turned down the hallway toward Lois Rogers' room. Number 15. A fall wreath with yellow and orange silk flowers hung on the door. Pat knocked.

"Lois? Dear, it's Pat. Are you awake?"

A pause, then a voice from within the room. "Just a minute. I'm coming."

"Don't rush."

Pat heard a shuffling, and the door slowly opened. "Pat, how nice to see you!"

"I was going to take a little walk outside. Breathe in some wonderful autumnal air. Would you care to join me? You can use your wheelchair, and we can bundle you up so you'll be nice and snug."

"Oh, that sounds pleasant. But I think I'll rest this afternoon. You are so kind to think of me. Do you want to come in for a minute?"

"Of course." Pat stepped into a space that could pass for an oven. Even though Lois's room got the afternoon sun, the tiny woman still wore heavy, sea-green sweatpants, a matching top, and fuzzy slippers.

"Please sit down over there." She motioned to a drop-leaf table by the window. "Would you like a cookie?"

"That would be delightful if it's not too much trouble."

Using her walker, Lois stepped carefully to a counter that held a mini-fridge, microwave, and sink. She reached into a cabinet above it all and brought out an opened package of shortbread cookies.

She placed four cookies on a paper plate. Carefully carrying the wobbling plate to the table, Lois presented it to her guest. The cookies had slid to one end.

"Shortbread — my favorite!" Pat exclaimed.

"Tea?" Lois inquired.

"No, this is just perfect. You need to sit down, also, Lois." The two women munched on the crunchy, buttery cookies for a minute.

"I heard that Maisie left. I'm sorry to see her go. She was what we used to call 'a hoot.' " Lois smiled.

"She had great energy, didn't she?" Pat returned the smile. "But she'd recovered well enough to return home to her apartment." Pat took the last bite of her cookie. "I didn't realize you two had become close."

"We weren't, really. She just seemed so … plucky." Lois sighed. "She's fortunate to have a home to go to. You know, Maisie doesn't have any close family, either."

"Oh, Lois. My dear, you know that this is your home now. We are all your family." Pat leaned across the table and took Lois's veined hand in her plump one.

"I know. I don't mean to be ungrateful. You and Dr. Tracy have been so kind to me. And Ricardo and the staff are sweethearts."

"Well, if you need anything, anything at all, you have to let us know." Pat leaned back in the wooden chair. "In fact, Ricardo was speaking to me earlier about what kind of foods would tempt your appetite."

"Really? Oh, I don't want to be any bother."

"Some treat you may like?"

"Well," Lois paused, "Do you think he could fix a nice

custard? With cinnamon?"

"Certainly. Consider it done! He can bring it to your room with tonight's dinner."

Lois grinned. She was missing some teeth, but two dimples still showed through her wrinkled cheeks. "Thank you!"

"Well, I'm going to go for my promenade. I'll check on you later."

Pat walked to the door and then turned. "Oh, and don't forget the notary is coming tomorrow. Just a formality. For those papers that you said you wanted to sign."

"I wrote it down there." Lois gestured to a wall calendar of serene nature photos.

"See you later, then." Pat walked quickly, almost running, to the nearest exit doors.

The air outside was bracing, and a bit of a shock. She wound her way past the back gardens and the hothouse until she had circled the paths once. She sat on a bench dedicated to long-ago, past residents: *"To Sherry and Bernard"* the bronze plaque read. Pat sat straighter. *That was an idea.* She would tell Lois that she would have a memorial created for her. *A bench? No, a birdbath or a fountain. Lois liked birds and butterflies. Really, it was the least she could do, since the woman was bequeathing her comfortable estate to The Manor.* To Pat.

TWENTY-TWO

A Mysterious Stranger

WHO VENTURES OUT SO LATE under a waning moon? A few
bats flew through the dark, roused briefly from their winter
torpor to search for moths or termites. A great horned owl
swooped silently from her perch in a redwood tree. A stray
mouse or two would do nicely for her dinner.

The slender, tall human dressed in metal grey with a black
cap walked along a path beneath them. With little light from
the moon, the person blended in with the shrubs and low
trees. Their stride was purposeful, if slow, and they tread
quietly in the low fog. They carried no flashlight, no light to
flush out an unsuspecting rat or gopher — much to the owl's
disappointment.

The pathway the person traveled curved past a bench
and dormant rose bushes, to a hothouse in front of a long
fence. Reaching the building, the solitary figure tapped at
the keypad, the faint clicking noticeable only to the night
creatures. Slipping the opened lock into a pocket, the person
entered and carefully shut the door behind them.

Only the faintest light was now visible within the structure. It wavered and bobbed. If anyone had noticed, they might have been persuaded the glow was a firefly, if such flashy creatures existed in wine country. Or a trick of the eye — a reflection from a car on the main road.

The light steadied and held for a minute. Then it went off as suddenly as it appeared.

The figure barely opened the hothouse door, and exited, sliding past it easily. They placed a tote bag on the ground. Then, they removed the lock from a hip pocket and wiped it with a handkerchief as dark as the surrounding night. It clicked shut as they replaced it on the door handle.

Now, slightly off-balance, the individual retraced their steps. The tote bag they carried was a darker shade than their grey clothing. It was heavy enough to throw their stride off a bit. The figure moved past the lattice bench, and bare roses, toward the side of the large, sleeping building, and disappeared from sight (if anyone had been watching).

The bats and owl resumed their pursuits. A human would not deter them tonight.

TWENTY-THREE

The Necropsy – Part One

ROBIN AWOKE IN A TANGLE of sheets. Wild dreams roiled in her sleep — not quite nightmares, but disturbing, nonetheless. She could recall only snippets of them: carrying a helpless, heavy child, and being lost in the skyscraper corridors of San Francisco. *A disturbing way to begin the day.*

She sat up and took a drink of water from the glass by her bedside. The matching flowered carafe was her mother's, and she liked having it nearby. Rupert, realizing she was awake, meowed loudly for his breakfast.

"Okay, Rupert. I'm coming." She served "the master" some kibble and canned cat food and freshened up his water. Then she made herself a cup of coffee. *The first of the day.* Checking her messages, she saw that both Lucia and Yvonne had texted. She had been playing phone tag with Lucia, and planned to meet her later that morning at the bakery; Lucia's text confirmed it, with an accompanying happy face emoji. Yvonne's was short and to the point. Her text read:

See you at 10am @ bakery? News of the necropsy.

Robin smiled. No emoji. Yvonne was not given to verbose or flowery missives.

The sky hadn't decided yet if it was going to rain, or bestow some afternoon sun. Whichever, it was now chilly and grey, so Robin dressed accordingly. She patted Rupert goodbye. He was already at his vantage point on the living room windowsill, looking out to the street; the block was his fiefdom.

Should I walk to the bakery? Yes, Robin decided. *The exercise will do me good and clear my mind.*

Thad was already at the bakery when she arrived. *We'll have to meet later today about the holiday orders,* she mused. Things would be crazy-busy from now through New Year's. Next week was the last happy hour until January. Customers were disappointed, but it was too hectic to juggle it all. She didn't want Thad to quit. His hefty raise had been in place for two weeks, so she prayed that would help ease the stress.

A few early morning regulars were sitting at tables, nursing mugs of coffee and cheese Danish. Only two Dots were playing a game of dominoes, the tiles clicking softly on the tabletop. The bakery's overhead lights were pools of sunny yellow, a contrast against the grey fog layered outside. Robin chatted briefly with the customers and said a few words to Mateo, her new manager. He was working out fine, thank God. She walked to the back to set up an afternoon meeting with Thad. He seemed in good form, so Robin was relieved. *One less thing to worry about.*

Robin poured her second cup of coffee of the day and stepped into her compact office, the scent of brown sugar and baking apples following her inside. She opened the laptop, preparing to go over the books and review holiday orders and supplies. Instead, she put her coffee down and sat back. *One less worry? Where did that come from? Those dreams? Am I worried about something?*

She mentally ticked off possible concerns: the bakery? No, Mateo and Thad were working well together. Her regular crew was dependable. And she had the usual seasonal help lined up, college students on their winter breaks. Patrick? Of course, she missed and mourned him. Glancing at her left hand, she noted that putting her wedding rings away had created a shift for her. Time to move ahead, to find her way through the grief without him. *So, that wasn't it.* The murder? Disturbing, for certain. But there was nothing she could do about it, other than be vigilant about her safety. The dead animals? Yvonne was covering that situation. She had offered to help if needed.

Robin took a sip of her black coffee. Her mother? *Ding, ding, ding!* Her mother! That was the nagging and now not-so-muted worry. Lucia mentioned in one of her voicemails that she had seen Charlotte, there was some issue with the food, and she would fill Robin in today. And that odd heart ailment. Yes, that was definitely a concern. Ever since Charlotte's regular doctor retired, she had relied on the physician there, Dr. Tracy. Charlotte seemed to like him well enough. But Charlotte liked almost everyone. Robin wasn't so sure of the man, herself.

Finally, it came down to this. She wanted her mother back at home. Where she could keep a better eye on her. And Charlotte would be able to resume her old social life, see friends, go to church, and to the bakery. The old customers missed her. So did Robin.

And, Robin thought, *I truly believe that Mom wants to be back, too. Well, there are a few things I can do to accomplish that.*

She picked up a lined tablet and pen and made a list. First, talk to Lucia and find out what was going on about the food. She wanted to get that straightened out right away. It was an immediate issue. Second, go to The Manor and speak with Dr. Tracy or staff about her mother's current condition and get her medical records. Third, find a new doctor for Charlotte. *Who are the top cardiologists in the county?* She'd start making some calls today. Fourth? Get the house comfortable and ready and bring Charlotte home. By Thanksgiving.

Okay! She had a plan. *Mom will be home soon.*

Robin relaxed into her chair and pulled up the list of extra ingredients and supplies the bakery would need for the holidays. People were already placing orders: for gingerbread, cranberry scones, yule logs, and pumpkin pies. So, so many pies.

At ten o'clock, there was a knock on Robin's office door.

"Come in."

"Hi. Good time or bad? Can you take a break now?" Lucia stood in the doorway. She wore a sienna-colored turtleneck, dark jeans, and her favorite boots. A mustard, rust, and black paisley pashmina scarf was draped loosely around her neck.

"Is it ten o'clock?" Robin glanced at her watch. "Sure, I can stop now. And don't *you* look like the poster child for autumn in the wine country."

"Aw, this old thing?" Lucia swung the shawl over one shoulder. "You look chic, as always."

"My basic black." Robin laughed.

"Listen, Yvonne is already here. With Scott."

"Scott? I didn't know he was coming."

"Yeah, well, he did. And he's sitting *right* next to Yvonne." Lucia fluttered her eyelashes.

"No! I think you must be seeing things. Are you seeing things?"

"Come out and judge for yourself."

The two friends walked through the main part of the bakery toward the farthest, quieter room. Robin stopped and asked Mateo to bring a carafe of coffee, cream, and a couple of mugs to their table. "Oh, and a plate of chocolate chip, walnut cookies, please."

TWENTY-FOUR

The Necropsy – Part Two

GREETINGS WERE EXCHANGED AND COFFEE was poured. Appropriate *'ooohs and ahhs'* were exclaimed over the still-warm cookies.

Lucia and Robin sat across from Yvonne and Scott. In front of him was a printed, stapled copy of an email.

Yvonne began. "So Scott called me last night." She glanced at him and he nodded. "His uncle finished the initial necropsy report of the rabbit and got it to him pretty quickly."

Scott continued. "He's a good guy — Uncle Rick — and he rushed this through for me. For us." He turned the papers to face Lucia and Robin. "I called Yvonne after I spoke to him, and filled her in on what wasn't covered here in the analysis."

Lucia and Robin peered at the report. The University of California Davis School of Veterinary Medicine logo was stamped clearly in the top left corner. The first page listed basic intake and contact information, diagnostic tests, and a section for 'Clinical and Pathological Report.' The language there was mostly unfamiliar to Robin. Lucia recognized a few terms, from a lifetime of dealing with animals on the ranch.

Robin flipped through it but stopped quickly when she came to the pages of the necropsy photos. She turned the email back to Scott.

"Can you translate this for us?" Robin asked.

"Yeah. This is only the gross necropsy," he said. "The ancillary takes longer. According to Uncle Rick, the short version is that the animal didn't have outward, visible signs of injury. Nothing congenital was found. No broken bones. It wasn't hit by a car and it didn't have any marks caused by an attack, like from a hawk or owl. Those kinds of things were not the cause of death."

"The necropsy ruled all that out first," Yvonne added.

"The initial tests did show a white streaking indicating damage to the heart muscle. That was suspicious. There were remnants of something it ingested in its stomach that still need to be analyzed," Scott explained further.

"Is that good news or bad news?" Robin asked, looking across the table at them both. She felt like she should be taking notes, and glanced around briefly for a non-existent pad and pen.

"Depends," Yvonne answered. "We know what it didn't die from. But that doesn't rule out poisoning."

"I was afraid you were getting to that," Lucia said.

"The ancillary report will take another two or three weeks, at the earliest," Scott said. "They'll test liver and kidney tissue, really do a full microscopic analysis. The postmortem toxicology will look for poison."

"What are the odds that it *is* poisoning?" asked Robin.

"Any guesses?"

Yvonne and Scott looked at each other. "Pretty good, right now," Scott replied.

"Well, great." Lucia sat back in the wooden chair. "So, maybe, just maybe, someone is out there poisoning our animals."

"That's not certain. We need … I hesitate to say evidence … but yes, more evidence," Yvonne replied. "Have there been any other problems with Flossie or the other critters?"

"No, thank God. That was enough of a scare for us. And I checked with Frank. Nothing odd has turned up at The Manor."

"And you haven't heard of anything like this elsewhere in the county, right?" Robin asked of Yvonne.

"Nope. I even checked in with my dad." She turned to Scott. "He was a county sheriff. I hated to bug him; he's a worrier." Looking at her friends, she said, "Whatever is going on seems to be centered here."

They were quiet for a moment. Then Robin had a sudden thought. "Scott, not to be indelicate, but how much is all this costing? Can we chip in?"

Scott laughed. "Thanks, but no. I'm getting the 'family discount' from my uncle. He's always liked solving the odd vet mystery."

Scott stood first, scooping up the report. "I need to open the store. But do any of you want a copy of this?"

They all nodded 'yes.'

"Why don't you email it to me," Yvonne replied. "You have my info. And then I'll forward it to them." She gestured toward Robin and Lucia. Looking at her watch, she said, "I have to run, or I'll be late for Kiwanis."

Lucia said she was staying for a few more minutes to talk to Robin about Charlotte. "But, wait, before you go," Lucia said, addressing Yvonne, "you know you're invited to Thanksgiving at the Ricci home, right? Robin and Charlotte are coming. You too, Scott, please join us. We're kind of a big, noisy family, so be warned."

Yvonne spoke first. "Thanks, Luce, but my kids are coming down from Mendocino for a long weekend. We'll be with my folks."

"It sounds fun, but I have to decline, too. I plan on going to my parents' house," Scott responded.

As they walked out together into the still-foggy day, he turned to Yvonne. "Your kids are coming? That sounds great."

After they left, Lucia shifted seats and sat across from Robin. "I need to get to the winery soon, too. That's not good news about the necropsy, though, is it?"

"I'm afraid not. I don't like it. That … and the murder still unsolved."

Lucia nodded. "I suppose it's a waiting game until those other results are in. Or something else happens."

"Yes," Robin sighed. "So about Mom?" she asked, changing the subject.

Lucia quickly explained about Maisie, what she overheard, and how some residents were evidently getting preferential treatment and meals.

Robin was incensed. "How dare they! And at what we pay them. Maisie did us a favor, by telling us. You know my mother. She never complains. God, what about the poor people there who don't have anyone to speak up for them? What do they do?"

"I knew you'd be upset. Are you going to talk to someone there?"

"Oh, yeah. Today I decided to find a new doctor for Mom and spring her from that place. Get her home by Thanksgiving."

"Good! Let me know if I can help in any way, or if you need backup. I can drive the getaway car." Lucia stood up and then hesitated. "So didn't you get a something-something vibe just then? Between Scott and our pal?"

Robin gathered the empty carafe and creamer. "Hmmm, maybe, from Scott. But you're more of a romantic than I am."

Lucia laughed and hugged her friend. She took the last cookie and wrapped it in a napkin. "For my afternoon break."

TWENTY-FIVE

Robin's Confrontation – Part One

WITH THE EXCEPTION OF TWO phone calls from a hysterical bride-to-be, the rest of Robin's day was quiet.

Thad re-directed those sorts of problem calls to his boss. His role as head baker, as he often told Robin, was to be 'creative.' As the owner, she fielded any complaints, vendor, plumbing, and equipment issues, bills, payroll, staffing, events, and ordering. She could, and did, easily run the front counter, if needed, too. Her parents had purchased the building years ago, so at least she didn't have to deal with a landlord and rent.

That afternoon, she deftly reassured the hysterical bride that, *yes*, they had received the color swatch she sent. *Yes*, they could match that particular shade of deep plum for the icing on the vanilla cupcakes for the bridal shower. *Yes*, the bakery would use gold leaf, instead of the silver dragées for decorations, since those little balls were now illegal in California. *YES*, they'd have one cupcake iced only in frosty white for the bride.

Once more, Robin blessed her mother for her decision years ago *not* to bake wedding cakes. Celebratory cupcakes were enough.

In between the bridal dilemma demands, she made calls to friends, familiar customers, and tennis buddies, asking for referrals for a new doctor for Charlotte. She gathered together a list of physicians in nearby towns, all of whom came highly recommended. If there was one thing Robin knew how to do, it was research.

At the end of the day, Robin walked home to the ever-demanding Rupert, her dinner companion. *Tuna Delight* for him, mac and cheese, and a salad for her.

Over her simple dinner, Robin decided she would show up at The Manor during the next morning's breakfast hour — not call ahead or tell her mother she was coming — and try to catch the staff and Dr. Tracy before the day's activities began. It would be a tactical maneuver to see what food was served. *Surprise!*

She texted Thad and Mateo to let them know she'd be late. And if the bride called again, to *"take a message."*

Robin loved that drive over to The Manor. It wasn't far, and today the fall colors were vibrant and the air held lingering earthy scents of recent harvests. Both humans and animals were getting ready for the next season. Roofs were repaired and gutters were cleaned. Acorns were surely stashed away, and burrows made tidy for the winter. Foxes and coyotes were growing their lush underfur. Even Rupert seemed fluffier.

Robin had loved her life in the city with Patrick. But now, the quieter, softly paced countryside of her youth suited her.

She pulled into the lot and parked close to the entrance. The lot was sparse this morning, with mostly staff cars hopscotched throughout the spaces. She had stopped at the bakery first, and put together a large box of scones and pastries, a treat for her mother and friends.

Walking in, the warmer air immediately felt heavy. Muted music played in the background. She signed in and went directly to the dining room.

"Hi, Mom."

Charlotte was seated at her usual table, with Jack, Bev, and another gentleman Robin didn't recognize.

"Robin, honey! I didn't know you were coming this morning."

"Well, I decided to surprise you." Robin pulled over an extra chair and opened the bakery box, full of its sugary treats. "Can I interest you in a Danish or scone to go with your coffee?"

"Oooh," Bev spoke up first. "Yes, I'll take a blueberry scone, if you have one."

"This one has your name on it, Bev." Using the tissue in the box, Robin placed the pastry on Bev's plate.

Charlotte and the others expressed their preferences and thanks.

"How is everyone doing today?" Robin smiled and looked around the table. She extended her hand to the new man and introduced herself. "Hi, I'm Charlotte's daughter."

"Saul," he responded. "I'm in rehab here temporarily

because of a hip replacement. Your mother, Jack, and Bev have made me feel welcome. This sure is tasty," he added, munching on a jelly Danish. "Better than this," he pointed to his plate.

"What's for breakfast today, Mom?" Robin asked, looking at her mother's dish of monochromatic food.

Jack was the one to respond. "Here's the menu," he said, handing Robin a slip of paper.

The half sheet of white paper had the date and the words *TODAY'S BREAKFAST MENU* scrolled on the top. Underneath was typed:

Creamy Scrambled Eggs

Toast and Butter or Non-Dairy Spread

Jams

Ham or Vegan Breakfast Sausage

Fresh Fruit

Decaf Coffee or Tea

Robin looked twice at the menu and her mother's plate. It didn't match.

"Mom, how does that taste? That doesn't resemble 'creamy scrambled eggs' to me." The supposedly fresh fruit looked like hunks of dry cantaloupe.

"It's not," Jack replied instead. "These are reconstituted eggs, I'll bet. Powdered. You'd think that with all of the farms around here, they could get fresh eggs. And this fruit is hard as a rock. Not even in season, and not good for old teeth." He grimaced.

"Well, the ham *is* kind of tough," Charlotte admitted. "They give us lots of jams, though." She indicated a bowl holding small plastic containers of grape jelly. "I do miss our bakery's bread and rolls," she added quietly.

Saul spoke up. "I was in here two years ago after my first hip surgery. Things sure have gone downhill. Breakfast then included waffles, pancakes, and those pie things."

"Quiche," Jack said. "Yeah, those were good."

"Oh, quiche," Bev repeated.

"When did it get so bad?" Robin felt embarrassed. How could she have not noticed it before? Or listened? She had thought … what? That it had been just Jack complaining and being a grumpy old man?

"Well, I wouldn't say it's *bad*," Charlotte replied.

"You're being too gracious, as always, Char," Jack said. He turned to Robin. "It's been like this since that Pat took over. And she brought a new chef with her, Ricardo." He shook his head. "At least I can go to my kids' for dinner, or eat out. Some others," he looked around, "are stuck."

"I can tell you, I'm not staying a day longer than I have to," Saul added. "And that doctor here gives me the creeps."

"Well, let's see what I can do about the menu." Robin stood up.

"Good luck," Jack said.

"Don't cause trouble, dear," Charlotte said nervously. "What will you say?"

Robin took a close look at her mother. Really looked. Charlotte was pale, fading into her tan sweater, which swam around her small frame. When had she gotten so frail? Or scared? Her mother had always been strong under her genteel exterior. She had run the bakery with Robin's father, and taken care of him *and* the business while he was ill. Over the years, she chaired numerous social and civic organizations and volunteered with many others. A quiet, but capable woman. Had a broken, fractured hip changed her that much?

"Don't worry, Mom." She kissed her mother's cheek. "Everything will be fine."

TWENTY-SIX

Robin's Confrontation – Part Two

DR. DENTON TRACY CAREFULLY UNSCREWED the blue cap from the amber-colored vial. His hands shook slightly as he placed one long, white tablet in his mouth. He took a couple of sips of room-temperature water from the glass on his desk. He swallowed, leaned back in his chair, and briefly closed his eyes.

It will be a long day, he thought. He looked once more at the tall pile of resident folders on the chair closest to his desk. They threatened to tumble to the floor at the slightest nudge. He had begun the project of sorting them last evening but had made little headway and gave up.

He *knew* that all the residents had received their flu shots ("*100 percent compliance,*" he had proudly reported to Pat). Now he couldn't find all of the appropriate paperwork. Also, the folder on Lois Rogers had been misfiled.

That's Pat's fault, he grumbled to himself. She had pulled it from the cabinet the other day. *And tossed it back on my desk when she was done, mixed up with the other files and reports.* At least Lois's information had finally floated to the top and was now open in front of him.

"I miss Sandy," he whispered.

The deceased CNA had been helpful with his small filing projects and other duties. She was sharp and had been attending nursing school at the time she died so suddenly. Pat didn't approve of Sandy helping him, but wouldn't hire anyone else. So she allowed Denton to employ Sandy, in a limited capacity. *Not that Pat ever paid her extra for it, of course.*

And on days when he was not quite up to par, he let Sandy dispense the meds to a few, select residents. Of course, Sandy wasn't licensed to do so. But she got along with the people there and was so capable, and well-liked. He calculated the risk and swore Sandy to secrecy. He paid her a little extra under the table. Pat would have thrown a hissy fit if she had known. Or worse.

Sandy was so good at organizing my files, he mused. Denton acknowledged he didn't have those skills. *Numbers. Now, that is where I excel.* Risk management, and columns of figures. Calculating odds and chance. No, definitely not filing. He should have a formal assistant. *Ha.* That was never going to happen.

Well, there's no avoiding it now. Denton sighed and reached for the top few folders on the chair when there was a knock on his door.

"Yes?" he answered, somewhat annoyed.

The door opened and a woman walked right in. The white streak in her reddish hair was remarkable, and he stared for a second.

"Dr. Tracy? I'm Charlotte Hill's daughter, Robin Hill

O'Connor. I've seen you in passing. Do you have a minute to speak with me about my mother?" Robin was already walking to the only available chair in the office.

Denton stood. "I, uh, Miss O'Connor, I'm rather busy right now." He motioned to the files. "Perhaps you can make an appointment for later this week."

"This won't take a minute, and my week is full, Doctor."

Robin sat, as did Denton. She observed him at close range — and he appeared to Robin to be all angles, except for his shiny, round, balding head. His face was glinting slightly with perspiration.

Well, it is stuffy in here, Robin acknowledged. She felt too warm in her windbreaker now. She slipped it off and got right to the point.

"I am preparing to remove my mother from this facility, and would like copies of her medical records and files to be ready by the time she leaves."

"Remove her?" The doctor looked shocked. "Why? To where?"

"Back to her home. Our home."

"I don't recommend that at all. Charlotte has acclimated very well here, and her condition requires more care than you can provide at home. No. And besides, I can't discuss her health or release her records to you."

"I can provide in-home care for my mother, if she requires it, Doctor. And you'll note that she gave permission for me to access all of her medical records. *And* I have a Power of Attorney that she signed. Those documents should be in her files. Would you like me to fax or email copies over to you? If you can't find them?"

Denton's face was getting moister. He took a handkerchief from a drawer and dabbed at his brow.

"No need. If you say they're here, I'll look for them. But again, I cannot sign off on her leaving."

"I believe you can, and if not, no matter. I'll have a physician lined up for her within a few days, to oversee this new heart condition she apparently has developed. My mother has healed well from her fall and hip surgery, and often only needs a cane, now. A general, family medicine doctor or her orthopedist can follow up on that."

"There … there may be rent due. She signed a contract."

"If my mother owes rent, have the accounting department bill me."

Robin stood up. "I really don't see that we need your permission. This is just a courtesy visit to advise you. I expect that you'll have all of her records in order and ready. It should be within one week, no longer than two. I'll let you know."

She reached for Denton's business card in a wooden holder on his desk and glanced at the open file lying there. *Not too discreet of him. Very poor HIPAA procedures,* Robin thought.

Denton quickly flipped the file closed. "I'll report your decision to Pat. To Ms. Breward."

"Oh, no need. I am going to speak with Pat right now, and also to the chef about the quality of the meals here lately. They seem too skimpy, and not nutritionally sound for people who have so many health issues." Robin turned around as she got to the door. "I'll be in touch soon. You have my contact information on file."

Denton shut the door as soon as Robin left. He picked up

the phone and dialed a private number.

"Pat," he said when she answered. "We lost another one."

<hr>

Robin felt giddy and relieved. Now she had to let her mother know of the decision — the *big* decision — that she had made on her behalf. Charlotte was expecting her daughter to check in before leaving The Manor. Her mother should be in her room now, reading and resting.

From Dr. Tracy's, Robin walked through the lobby and down a corridor to Pat's office. The brown, plastic blinds were shut on the half window. She knocked, but there was no answer. She turned the doorknob. It was locked. *Damn.* Robin swore quietly. She had wanted to talk to this woman face to face.

Okay, next stop the kitchen. Even if she hadn't been familiar with the facility's layout, she could have found her way there by the sound of voices, and clanging dishes. It was a definite sign that breakfast was over. The scent of coffee still filled the dining room and beyond it. She stood in the kitchen's open doorway and was jolted by the sounds and smells. It was muggy, steamy, and noisy in there, with a dishwasher whooshing, and the smell of detergent overtaking the one of coffee in the adjoining rooms.

"Hello? Hello!" she shouted above the din. "Sorry to bother you. I'm looking for Ricardo."

A black-aproned staff member approached her. "He just left." She wiped her hands on a towel, adding, "You can't come in here."

"Do you know when he'll be back?"

The woman shrugged. "No idea. I guess you can try to call him."

"Is he the only one who handles the menus, and makes the meal decisions?"

"Yeah. He and Pat."

"Okay. Well, thanks." Disappointed, Robin exited the area.

Before seeing her mother, Robin stopped in the lobby and picked up more business cards at the reception desk. All of them were stacked neatly in a plastic rack next to a lavish white orchid. This time she picked out the ones for Ricardo and Pat and put them in her pocket for later.

It was a short walk to her mother's room. The floral swag on the door was a nod to fall. She knocked but the door was already unlocked.

"Mom?" She called out to the small room as she walked in. Charlotte was sitting in a stuffed chair, one of a set from her house. Her stocking feet were up on a matching ottoman. Framed photos of family and friends crowded a nearby table.

"Hello, honey. How did it go?" Charlotte asked, an anxious note in her voice.

"Well, fine. Fine." Charlotte moved her feet and Robin sat on the ottoman, facing her mother.

"Mom, I hope this is okay, I made a major decision for you today. I'm bringing you home. You're leaving here. Soon. I already spoke with Dr. Tracy."

Charlotte's mouth dropped open. Then she began to cry.

"Oh, Mom, what's wrong? I should have talked to you

first, I know. Did I do something terrible?" She took her mother's hands in hers.

Charlotte took a breath. "I'm sorry. No, I … I didn't realize how much I wanted to go home." She sniffed and Robin handed her a tissue. "Do you really think I'm all right enough to go back home again? It won't be too much for you to handle?"

"Mom, I'm so, so sorry. This should have happened a long time ago. I was in a fog, I guess. Please forgive me. I'll arrange for a good physician in Santa Rosa or nearby to check you out. We absolutely can make this work. You'll be happier there, won't you?"

Charlotte nodded.

Robin continued to explain the plan. "I'll contact Cory. You know, the handyman we've used at the bakery? He can put safety bars in the downstairs bathroom and shower. We'll move your bedroom set into the guest room next to it, so you won't have to use the stairs and can be close to the kitchen, living room, and front door. And maybe buy a stair lift."

Robin could see the new arrangement in her head. "We can get a caregiver to come in and fix your meals and help you out when I'm at work. Lou and your friends can walk over and visit. Whatever you need. I can guarantee the food will be better at home. And Rupert will be so happy to see you."

"Rupert. My best boy." Charlotte smiled. "Are you sure?" she asked again.

"Yes! I've missed you, Mom. And so has Rupert."

TWENTY-SEVEN

Maisie Returns Home

MAISIE THREW THE FOLDER FROM The Manor into the trash bin under her sink. She still had good aim.

"Quacks!" she muttered to herself. "All of those people there are quacks!"

It had been two days since Maisie returned to her apartment; she was slowly getting organized.

"I feel better already," she said more loudly, as she watered the one semi-dead plant on the counter. Stronger, more like her old self. *And no more of those damn heart pills.* The few that Dr. Tracy had given her as a "parting gift," she had washed down the sink. "Good riddance." Okay, maybe she still needed an aspirin or two. *That was it!*

Besides the broken clavicle, Maisie had ended up with an egg-sized bump on her head from her fall. It was barely noticeable now. She was "lucky," the doctor in the emergency room had told her then; there was no concussion. *Good thing I have a hard head*, Maisie laughed to herself. *In more ways than one.*

Yes, Maisie had been accused of being stubborn, but she wasn't a fool. That fall had left her feeling vulnerable, but she was *not* going back to The Manor under any circumstances. *No sir!*

She called the physical therapists to let them know she was home and to set up her next appointment. She had only a couple of weeks of PT left, anyway. Maisie assured the young receptionist on the phone that she was faithfully wearing the sling, as was directed.

Next, she called the orthopedic surgeon's office and confirmed that appointment. *Maybe the doctor can check on my ticker when I go in.*

She hung up the phone and squinted as she surveyed her apartment. *Eh.* It had gotten dusty the few weeks she had been gone. Maybe more than a couple of cobwebs appeared. It didn't matter. She was home! And she would have returned from rehab before now if Doc Tracy hadn't told Medicare that her heart was acting up.

I can heat something to eat. Can still take care of myself. As long as I don't have to lift anything heavy, I'm good. Yup. I'm okay.

While Maisie had called a cab to bring her home, it hadn't taken long for her neighbors, Buddy and Vicky, to learn she was back. Vicky was soon at her door with a bag of groceries.

"Here are a couple of necessities to tide you over," Vicky greeted her, stepping directly into the living room/kitchen area. She set the brown bag on a drop-leaf table and unpacked the items.

"We're so glad you're home, Maisie!" Out came one loaf of bread.

"You were missed here around The Bird." A dozen eggs appeared next. That was followed by jars of peanut butter and jam, two cans of tuna, a mini container of instant coffee, some low-sugar canned peaches, a quart of non-fat milk, two cubes of unsalted butter, and three cans of chicken noodle soup.

"We didn't expect you back so soon." A bag of lettuce emerged.

"Buddy would have picked you up, you know." A bottle of Italian dressing was the last to materialize.

"Is there a rabbit in there, too?" Maisie asked, peering at the food covering her small table.

Vicky laughed. "Do you want one?"

"What do I owe you for all this?"

"Oh, Maisie. Nothing! Just wanted to get you started."

"Well, I appreciate it." Maisie tried to shrug and winced a little. "I, uh, also appreciate your visiting me at that place."

"Of course. Sorry I couldn't get over to The Manor more than once. It seemed nice enough."

"Hmmph. Have a seat."

Maisie motioned to a chair by the window. Vicky sat across from Maisie, who had now settled into her comfortable, tweed recliner.

"Looks can be deceiving," she started. "I found out that director is cheap! Stingy with food for some of us, but I guess the *elite* residents there got fancy meals. The 'chef' was always lurking around, watching what we ate. If he wants a review, I'll give him one! And let me tell you, that doctor is an odd duck, too."

Vicky shook her head. "That's too bad. I didn't realize it was like that."

"I couldn't get out of there fast enough. And I already feel better." She reiterated her private thoughts.

"Well, being home will do that. You *look* better. What about your heart ailment?"

"Pfft. I wonder if that snake oil doctor was even right."

"Well, you should have it checked out anyway, to be sure." Vicky looked around. "Do you want me to put the food away? Need me to dust or mop for you?"

"No," Maisie shook her head. "No, thanks. I'll manage."

Her neighbor stood up. "If you need anything, let me know. And you stay put, I'll let myself out."

Maisie took her time placing the groceries in the refrigerator and cupboard. *Yes, that was thoughtful of her. Vicky. And Buddy's a good neighbor, too, in his own stoic way. Always ready to give me a ride downtown.*

She reflected that the only things she'd miss about being at The Manor were not *things*. Not that food. And God, not Bingo, or the forced activities. No, it was Charlotte and Jack. And Bev. She felt they were all together in the trenches over there. Comrades in arms, so to speak.

Char kind of reminds me of my sister, too. And Jack was a character. *He made us all laugh at the absurdities there.*

She had even been invited by Charlotte and Robin to Thanksgiving dinner at the Ricci's house. Imagine that!

Charlotte had called Maisie the previous evening, to check

that Maisie was doing all right. And to say that she, too, was going home soon. There was delight in Charlotte's voice.

"Lucia and her family love a big crowd." Charlotte told her about the Thanksgiving plans. "Lucia said specifically to invite you to dinner. You can come with us."

Maisie heard Jack's voice in the background. "Or if she needs a ride, we'll find one. No need to be alone."

Surprised, Maisie thanked Charlotte and said she'd let her know.

As she placed the three cans of soup alongside the two tunas in the cupboard, Maisie pondered that conversation. Every Thanksgiving since she lived at the Hummingbird Apartments, Senior Center volunteers had dropped off a to-go container of turkey with stuffing, cranberry sauce, and green beans. She presumed that was going to be her holiday meal again.

But a *real* hot meal? With *all* the fixings? And pies?

Yes, she just might go.

TWENTY-EIGHT

Yvonne Plans a Party

YVONNE WAS SITTING IN HER home office. *My only office since retiring.* Awards and plaques hung on walls painted a soothing café au lait color.

There were tabs, and emails open on her laptop and second monitor, and she felt a headache coming on. Yvonne had been going through the Kiwanis holiday party files for over two hours and needed a break.

Maddie was asleep on her plaid dog bed, next to the Craftsman desk. Yvonne stepped over her dog and walked the few steps into the neat kitchen of her older ranch-style home. Two aspirin and one glass of water later, she was back.

She opened a window to let some cool, late afternoon air inside. There was more than a breeze, but not a full north wind blowing outside. The wooden blinds clicked back and forth, bumping the sash lightly. Maddie stirred but didn't open her eyes.

"Oh, you heard that, did you?" Yvonne smiled at her doggie companion. More and more grey fur was showing every day around Maddie's muzzle. Yvonne hoped and prayed that it wouldn't be a tough winter for the old gal. She placed a throw blanket over the dog, who resumed her snoring.

Back to the project, and the many, many lists. *How did I, of all people, end up in charge of the holiday party,* she asked herself for the hundredth time. *Why me? I'm the least suited for this.*

She knew the answer. The chairperson, Arnold, had broken his femur. He would be recovering at his son's home in Humboldt after he was released from the hospital. The next in line, Felicia, had decided abruptly to retire to Nevada and a drier climate. Alonso was in retail, and this was his busiest season. Somehow, the event trickled down to Yvonne. And the venue the club had previously chosen closed suddenly a week ago when the owner went bankrupt. So that was out. The usual places had been reserved months prior, she knew. Yvonne had called every possible spot in Miller's Creek, and the next two towns over. Even the bakery was booked for that night, for their employee and family party.

She rolled her shoulders. Her usual duties in the club were organizing the setup and cleanup crews. Distributing beverages at the golf tournament. Things like that. Yvonne would never consider herself the typical harbinger of *ho, ho, ho* glad tidings. And yet. And yet, here she was, with Arnold and Felicia's notes and files from past parties in front of her.

Lucia would be better at this. Lucia, who never met a holiday she didn't like. Except Lucia wasn't a member of Kiwanis. *Darn.*

Wait! Yvonne had a brilliant idea.

She started to text and then decided a phone call was more appropriate. She scrolled down until she found the number she wanted, and hit 'send.'

"Hiya. What's up?" The voice on the other end responded.

"Lucia! I'm glad I reached you. Are you with a customer or do you have a minute?"

"It's a lull, I have some time. Is everything all right?"

"No. Well, yes. But no. I'm in a jam."

"Okaa-ay. Want to explain?"

"Luce, I ended up in charge of the Kiwanis' holiday party. Arnold is in the hospital, Felicia split, Alonso is slammed, and the hall that we had closed down. There's no place to have the party. Can we use the winery? Please?"

She gave Lucia the date and times. And begged.

"Wow, that's just around the corner! Here at the winery? We don't usually have outside events here, you know. I should probably run it by Dad. Get his imprimatur. We wouldn't be able to cater it, though."

"That'd be okay. The caterer is still lined up for the night; you know Misty, she's great. And it's only hors d'oeuvres and her famous tiramisu cupcakes. She'll supply plates and utensils. We'd pay for the wine poured, of course. And do cleanup. Whatever you need from us. I know how beautiful the winery looks in December. It's magical! We could bring in some decorations, though, if you want."

"No, thanks." Yvonne pictured Lucia shuddering at the idea of plastic trees amidst her natural, winter woodland scape.

"It's for a good cause." Yvonne wheedled a little. "All those toys we collect for the kids … ."

"Oh, play on my heartstrings, why don't you." There was a pause. "Have you tried the church and Father Art? You do have an in there."

"I called my cousin first. Unfortunately, the hall is already booked that night for the kids' Christmas pageant."

"No room at the inn?" Lucia chuckled. "Sorry, I couldn't help myself."

"Har, har."

Yvonne could tell Lucia was warming to the plan. She laid out the logistics and other details.

"Okay, you sold me. Listen, let me phone my father and break it to him. I'll call you right back. I think he was in the club a long time ago. So he may feel benevolent."

"Thank you! You could become a member, too. Join up before the year ends?"

"Nope, I have enough to do with the winery organizations I belong to. And please note that I am *not* a board member or chair there, either."

"I know. It was worth a try."

"Oh, before I hang up, and forget to tell you, Robin is bringing Charlotte home from The Manor. Probably in the next week or so. By Thanksgiving."

"That's so great."

"I know. There was a problem with the food there, per one of the other residents. Maisie – do you know her? Not enough or a poor quality of food. I don't have all the info. Only that Robin has had it with them, and is pulling Char out. She has to do a few things to make the house safer first. Robin's getting a new doctor for her, too."

"This sounds better for both of them. They need each other," Yvonne responded.

After the goodbyes, Yvonne sat back in the chair. Her headache was much better.

She worked for another twenty minutes. The wind had picked up and the blinds were chattering now. She got up to close the window, just as her phone rang.

Reaching with her free hand, she pushed the green button.

"Hi. Are we ready to party?"

"Excuse me?"

It wasn't Lucia.

"Hello?" She looked at the readout: *Scott.*

"Scott? I'm so sorry. I thought it was Lucia calling."

"And ready for a party, it sounds like."

"Well, the Kiwanis holiday party. Long story."

"I'm sure it's an interesting one."

"A frustrating one. But resolved, now. I hope. Oh, have you heard from your uncle?" There was an upbeat tone in Yvonne's voice.

"Well, that's what I'm calling about. I talked with him. The ancillary reports aren't in yet."

"Oh, darn."

"Right. And my employee, Pedro, found another feral cat. Dead. I let my uncle know, and thought I should tell you, too."

Yvonne sighed. "Thanks. I've been a little distracted lately." She looked at the files on her computer. "But I haven't forgotten about the poisonings. *Hypothetical* poisonings." She corrected herself.

"In fact," she told him, "I've been thinking about hiking behind your place and the winery, near the creek bed. See if there is anything out of the ordinary. Anything odd. Or suspicious. I don't even know what I'm looking for."

"I'd like to join you. I mean it's happening in my backyard, on my property. I've checked before, of course. But you're the professional."

"Okay." She looked at her watch. "It's already getting late and will be dark soon. Want to meet tomorrow morning around eight o'clock? At your store?"

"Sounds like a plan. It's pretty muddy back there now."

"I've got boots. See you then. Thanks for the call."

TWENTY-NINE

Pat's Losses

THE GREY AND MISERABLE AFTERNOON matched Pat's grey and miserable mood. She had just hung up from speaking with the two retired tech gurus from San Francisco. They were *supposed* to be investing in the facility in nearby toney Marin County that she wanted to buy. Now, they were backing out.

"We wish you luck, though," the older one (*what was he, all of thirty-five years old?*) had told her.

Luck! Apparently, investing in a craft, whiskey distillery startup was more glamorous than using their multi-millions for an "old people's home," to use their phrase. *Luck.*

Pat missed being able to slam down the phone. Pushing a red button on the device was not nearly as satisfying. Although, she did forcefully close her office door on the way out. Pat passed the reception desk and brusquely told the young woman there to take a message if anyone wanted her.

Deciding against a walk in the heavy mist, she drove straight to her apartment. It was located in a modest three-story complex on the outskirts of town. There was a neat, concrete inner courtyard, with a salvia ground-cover border.

Pat walked up the three flights to her corner apartment; it was the only concession she had made when she rented it. The corner was more expensive but gave her some semblance of privacy. Like the car she drove, nothing about the building's exterior was ostentatious or flashy. There was a lot of tan and beige, like she wanted. No need to call attention to herself.

It was the middle of the day, and she assumed most neighbors were at work. It was always a quiet building, where people were too busy, or introverted to snoop around.

Pat turned the key and switched the alarm off. She placed her large black, serviceable purse on a bench in the short hallway, next to a pale-yellow orchid. Removing a flash drive and file folder from a zippered compartment in the handbag, she walked into the extra, back bedroom, turning on lights and lamps as she went.

The room smelled slightly musty. Pat pulled the blinds closed; she needn't have bothered. The room overlooked a wide alley, and aside from the street sweeper's truck rolling by and scooping up soggy, fallen leaves, nobody was near.

The office space was basic, with no photos, or knick-knacks adorning the scant shelves. She unlocked the bottom right drawer of the desk; it slid open easily. A ream of copy paper and a few lined notepads sat there.

Pat took those out and tossed them on the tan-carpeted floor. She jiggled the false bottom loose. From under that, she pulled out a manila envelope with two passports, and two matching driver's licenses. The top set was for her given name: Patricia Ann Breward. The second set had the name shown as "Anna Del Bosque," a wry twist on Breward. Her last name meant 'a wood on a hill' in Old English. And bosque was the Spanish word for woodlands. It was her little joke. The Del Bosque passport had come in handy in Mexico and Guatemala.

"Hello, again, Anna," she chuckled. Her first laugh of the day.

A burner phone and a hefty envelope of cash were placed neatly beneath, along with bank statements and credit cards matching both passports.

Reassured, Pat added the new file folder and flash drive to the drawer and replaced the false bottom and other contents. She locked it, walked into the living room, and sat on her brocade sofa, a leftover from The Manor.

She sighed. *Well, what's the body count?*

She knew that Charlotte was leaving soon. Denton had reported the conversation with the "pushy daughter" who was asking questions about the food, Charlotte's condition, and wanting medical files. *Too nosey.* Maisie was gone but she had been a troublemaker, so no love was lost there.

She reflected on the year's losses: Edith, Ralph, and a handful of others; Saul had just left for another facility. Charlotte had been a "private pay" resident, a guaranteed, higher monthly income for them. *Damn.*

Now? One new rehab patient was arriving; he'd be there a while recovering. Another one or two were anticipated. That could change.

But the anticipated cash from those tech investors had gone 'poof,' upsetting her private plan to inject money into

The Manor and to set up a grander place in affluent Marin.

Well, at least there's Lois. Pat glanced back at her office. The notarized copy of Lois's trust and Last Will and Testament was secure in the bottom drawer, as was the flash drive with the scanned versions.

After the signing, Lois had expressed comfort knowing that her (substantial) estate would go toward assisting less fortunate residents.

"It's like a charitable fund, an endowment that I'm leaving, so to speak. Isn't it? To help other seniors without a family," she had said, a little teary-eyed. "Not that I'm ready to go, yet."

Pat would administer the money, of course. *I do like Lois,* she thought. However, any real sentimentality had shriveled in Pat long ago.

Now what? She reflected again. Things hadn't worked out in Miller's Creek like she had thought. Her fault, maybe. She had forgotten how small towns were, with everybody in your business. Fewer opportunities.

Ricardo's still following the game plan. She snorted. *He should be. He's paid well enough.*

But Denton. Denton was acting squirrelier lately, ever since the move from Reno. *The old fool should be grateful to me for saving his ass. Maybe I'll have to remind him and reel him in a little.*

She shifted around on the lumpy sofa. *If I stay.*

THIRTY

An Advocate

IT WAS THE "HOUR OF the wolf," and Robin awoke with a start. She looked at her nightstand clock: *2:18 a.m.*, it blinked.

She had been used to waking up in the middle of the night. After Patrick was killed, she barely slept. But lately, she'd been able to get a good night's rest, even for an early riser like herself.

She tossed around the bed for a while, then, giving up, walked into the kitchen, with Rupert padding quietly behind her. Robin rummaged in the back of the pantry for a box of chamomile tea.

"There must be one in here. Somewhere," she muttered to the cat. He had no comment and was of no assistance.

Finally, she found it behind an old box of instant cocoa mix. Robin microwaved a mug of hot water, added the tea bag, and sat at the kitchen table, wrapping a plush bathrobe tightly around her. Rupert wandered back to his bed since no snack was forthcoming.

It wasn't Patrick's ghost that had disturbed her sleep tonight. She was sure of that. What was bothering her? She took a sip of her tea; it was mild and soothing.

It had been a busy couple of days, maybe she was still wired. Between the holiday demands at the bakery, and getting ready to move her mother back home, there had been a lot going on. The handyman had installed the grab bars in the downstairs bathroom and switched out the guestroom bed with her mother's. Clothing could be moved into the closet and drawers as needed. Slippery throw rugs were washed and stored away. The chair lift company was due in a week, but for now, her mother could manage without that appliance. Robin had stocked the fridge with her mom's favorite foods and had ready-to-eat meals in the freezer. She had a referral to a top cardiologist in Santa Rosa, and an appointment for next week.

Yes, it had been hectic, exciting, and the right decision. She was sure of it. Still, she felt uneasy. Robin got up, found a lined tablet by the phone, and decided to write. What flowed from her mind to the pen, then to paper was:

There's something weird going on at The Manor. Who is Pat? Where did she come from? What is Dr. Tracy's background? Who can I call and check on this — city, county, or state agencies? The Senator? Make a list!

So. That was it. Her reporter's instincts were working the night shift, nudging her awake.

I know that Mom will be fine here at home. But what the hell has been going on there? I think it's been problematic since Pat took over. Mom seemed content with the old owners. I should have seen this all before now. And dealt with it.

Berating herself once again, Robin closed her eyes, breathed deeply, and thought back. Yes, she had surely been immersed in her own heartache. After Patrick's death, she went to a grief counselor, upon her mother and Lucia's urging. She lived in the city then, and every neighborhood coffee house, restaurant, and theater became off-limits to her. Too many happy memories now were shattered. Grocery shopping was an agony. Seeing people, anyone, was like a slap in the face. *Why were they alive and Patrick wasn't?*

On one level, Robin knew it didn't make sense. But she couldn't seem to help her feelings then. Her journal entries from that period were raw, too painful to read now. But writing had helped. At least, it clarified for her that the temporary leave from her newspaper job must become permanent. So she sold their home and moved back to Miller's Creek.

She had done a good job managing the family bakery; it was almost by rote. And she thought she was taking care of Charlotte well, too. But was she?

Well, she could make some amends now. What about those other residents at The Manor who didn't have anyone to watch out for them? Charlotte's friends over there? They needed an advocate.

They had one now.

THIRTY-ONE

Yvonne and Scott Investigate

THE RIVER WAS STILL LOW, but turbid from the recent, early rains. After a few years of drought, everyone in the county was eagerly awaiting the predicted December downpours. The creeks, river banks, and hillsides were muddy enough, though, creating a happy haven for frogs.

It was a mostly clear morning, with the fog having rolled back to the coast. At 39 degrees, it was still "see-your-breath" kind of weather, though. A few cranky crows perched in the nearby oak trees, arguing amongst themselves, and eliciting faint rebukes from the chickadees.

Scott greeted Yvonne with a cup of coffee when she arrived at the feed store, a few minutes early.

"Hi. You take it black, right?" he asked, handing her a thermal cup as she stepped out of her SUV.

"Yeah. Thanks." She wrapped her gloved hands around the steaming cup. "How did you know?"

"I might have noticed from the other day at the bakery. I made it at home. Hope that it tastes okay." He held a similar cup. "Glad to see you're bundled up."

She was, too. Her Eddie Bauer fleece-lined jacket, gloves, and wool beanie felt just right. Jeans, navy turtleneck, wool socks, and old boots completed her poison-hunting ensemble. She noted that Scott was also dressed warmly, although flannel seemed to be his preferred style choice. His black boots were scuffed and worn and had remnants of dried, red adobe mud on them.

"I suppose Maddie is asleep at home?" He glanced toward her SUV.

"For sure. She's been fed, emptied, and was snoring on her bed when I left." Yvonne took a sip of the coffee. "Cinnamon?"

"Well, 'tis the season, huh?" He shrugged. "So where do you want to start? I don't have to open up until nine-thirty today."

"Let's go to where you first found the dead cats."

They walked to the right, and behind the feed store, their boots crunching on frosty bits of gravel and rock.

"Here we are. The first one was over there, under that scrub bush." Scott pointed. They had reached the farthest end of the property which ran parallel to the creek. "I've searched and looked around, as you know," he said. "And yesterday I installed cameras aimed back here. I'm pissed that I … we … can't figure out who is doing this."

"Or 'what' is responsible." Yvonne had pulled her phone from a side jacket pocket. She scanned the area and began to take photos.

"Here, let me hold your cup. Spot something special?"

"Thanks. No, it's a habit from when I was a detective.

Maybe I'll see something later that I don't catch now." She aimed the phone's camera nearer to the bush, did close-ups, and then focused further to the east.

"So do you think the poisonings are, like, organic? Is that your theory?"

"I don't know what to think. I mean, the local vets haven't sounded any alarms about new diseases. No other towns that I checked with have upticks of poisonings."

"I've probably been more focused on these poisonings," Scott said. "Still, can't ignore that murder, either. I mean, I do realize they could be connected, somehow."

"I know. Miller's Creek isn't usually a crime-ridden town," Yvonne answered.

"Well, I guess we have three possibilities." Scott ticked them off. "One, there is a sick bastard who murdered a woman and is killing animals. Next, two separate people are committing these crimes. Finally, there is one murderer, and the animals are dead by some other means. Like ingesting something they shouldn't have."

"The problem is, which one?" Yvonne responded.

"I know from growing up on the ranch, and from the feed store, that critters can get into foul stuff sometimes. But," he laughed, "my professional background was more about plankton than poppies."

"Right. Marine Science guy. I guess we have to wait to hear from your uncle."

They walked along quietly for a while, Scott looking right and left, Yvonne snapping pictures as he pointed out where the other animals were found.

"How about we head to the winery next?" she suggested, as they approached a neighbor's fence line. "Lucia said we could snoop around where Flossie was poisoned."

"Sounds good to me." He checked his watch. "I have to be back in about an hour, though."

"Let's drive to the winery, then, instead of hiking," Yvonne suggested. "And maybe stop near The Manor, and check out the area behind there — if we have time afterwards."

"The Manor? Was there an incident there that I haven't heard about?" They made their way to the store's entrance.

"Not that I know of. Lucia's cousin Frank, who works there, said he hadn't seen anything odd. But it's in a straight line along the route, you know? And close. It sits between you and the Ricci property. Checking it out seems … ."

"Thorough," he added.

"Yeah. Thorough."

"Want to take my truck? It's already covered in mud." Scott indicated an older model Chevy parked in front of the feed store. It had the dents and dirt to prove it was a genuine, country vehicle.

"Sure. Okay."

Scott was already opening the doors; the passenger one creaked loudly. Yvonne was used to driving and it felt weird to be a passenger. She climbed in and pushed aside some hay on the seat.

"Sorry," he said.

"It's fine. I'm used to Madison's fur. Hay won't hurt."

Scott turned the truck to the east, and drove on the almost deserted road, past The Manor, until they reached the

Ricci property. Two roads diverged beyond the main gate; one paved, and one covered with pea gravel. A large sign proclaiming *Ricci's Redwood Grove Vineyards* was posted next to the smoother road. Yvonne directed Scott to the other side, taking them to the main family compound.

"Lucia said her mom would be home this morning, and to check in with her first, before we trek around."

He nodded and guided the truck over a few minor potholes. Two cattle dogs met them as they neared the house, barking an alert to the resident inside.

Carmen Morales Ricci opened a side door of the two-story home, shushed the dogs, and waved hello. In her late seventies, she looked like a shorter version of her attractive daughter.

"Yvonne! Come inside with your friend, and have some coffee and pan dulce before your hike."

"I should have warned you," Yvonne leaned over and whispered to Scott, before unlocking the door. "There's no use refusing, and whatever she made will be delicious, anyway."

He smiled, and they walked together into the warm kitchen.

Yvonne introduced Scott, and at Carmen's urging, they sat at a large table covered with a royal blue patterned oilcloth. Carmen placed two heavy mugs of coffee in front of them; napkins and a plate of assorted pastries appeared next.

The hostess sat across from her guests, eyed Scott up and down, and said, "So you're the new bachelor who's breaking hearts in town."

Scott nearly spit out his coffee. Yvonne smothered a laugh.

"I ... I'm sorry," he answered, wiping his chin. "What?"

"Small town," Carmen shrugged. "Word travels fast about a newcomer."

"I haven't broken any hearts, Mrs. Ricci," he said, gathering his composure. "I promise. Really. I'm just putting in long hours at the feed store and getting settled here."

"Hmmm. Well, I have a niece — a wonderful girl — who I could introduce you to." Carmen glanced over at Yvonne. "Unless?"

"Oh, no! No, Mrs. Ricci. We're, uh," Yvonne waved her hands. "Scott and I are working together on these possible poisonings."

"Well, keep my niece in mind, then," Carmen instructed Scott.

Blessedly for him, the conversation turned to Flossie's close call, how the old sheep was faring, and finally, to the unsolved murder in town.

"I worry about Lucia living alone, but she's stubborn, you know. Is there any news? Are there any suspects?"

Yvonne shook her head. "Angelo and his department are working on it day and night. The county sheriff, too. No leads. Yet. Please don't worry about Luce. She's careful and has Annie with her at night. For all we know, it was committed by a transient who is long gone." Yvonne tried to reassure the concerned mother.

"I hope you're right." Carmen sighed. "Well, I'll wrap some pastries for you to take home. Pick them up on your way back from the paddock. You know the way there, right?"

"I do. Thanks, Mrs. Ricci. We'd better get going."

They left the coziness of the kitchen for the chilly air and took a pathway that led them to the double-gated paddock and grazing area.

Yvonne gestured. "Lucia said she found Flossie over by the far side of the shelter." As before, Scott searched the ground while Yvonne photographed. After twenty minutes, no magical answers appeared, and they walked back to the house. They picked up their pastries from Carmen and drove back to the main road.

"We can still swing by behind The Manor if you want. I can be a few minutes late opening up."

Yvonne nodded. "Okay. But we can't access the land via the facility anymore. They fenced it off. I know of an old haul road that could take us there, though."

"Point the way," Scott said.

They turned onto a narrow, dirt strip to the left of The Manor. It dead-ended at a large field, now faded to pale winter whites, with spotty patches of green. They concentrated on walking the creek bank first.

"Not much sign of humans around here," Scott commented. "We haven't seen old bonfires, trash, or even transients."

"Well, when I was chief, the worst thing that happened was high schoolers skinny-dipping in summer. Or a New Year's Eve party on the beach with booze and fireworks. Otherwise, this stretch is pretty quiet. Maybe an occasional fisherman."

"All I see are plants, scat, and evidence of wildlife." Scott stopped and pointed toward the fence. They had reached the edge of the property. "Looks like a bench of some kind up there."

"Oh. That was built a long time ago for the residents to use, for them to sit and enjoy the water and meadow. It's a shame it's blocked off and they can't use it now."

"Take a look?" Scott suggested.

"Yeah."

They cut through the field, with the creek's effluvial scent at their backs. A dormant rose bush was planted next to the weathered bench; other straggling, forlorn plants were on the opposite side.

No dead animals, no bones, no bodies.

It was time to call it a day. Or a morning, at least.

THIRTY-TWO

The Stranger Admires Their Handiwork

WHAT A TREASURE!

They seemed so innocuous to the untrained eye, these items purloined from the hothouse that November night.

Liberated is a better word. Because they could provide some freedom if used correctly.

And they were now tucked away carefully where no prying eyes would ever see them. Nurtured. Cosseted as they should be, given their potential value.

Nobody had seen "the theft," except the nocturnal creatures scurrying along the ground or who were flying overhead. Although, this was a far lesser crime than others committed recently.

Wouldn't Pat be livid if she knew they were missing? That they had fallen into the "wrong hands?"

No cry of outrage had been forthcoming. So she didn't realize it, yet. *Would she?*

Yes, there was some deep satisfaction in knowing that Pat would be apoplectic. More in the idea that this could be her undoing.

She thinks she's so clever. That nobody else knows the code to the hothouse. Or about her secret accounts. She's always thought she was smarter than everyone else ... the staff, residents, the people in Miller's Creek. The people in those other facilities, too.

If the citizens here knew the truth, well, they'd run her out of town on a rail.

I know the truth. I know it all. The dirty schemes, the illegal tricks, and fraud. The misery caused.

"Pride goeth before a fall." *And Pat was certainly full of pride.* And headed for a fall.

Me, too, I guess. Mea culpa. But this will be on my terms.

It will be a laugh, a delight, to see her get what she deserves. And what did she deserve? Ridicule, hate? Of course. Destitution? Prison? Most certainly.

No cell block for me, though. I'll be long gone before it all plays out for Pat. Dear, dear Pat.

THIRTY-THREE

Pat Makes a New Plan

FRANK WAS LOATH TO KNOCK on the office door, but it had to be done. He could hear some noises beyond, so he knew she was in there.

Here goes.

"Pat? Pat?" Frank rapped on the wooden door.

"Yes, what is it?" A voice from within.

"It's Frank. I, uh, need to talk with you about a problem."

There was the sound of a metal file drawer being slammed shut.

"Just a minute."

Pat opened the door and stood in the frame. "Yes?"

Frank was a head taller than Pat. He took one step back, cleared his throat, and began.

"I'm sorry to have to tell you this." *Boy, she doesn't know how sorry I am.* "But the main water heater is going. It gets a lot of use, and, well, it's old. We've patched it up as best we could in the last few years. It won't last much longer."

Pat's eyes narrowed. "What does 'not much longer' mean,

Frank?"

"Well, not through this winter, for sure. Maybe not even through December."

"December. And what do you estimate a new water heater will cost me?"

Frank had already done some calculations. "Could be anywhere from $10-20,000, depending upon the model and quality."

Pat blinked. "Outrageous! That's much too high. Get some other quotes. In the meantime, figure out ways to keep this one running."

Pat closed the door before Frank had time to respond.

"Yes, ma'am," he muttered, now alone with his marching orders.

———————

This is it. Really, a sign. Pat pondered the situation. She crunched down on a butterscotch candy, grinding it to fine amber crystals.

The news about the water heater followed what had been a disturbing morning phone call. An old contact with the state, an insider who worked with Medicare was on the line.

"Pat, I think you should know someone has been calling around, checking on your license and work history. Looking for any violations or irregularities," the woman said. In the background were traffic noises, car horns, and the hum of motors.

"Who?" Pat raised her voice to be heard. "Who is it?"

"I haven't found out yet. I can't dig around more until next week."

"Not sooner?"

"Sorry, no."

"All right. Let me know what you discover. And anything else you hear."

"Certainly. And as always … ?"

"Yes, you'll see a deposit in your account by tomorrow."

Pat had hung up shortly before Frank's intrusion. Now she had two troubling things on her mind.

Yes, the water heater was one. But the more urgent issue was someone snooping around. Pat locked the office and left for a walk. She needed to clear her head.

Think! Always have a Plan B.

Pat once had a fleeting notion that The Manor might be the first in a group of assisted living and nursing homes, a little empire all her own. Then the deal in Marin went sour, and with it, the cash injection for The Manor. And that upscale place would have been her showcase, the link to purchasing others and impressing investors. Through her contact, she knew of a couple of facilities in the state ready to go under, and available to be bought on the cheap.

I could have done this. Now, somebody is on my tail. Is it someone in town? Or from the past?

She found herself walking toward the hothouse. Once there, she looked left and right before entering the code. Nobody else was out on the grounds on this foggy morning.

Pat flicked on the light. The moister air of the hothouse made her glasses steam up, and the earthy scent was more intense in here. Plants were lined up neatly, orchids on the left, others on the right. Separate. Distinct.

Pat ran her hands gently over a blush pink orchid. She picked it up.

"I choose you," she whispered to it. Carrying it carefully, she turned and flipped off the light. Doing a double take, Pat turned the light back on and looked around.

Was something different? Out of place? No, that's impossible.

She locked the door and walked to a nearby bench, placing the orchid beside her.

"Plan B," she said aloud. It wouldn't have been the first time she had to pivot.

She had begun her career as an altruistic young nurse in Nebraska. However, old age was big business. And she was a quick learner. Such unwitting mentors she had.

First, she saw how staff would purchase second-hand wheelchairs, add fancy cushions, and charge Medicare and patients the full rate for a new chair. Cutting corners on food — that was easy. It was a little harder billing for doctor visits when there were none, but it could be done. Creating a cozy relationship with certain shady for-profit hospice companies was another trick, yielding a kickback for every resident who signed up for services they didn't yet need. There were ways to charge rehab residents extra and to extend their stays, too. She knew the ploys by now.

When she was younger, Pat was attractive in a Midwestern

girl-next-door sort of way, or so she was told by the lonely elderly men in the facilities where she worked. Some gentlemen were more than happy to leave their pensions to a pretty girl who gave them attention in their last days.

As she grew older, she saw it was advantageous to get a few more credentials and licenses. She was smart, and it wasn't hard. Those extra degrees got her hired without much of a background check.

In these later years, she took on the role of a daughter to those souls without family. Why not? It made them content in their dotage. And eventually, Pat was compensated, too.

Lois, though. Lois's "endowment" would be the largest windfall so far. It would be the icing on the cake if Pat could leave with that nest egg.

No, she couldn't walk away yet. Not without sweet Lois's bequest.

Pat picked up the orchid and walked toward the side doors. Perhaps a visit was in order.

How are you feeling, Lois?

THIRTY-FOUR

Bringing Charlotte Home

ROBIN REMOVED HER RED-FRAMED reading glasses and placed them next to the laptop.

"Your mama is coming home today," she said, turning to Rupert. The cat was dozing on the hardwood floor, having found a triangular patch of winter sunlight.

My mama, too.

Robin turned back to the computer and printed out the spreadsheet she had organized for the following week: which friends were stopping by and for how long, who was bringing lunch, and who was dropping off a casserole for dinner. Charlotte would insist she was fine alone, but Robin didn't want to chance it. At least, not at first, until she could gauge how her mother was doing.

Everything was in place for Charlotte's return. All would be right in their little world again, and before the holidays, too. In time for the bakery's party, also, where Charlotte would surely be fêted by the staff members and their families.

Robin checked her watch. Nearly ten o'clock and time to

leave for The Manor. She wanted to spring Charlotte before lunch, pick up her medical records, and have her mom back home by the afternoon. She had taken the day off from the bakery, despite it being their busiest season.

"Call or text me with any questions or problems," she had told Thad and Mateo. "I can run in, if necessary."

They had harrumphed and assured her they could handle things for the day. So she was off duty, and free to spend the time with her mother.

She turned on some lamps to give the house a welcoming feel, fed and petted Rupert and checked her phone for messages before she closed and locked the front door. Nobody had called. Not the bakery. Not Lillian, a colleague from her days at the *San Francisco Tribune & Times*.

Googling Patricia Breward had turned up precious little. There were a handful of local blurbs from when Pat had become the new owner of The Manor, citing her "extensive experience," but without specifics. There was a press release from the Garden Club announcing Pat as that month's featured speaker, and extolling her "love and appreciation of orchids and the entire family Orchidaceae." The white pages sites that Robin found showed scant personal information, other than Patricia was single, and had lived in the Midwest, Nevada, Southern California, and Mexico. No family members were listed. Robin couldn't even find a traffic ticket or late library book fine linked to Pat. Next, she tried searching for Dr. Denton Tracy. His license was active in California, and he, also, was currently single (divorced) and had lived in Nevada.

Hitting a wall, Robin placed a call to her friend Lillian's direct line at the newspaper.

"Lil? Hi. It's Robin."

"Hey, stranger," was Lillian Chang's response. "How are you doing up there in the hinterlands?"

Robin laughed. "I'm okay. You know, busy with the bakery, and my mom. Settled in."

"Well, we miss you here. You should come down to the city sometime after the New Year, and we can go to lunch in North Beach."

Robin could hear the newsroom chatter in the background and felt a quick pang for her old life.

"I'd like that. Or you could come to Miller's Creek and go wine tasting with me. I'll play tour guide and take you to some great spots. You still like a good Pinot?"

"You know I do. Twist my arm. We'll get together one way or another soon. But I know you. And *you* didn't call just to chat. Right?"

"True. Do you have a minute now, or are you on deadline? I'm hoping you can go through old files in 'the morgue' and do a little digging for me."

Robin gave Lillian all the information she had on Pat and Denton, which wasn't much. And more importantly, she provided the 'why.'

Wrapping it up, Robin told Lillian, "Thanks, I have a hunch something isn't right." Lillian promised to see what she could find."

Now it was time to pick up Charlotte; there was no news

yet from Lillian. *Soon, though,* thought Robin. *If there is anything to be found, Lil will latch on to it.*

When Robin arrived at the facility, she signed in at the front desk (with yet another new receptionist), and went straight to Denton Tracy's office. The door was ajar. Denton was seated behind his desk and raised his head as Robin knocked. It appeared that nothing had been moved since Robin was last there. Folders still sat precariously on cabinets and chairs.

"Dr. Tracy. I'm checking my mother out now, and would like her records."

Denton stood. His eyes looked left and right. "Ms. Hill. Uh, O'Connor. This is abrupt. I can't pull them at a moment's notice."

"You were given considerably more than a moment, Doctor," Robin responded. She gestured to the disarray around them. "Don't you have an administrator here to handle these requests?"

Denton cleared his throat. "There was. She left a few months ago. We're hiring someone new in January." He sat down but didn't invite Robin to do so. "The girl who died, Sandy, had been assisting me. Then there was her unfortunate accident."

"Accident?" Robin asked. She sat down anyway on the closest empty chair.

"Demise. Whatever it was." Denton waved his hands. "That is neither here nor there. The point is that I simply cannot provide the information that you are requesting today. I'll put something together and mail it to you within a week or so."

Robin stared at him. It was the look that had brought

recalcitrant interviewees to spill all. Denton coughed and turned away.

"I believe it is our legal right to have those medical records available upon discharge," Robin said.

"Well," Denton pushed some papers around. "Well," he repeated, "as you can see, I am overwhelmed. I have patients to attend to. And more important things to do here than filing, or paperwork."

Robin slowly stood. "I'd like those records to reflect that my mother is leaving today. Without the necessary files. There is no need to mail them, Doctor. I'll be back the day after tomorrow to pick them up. Surely you can have them ready by then."

She left without another word and strode down the hall. *Arrogant jerk! This place is a mess. Where's the admin staff? Having up-to-date records is vital. Vital!* Robin was huffing like an indignant steam engine by the time she reached her mother's room. *I should file a complaint today with the county or our Senator. Maybe I will.*

She stopped, took a breath, and put a smile on her face. "Mom," she called as she knocked. "It's me. Are you ready to go home?"

THIRTY-FIVE

In the Ricci Kitchen

THE KITCHEN SMELLED HEAVENLY. LUCIA stood next to her mother, creating the tamales that would become only a *part* of the upcoming Thanksgiving feast. She breathed in the scent of onions, garlic, broth, chiles, and her mother's magic.

"Mama," Lucia said, pushing up the sleeves of her sweater. The teal blue wool had dustings of flour and masa after a half-day of cooking. Her apron had even more traces. "Mama, I'm almost afraid to ask, but don't you think we have enough tamales here?"

Lucia looked over at her mother's kitchen island. Pale yellow corn husks were piled high — some filled with the long-simmered tomatillo-chile sauce and chicken, others with corn and cheese for the vegetarian guests. The stack, to Lucia's eyes, was growing exponentially.

Carmen turned to her daughter. "Really? Enough? You're the first one to ask for leftovers."

True. "I know," Lucia responded. "But there's going to be the turkey, stuffing, salad, green beans with pine nuts, mashed potatoes." She ticked off the list. "Frank and Gabrielle are making manicotti. Robin said she was bringing the rolls and pies. I know somebody else is down for fresh crab if it's available. Or calamari, if not. I forgot who has appetizer duty."

Lucia gestured to the list that Carmen had posted on the refrigerator. It noted the dishes to be served, the preparation schedule, and who was bringing what. While it wasn't on that list, Lucia knew her mother would inevitably make a flan or two.

"I won't have anyone starve at my table," Carmen huffed. Lucia rolled her eyes.

There was a slight commotion at the kitchen door, as Lucia's father, Roberto, and her brother, Sal, trudged into the kitchen, carrying two folding tables. Lucia could hear Annie barking outside, accompanied by the other family dogs.

"Smells good!" Roberto sniffed the spicy air. "Make plenty of tamales this year, honey. We hardly had any leftovers last Thanksgiving."

"See? See?" Carmen said, elbowing her daughter. Lucia groaned. It was going to be a long day in the kitchen. She had slipped off her boots an hour ago.

Carmen directed where everything should be set for the upcoming dinner, pondered, and then decided they would need at least one more table.

"Don't forget the card table. I'll need that for serving. And you might as well bring the wine in, now."

The men trundled out, in search of more tables from the barn. Lucia could hear them discussing how many bottles of wine and which vintages, as they left.

"Bring in some of the Estate 2017 Pinot," Lucia called after them, just before the door closed. She saw her father wave.

Lucia and her mother continued to work comfortably in tandem, having cooked side by side since Lucia was a child. Ray, her middle brother (and Lucia's favorite one, if she were to admit it), also had a knack in the kitchen, and would usually join in for holiday preparations. But he was out of town on winery business and not expected back until Thanksgiving morning. So it was only the two of them.

When Carmen was satisfied that there were enough tamales, they quit.

"Sit down. I'll make us some coffee," Carmen told her only daughter.

"I can do it, Mama." The look Carmen gave her made Lucia plop her bottom onto the nearby wooden stool.

Carmen started the espresso coffee maker, then reached into the oversized refrigerator and pulled out an assortment of cheeses, salami, a small jar of cornichons, and butter.

"Get the bread," she told Lucia, who turned and pulled a loaf of crusty French bread from the counter behind her.

Soon, they were eating a late lunch, sipping hot coffee, and admiring the day's culinary handiwork.

"I'm so glad that Robin is bringing Charlotte here for Thanksgiving," Carmen commented, taking a bite of creamy, coastal brie. "It's good that she's home again. I suppose we'll see her at the bakery more often, now."

"I know that Robin is relieved. She said things are bad there at The Manor. Poorly run. She hadn't realized *how* bad."

"That's a shame. Well, Frank hasn't been happy since that

new owner took over."

"Robin is thinking of filing a formal complaint with the county authorities. I guess the food has been meager, and recordkeeping is a mess. Maybe neglect. Who knows what else?" Lucia spread some tangy goat cheese on a slice of bread.

Her mother shook her head. "It had been such a nice place. Frank's oldest sister, 'Aunty Cristina,' was there before she passed, remember?"

Lucia nodded, and stood to clear the island of the lunch remains.

Carmen walked around Lucia to the large farmhouse sink and began to wash dishes, pots, and pans. Soon, bubbles of lemon verbena soap frothed to the top of the sink. Lucia was at the ready with a clean towel.

"It's too bad Yvonne can't join us for dinner. I'll miss seeing her," Carmen said, scrubbing a plate. "Oh, and I met that good-looking man she brought with her the other day. Scott. The feed store owner. You know, he'd be a nice match for your cousin."

"Mama!"

"Well, he would. Yvonne said they weren't dating. Although a younger man like that might be good for her."

"Mama, really!" Lucia repeated. "Do *not* play matchmaker. Please."

"We'll see." Carmen handed Lucia a plate. "Did your friends find anything interesting in the field that day?"

"No, not that I've heard. Yvonne took lots of photos, but I don't know if she's had a chance to go through them yet. Or even if they'd show anything useful. Maybe it's a coincidence, you know — Flossie getting sick at the same time as those other animals."

Carmen raised an eyebrow.

"Yes, you're right, Mama," Lucia said in acknowledgment, as she stacked the clean dishes on the island. "I don't think so, either. Not a coincidence. There's something that doesn't feel right about it all."

"First, that poor girl's death. Then this?" Carmen made a quick sign of the cross, drops of water falling from her hand. "We're lucky Flossie is fine now. But … ."

"You know, maybe I'll call Doctor Lopez tomorrow, before the holiday weekend, and talk with him. See if our vet has any new opinions on what happened to Flossie. Other than she ate something she shouldn't have."

"Well, I don't think your father pursued it beyond that. It was kind of chaotic then, all those treatments, and we were just happy she pulled through. Sweet little Flossie."

"Sweet *big* Flossie! Let's face it, Mama, she's fat."

"Chubby," Carmen responded, giving Lucia a stockpot to dry.

THIRTY-SIX

A Threatening Note

ROBIN ARRIVED AT THE BAKERY before five o'clock in the morning and it was already "all hands on deck." They were opening early, and Robin braced herself for the thundering hordes to come.

The day before Thanksgiving was their busiest of the year, and it appeared that everyone in town had ordered pumpkin pies, apple tarts, loaves of cranberry bread, or buttery potato rolls. Sugar cookies iced like turkeys or pumpkins were also in demand.

Robin had stockpiled and labeled her stash, and the boxes were stored deep in the back of the third refrigerator; her contribution to the Ricci feast. She greeted the staff as she walked in, and gave a short "go team" pep talk that was mostly ignored by the busy crew. Then, she unlocked her office, and sat at her desk, a double espresso nearby.

Her manager, Mateo, swooped in and handed her yesterday's mail.

"I'll be out there to work the front, as soon as we open,"

she assured him. He had a bit of a deer-in-the-headlights look. His first holiday season with the bakery had begun, and it was a baptism by fire, flour, and sugar.

"It will be okay," she added for his benefit. "It always works out."

He nodded and kept going.

She sighed. *How did Mom and Dad do this for so long? They had been troupers, to be sure.* Robin had left her mother sleeping comfortably in the downstairs bedroom. Charlotte knew the holiday routine well and had to be dissuaded from coming along at the crack of dawn.

"Sleep in! That's what retirement is all about," Robin had told her the previous evening. Charlotte was appeased only when Robin had promised to pick her up after the morning rush.

"I'll swing by before lunch and bring you back to the bakery. You can help then." *Or maybe just sit and visit with the customers.*

"I'm fine, you know. The doctor said so. You heard her."

They had seen the cardiologist the day before, and Robin was still digesting the information. The physician *had* given Charlotte a good report, overall.

"From what I've seen, the EKG showed no tachycardia, AFib, or arrhythmia. No history of any of that either. Your lab tests from yesterday were in range." The doctor checked the computer screen. "You do have slightly elevated blood pressure. We'll monitor it. I can increase your Lisinopril dose a little. And you'll need to come in for regular blood work."

When the doctor questioned *why exactly*, they had been so concerned, neither Robin nor her mother had any tangible answers, nor any medical reports or paper trail from The Manor, either. There was only a vague diagnosis Dr. Tracy gave to Charlotte in the summer. He had told her she had some undetermined cardiac issue that he was watching. Even the Lisinopril prescription was from her old physician who had retired, not from Tracy.

True to her word, when Robin returned to The Manor to collect her mother's records from the doctor, he was nowhere to be found.

"Out ill," the latest receptionist told her. Pat's office was locked up tight, too. *Of course.*

This new cardiac specialist looked askance at their explanations and reiterated: besides recovering from her broken hip, Charlotte was doing well — for a woman her age.

On the drive home, Charlotte was relieved and ebullient. Robin was quietly furious. *No evident heart problems. Why were Mom and I led to believe by Tracy that there were? It's malpractice! Scaring an elderly woman like that. Are there others he misdiagnosed?* She feigned a happy appearance for her mother's sake and decided to deal with the good doctor and Pat in her own way. After the holiday weekend.

And now there was the bakery to run, with all the inherent issues of missing or late orders, frantic customers, and overworked staff. Robin checked the store's voicemail, opened her laptop, and scrolled through incoming emails, both hers and the bakery's. Only a couple needed her attention today.

Then she spotted one: *From Lillian Chang.* Her newspaper colleague. It was a short message referencing Pat: "*Sorry, I haven't found anything much on P.B. yet.*" Lillian noted that mostly what she saw was a record of a peripatetic job history: registrations and licenses in the Midwest, New Mexico, Nevada, and California. A gap in there, too, right before Nevada. Lil said that she would keep looking after Thanksgiving. "*Love to your mom,*" Lillian signed off.

Robin closed the laptop just as her phone pinged. There was a text from Lucia. She was an early riser today, too.

Hi. Talked to the vet about Flossie. He thinks Flossie may have eaten milkweed or oleander. Some kind of "cardiac glycoside." (What??) Hmmm, not sure of that. We haven't seen milkweed on the place in years and have NEVER planted oleander! But some similar plant, maybe? Talk more tomorrow. BTW, found out that when my mom was at Farmers Market, she invited Tom to come to Thanksgiving! Blessedly, he has other plans. But he may stop by on his way to his sister's. Ack! I texted him 'save yourself,' but he thinks it will be "fun" to meet everyone. Fun! Oh, Lord. xo

Interesting about Flossie, Robin thought. Interesting and weird. *Cardiac?* The rest was good for a quick morning chuckle. Lucia had been trying for months to keep her sort-of boyfriend, Tom Kikugawa, away from the force that was the Morales-Ricci clan. Carmen was just as determined to gather him into the fold. Robin's money was on Carmen.

She checked her watch. *Almost time to go out front. One more chore.* Robin had drunk three-quarters of her coffee by the time she got to the mail that Mateo had dropped off. She thumbed through the pile quickly. It was the usual collection of bills, vendor offers, and requests for donations. She'd open them later. One plain white envelope stopped her. There was no return address. Her full name was typed on the front: Robin Hill O'Connor. Under that line, before the bakery address, it read "PERSONAL!!" That was odd. A complaint? Maybe she should open it and check, in case a regular customer was offended that their scone didn't have enough blueberries, or the Danish was short on jam.

Not a complaint. The one-page note exploded in extra-large font:

The police and coroner are idiots. YOU'RE an investigative reporter – INVESTIGATE. Don't be a fool. Who do you THINK is responsible? No coincidences.

Startled, Robin dropped the letter onto the desk. *What the hell?* She looked again at the envelope. It was postmarked locally. The letter had no signature. *Who sent this?*

Mateo knocked at the open door. He cleared his throat. "Robin? I hate to bother you. There's already a line of customers waiting to get in."

"I'll be right there. Thanks, Mateo."

Well, now what? Robin stood and called the police chief but got his voicemail. She left a short message, took a screenshot of the letter, and texted it to Yvonne and Lucia.

Just got this! Creepy. Swamped here at the bakery. Yvonne, can you pls forward to Angelo? Talk tomorrow – or later?

Robin folded the letter and placed it back into its envelope. She decided it was probably safe in her office, but she locked the door on her way out. No time to deal with it now.

The clatter of pans and the scents of cloves, nutmeg, and vanilla accompanied her to the front of the bakery. Unlocking the glass front door, she switched the sign to OPEN.

"Showtime!" she called to Mateo.

THIRTY-SEVEN

Thanksgiving Day

MAISIE HAD ALREADY SHOWERED AND eaten her breakfast of oatmeal and milk, with a mug of decaf coffee. Now, she had one slippered foot wedged into her tiny closet, while she pushed the wooden clothes hangers first left and then right with a *clack, clack.*

She was searching for a specific sweater; one that she knew wasn't torn, worn, or stained. Her deep grey pull-on slacks were freshly laundered and waiting on the bed. But finding this particular decent top was proving elusive. She turned to the cedar dresser in her bedroom. The furniture there had once belonged to her mother, with nicks and dings reflecting its advanced age. Maisie bent down with a grunt and pulled open the bottom drawer.

It's here somewhere.

Bringing out two mufflers, one pair of wool gloves, and a sack of pennies, she finally found what she was after, a wool sweater with a blue and red Scandinavian design that zig-zagged around the collar. She shook it out and brought it close to her eyes.

No moth holes. That's cedar for you!

It certainly beat the sweatshirts that were her usual attire. *And just the thing for a Thanksgiving dinner at the Riccis.* She didn't want to embarrass her new friend Charlotte, after all. Pleased, Maisie finished dressing in time to watch the annual Thanksgiving Day parade on the television and waited for her ride. A 4-inch pot of marigolds was by the door, the hostess gift she had purchased at George's Market the day before.

Promptly at noon, her front bell rang. Maisie turned off the television, switched on a lamp, and opened her door.

"Hi, Maisie. Happy Thanksgiving. Are you ready to go?" Robin was bundled up in a maroon coat against the sunny, but crisp day.

"All set." Maisie handed Robin the plant, put on her jacket, and locked up. Robin's hybrid sedan was parked almost in front of the apartment, and Maisie could see Charlotte in the front seat, waving at her.

She climbed in the back, found the seatbelt, and they were off.

"You look good, Char," Maisie told her, leaning toward the front seat.

"And I feel well. So much better," Charlotte turned her head to the left to see Maisie. "You look great, too."

"Thanks. And Char, I've been itching to tell you my news. I saw my doctor and he said that there is nothing wrong with my ticker. Nothing!"

Robin looked quickly at Maisie from the rearview mirror. "Really, Maisie?"

Charlotte gasped. "I can't believe it. Me neither. I was going to tell *you* today. I went with Robin to a cardiologist this week. She told us the same thing. No heart issues. Isn't that something? Both of us. So lucky."

Maisie uttered a mild curse. "I knew it. That Dr. Tracy is a phony. They're all crooks over there."

"Robin, did you hear what Maisie said? Her heart is fine, too."

"I did. That is *wonderful* news for you. Something else to celebrate today, right?" Robin smiled at her two passengers. She kept her immediate thoughts to herself. Today was not the day.

Robin pulled up behind three cars and two trucks parked already in the gravel driveway. Her mother had insisted she could walk the short distance to the house. She had brought her walker today for extra stability, in case. But since being home, she was back to using a cane. The three of them crunched along the path to the farmhouse. Everyone used the kitchen entrance, so they headed in that direction. The door was opened without them knocking by a preteen girl who said "hi," and swept past them, running toward the barn.

"Who was that?" Charlotte asked.

"One of the many Ricci or Morales cousins, I guess," her daughter answered.

Once past the threshold, the cooler air gave way to a kitchen that was steamy and warm. It enveloped them in scents of thyme, sage, roasted turkey, and simmering gravy. Spoons clanged against pots, and the chatter here overrode the fainter cheers and groans accompanying a football game on the television in the den.

A cork popped — the unmistakable sound of sparkling wine about to be enjoyed.

"Hey! Happy Thanksgiving!" Lucia swooped over from somewhere in the kitchen. "Come in. Let me take your coats." She hustled the new arrivals through the kitchen, past the den, and into the larger living room. They dodged tables already set with china and fall leaf centerpieces.

"Maisie, we're so glad you could join us. And, oh, marigolds? We love them. So sweet. Thank you."

Robin and Lucia settled the two older women into comfortable dove grey armchairs, took their drink orders (white wine for both), and wended their way back toward the kitchen.

Robin kissed Carmen hello and greeted those aunts, uncles, and relatives she knew. It was elbow to elbow in the large kitchen, with spillage into the adjacent dining room.

"How can I help?" she asked Lucia.

"Can you get their wine? Help yourself, too. You know where everything is. I'll join you when I can."

"Sure. But put me to work, too."

"Okay, if you insist. After that, could you please take this platter of appetizers into the den for the football crowd? Good luck in there. The game isn't going well. And to make things worse, Tom is there. With my father. And brothers." Lucia looked wide-eyed.

"I'm sure it's fine," Robin reassured her.

"Oh, yeah, Fine. Just fine!"

"Lucia!" Carmen called to her daughter. The potatoes are

boiling over!"

"Fine," Lucia muttered.

Robin did as asked. She served Charlotte and Maisie their wine and slid the plate of appetizers in front of the football fans. Tom had been chatting with Lucia's brother Sal and his wife but stopped to say hello to her. *He looks comfortable enough. I'll report back to Lucia later.*

At the appointed time, like magic, the bustling kitchen chefs turned into composed hosts, and the guests were seated at long dining tables. The youngest relatives were installed in the living room — it was agreed that was better for everyone. Giggles and squeals could be heard from there.

Carmen said grace. Roberto gave a toast. Platters and bowls of food appeared and were passed down the lines, family style. Sterling silver forks tapped gently on china plates, and chatting was mostly of the "ooh" and "yum" variety. As the wine flowed generously, laughter and conversation picked up.

Robin looked at her mother, seated across the table from her. Charlotte was smiling, visiting with tablemates, and including Maisie in the lively banter. *Her color is good. She does look well.* Robin hadn't had time that afternoon to think about Dr. Tracy, and what Maisie had told them. Or what that meant exactly, except it was either malpractice or ... worse?

Later, she told herself. It will all be dealt with later.

THIRTY-EIGHT

Thanksgiving Day – Turkey and Dogbane

BETTER THAN ANY PARTY FAVOR or celebrity swag bag is the coveted container of Thanksgiving leftovers. Clear boxes were stacked and labeled in the capacious Ricci refrigerator, ready for guest departures.

The meal was, of course, a success, and the desserts had been served and eaten over guest protestations of "no room!" The cleanup was progressing well, too.

Lucia's brother, Ray, was in charge of loading the dishwasher. "It's my superpower," he explained to an aunt, as plates, cups, and silverware were arranged in a Tetris-like fashion.

A few older teenage relatives were recruited to hand-wash and dry the good china; a rite of passage for that generation. The roasting pan was set to soak in the laundry room sink. Enough was enough, and nobody wanted to tackle *that* today.

Charlotte and Maisie were in no rush to go home, and they joined Lucia's parents and the few remaining guests in the den to watch a movie. Some of the youngest cousins had taken a postprandial hike around the ranch, ostensibly to check on Flossie, but really to get away from the grown-ups for a bit.

Robin and Lucia walked out to the wraparound porch for some privacy and settled in the red Adirondack chairs. Italian pottery mugs held coffee for Robin and jasmine tea for Lucia.

"Do you need another blanket?" Lucia asked.

"No, thanks. This one is perfect." Robin gathered the soft plaid wool around her shoulders and lap. Fall was edging into winter.

She pulled her phone out from beneath the blanket and re-read the text aloud to Lucia. "Yvonne should be here any minute with the info from the toxicology report. Do you want to wait until she gets here to go over everything we know so far?"

"Yes. Let's unwind for now."

Five minutes later, Yvonne's SUV pulled into the driveway.

"Hey! Can I bring Madison over there with me?" She called to Robin and Lucia from the car window.

"Sure. The more the merrier," Lucia answered.

Yvonne lowered the old dog out of the car, and they walked toward the porch. The two were a matched set on this late afternoon, both sporting quilted navy jackets.

"Cute ensembles. Can I get you some wine or coffee? Pie?" Lucia asked as she stood to pet Madison. She handed a blanket to Yvonne and set another one down on the porch for the dog.

"Hey, we're cute *and* warm." Yvonne sat in a chair across from Lucia and Robin. "Nothing for me, thanks. My mom and dad had the full spread there."

Yvonne turned to Robin. "So," she began without fanfare, "I sent the screenshot of your anonymous letter to Angelo. He took a report but wants you to drop it off whenever you have a chance. Can you think of anyone who could have sent it? Any other strange letters that have come in?"

"Nothing. I mean when I was a reporter, I'd get threats, or even lewd mail. But not since I moved home. And this appears to be challenging me, more than it is a threat. They used my full name on the envelope, too: Robin Hill O'Connor."

"Well," said Lucia, "he or she slams the coroner, *and* our police. There's an arrogant tone to it, I think. Strident."

"Agreed," Yvonne said. "And it sounds like someone doesn't want Sandy's murder to be ignored. How about if I take a look at it tomorrow? Do you still have the letter at the bakery?"

"Yeah, it's locked up. Thanks. I'd like that."

"Okay. Next bit of news." Yvonne pulled some papers from an inside jacket pocket. "Scott called me earlier. He's with his uncle and parents for the holiday. 'Uncle Rick' had information for him. For us. Scott emailed me while I was still at my folks' and Dad let me print it out."

She handed the papers to Robin, who was sitting the closest.

"And?" Lucia asked. "The translation for the layperson, please."

Yvonne leaned forward. "They conducted ancillary tests. Microscopic analyses. It's pretty extensive. We already know from that initial report that there was damage to the rabbit's heart muscle. That white streaking, remember? His uncle had said it's difficult to identify a specific poison unless the animal dies with remnants of it in their stomach." Yvonne pointed to the papers.

Robin ran her finger down a list shown there. "It looks like they checked liver and kidney tissue. Something about vitreous fluid, too?"

"That's the eyes," Yvonne added.

"Lovely." Lucia took a sip of tea. "Is there a conclusion?"

"Yup. We're in luck. They were able to find some remnants of a plant in the rabbit's stomach. Something called dogbane. The plant acts like oleander. It's a … sorry, can I see that again?" Yvonne took the papers back from Robin. She turned to the second page. "It's something called a cardiac glycoside. Rabbits can go straight into heart failure if they ingest it. Cats and other mammals show gastrointestinal signs first, then the cardiac distress."

"That sounds like what our vet said. What about sheep?" Lucia asked. "Could Flossie have gotten into this dogbane somehow?"

"I asked Scott, and he put his uncle on the phone. Yes, it's possible. I explained Flossie's symptoms and your vet's treatment. Rick said it *could* be dogbane, and that you're fortunate. Death can usually occur in six to twelve hours after a sheep eats it. But they react differently than small mammals. Something about them being a 'ruminant.' I had to look it up."

"Wow. Just, wow," Lucia said. "So no psychopath purposely poisoned them? It was a plant? Our vet always thought Flossie had eaten something accidentally, and that she wasn't intentionally poisoned. He thought maybe it was milkweed, and he treated her based on that."

"I can forward this email to you when I get home. There's more. It's pretty technical. Might require some deeper reading on our part."

Robin had been sitting silently. Finally, she spoke up. "Cardiac. What did you call it, Yvonne? A cardiac glycoside?"

"Yes. Why?"

"It's just that I took Mom to the doctor this week, to that cardiac specialist. And she said that Mom's heart is fine. And then Maisie told us this morning that *her* doctor said *her* heart was fine, too. And they were each told by Dr. Tracy that they had a heart issue."

"That's weird," Lucia said. She put her empty mug on the porch floor and bent to scratch Madison's head. "I mean, they wouldn't have eaten that plant. Not knowingly. And how exactly would it even affect humans, if they did?"

"I can research that tomorrow," Robin answered. *Somehow. Or later tonight after Mom is asleep.* The bakery would be slammed the next day, she knew, with out-of-towners and locals shopping, dining, and looking for holiday treats. *Somehow.*

"Do we even know what dogbane looks like?" Lucia asked.

Yvonne removed her cell phone from a pocket and entered the search words. "Here." She held it out for them to see. "*Apocynum cannabinum.* Hemp Dogbane. It looks pretty innocuous for being poisonous."

Robin reached for the phone and read aloud.

"*Only small quantities of the plant need to be ingested to invoke the potent effects of the toxins. Poisonous to humans, dogs, cats, small mammals, and horses. Dogbane contains cardiac glycosides that have physiologic actions similar to digitoxin. All parts of the plant are toxic and can cause cardiac arrest if ingested."*

She handed the phone to Lucia. "No, it doesn't look all that remarkable," Lucia observed. "It's not something you'd really notice."

"You know, when Scott and I checked the properties, I took pictures along the creek, behind the feed store, The Manor, and here at the ranch," Yvonne told them. "I didn't see anything out of place then, but I'll check the photos again, now that I know what I'm looking for."

A gust of fall wind swirled around the porch. "Should we go inside now?" Lucia asked.

Before they could rise, the incoming dusk also brought with it the gaggle of young cousins, eager to return to the warmth of the farmhouse and leftover desserts.

They clomped up the steps. When the youngest girl, Nan, spotted Madison, she plunked down on the porch next to the dog.

"What's your dog's name? Can I pet her?" Nan looked up at the grown-ups. Upon permission, she began giving Maddie belly rubs.

"Well, I guess we're out here for a bit longer," Yvonne laughed. "I don't dare disturb Madison now."

"I'll show Daddy and Sal the photos later." Lucia folded her blanket. "See if they remember dogbane ever growing around the ranch."

Eleven-year-old Javier, Frank's grand-nephew, was sitting on the bottom step. He looked up. "Dogbane? I know what that is. I collected dogbane beetles last summer. For my Scout project."

Three heads turned toward Javier. Questions came in quick succession: "You know about dogbane?" "Where was it?" "What's a dogbane beetle?"

Not anticipating this reaction, Javier blushed. "Well, yeah, you know. I just found them. I needed a couple more hemipteran for my Insect Study Merit Badge."

"He got an award for it, too, at the Harvest Festival," Nan said, proud of her older cousin.

"Yeah. Well. I saw them — the beetles — in some plants behind the old people's home. Sorry. I mean that senior home. Down the road from here." He looked at Lucia. "Want to see a picture of them?"

Javier reached into his sweatshirt and pulled out his phone. He found the file of insect photos, stood, and handed the phone to Lucia. "See?"

She passed it to her friends. A glittery, jewel-like insect filled the screen.

"Well, I'll be … darned," Yvonne said.

"You said you found this behind The Manor? The senior home. In a plant?" Robin asked him.

"Uh-huh. In August. The creek was pretty dry, and I was looking around. I had almost all of the insects I needed. Then, I saw these near the fence. They were so shiny! They dug back into the plant really fast. The dogbane plant," he added, pleased with his knowledge.

"Pretty," Nan commented. She had craned her neck to see what it was the adults found so interesting.

"Yeah, pretty. And deadly," Robin said under her breath.

THIRTY-NINE

Jack's Discovery

JACK AWAKENED WITH A DEEP ache in his joints. Specifically in his right knee. *My barometer*, he thought, as he rubbed it. The grey light seeping in from the half-closed blinds validated his knee's predictions: it was going to be a damp day.

He lay in bed for a bit, getting his bearings. *Another day in Paradise, right?* He sighed. *I shouldn't complain. It had been a nice Thanksgiving dinner at my daughter's. Good to see all the kids.*

Jack eased out of bed, stepped into his taupe sherpa-lined slippers, and made his way to the bathroom for his morning ablutions. His knee got an extra dose of pain cream. He rued that day years ago when he took a curve too sharply on his mountain bike. Jack had landed hard on the gravel, right next to an old, wooden trestle bridge. *Historic and old. Like me now. Thought I was such a hotshot. Trying to impress you, Margie.* Limping out of the bathroom, he nodded to his wife's photo on the bedside dresser.

Jack pulled out clothes with the weather in mind — a nubby cardigan over a wool shirt. A newer pair of sweatpants.

He debated whether to lock the apartment door, hesitated, and decided 'yes.' *I never locked it when the old owners were here. But with this crew? Uh-uh.*

He put the lanyard and key in his pocket. *If it's not pouring rain, a quick walk around the grounds after breakfast might be nice.* Maybe stretching would help that knee.

It was a short distance between his apartment and the dining room. Jack had to pass three other rooms on his side, and then turn left to the common area and dining room. He could smell the coffee and something fried. Decorative fall wreaths adorned two of the doors he passed. The other had a Christmas stocking already tacked up. At the corner was a library table covered with a burgundy-red runner. A white orchid, in a creamy ceramic pot, was placed in the center.

Huh! Orchids. Pat and her orchids. He walked past the table and then stopped. Something was out of place — something bright blue-green against the white that even his 90-plus-year-old eyes could spot.

Jack leaned his tall frame down to see better. There, crawling toward the base of the plant was an insect. And one that Jack knew shouldn't be vacationing on an orchid. He hurried to his room and got a water glass and a paper towel. His bad knee was forgotten as he nearly ran back, hoping to catch the intruder.

Aha! It was still roaming the unfamiliar turf. "What are you doing there?" Jack asked, as he expertly captured the insect in the glass. "You are *so* lost!"

He carried it to his room, breakfast forgotten. Once there, he secured the paper towel with a rubber band, punctured a few holes in the top with a fork, and placed the glass on what passed for his kitchen table.

Jack opened a drawer and rummaged around until he found a magnifying glass. Next, he went to his closet and thumbed through some books from his teaching days at Berkeley until he found the one he was looking for, a dog-eared field guide to local insects. *Perfect!*

Sitting with the contained beetle next to him, he opened the book, its cracked binding falling first to the section on dragonflies. *Margie's favorites.* He soon found the chapter and photos of beetles.

"No, no, definitely not," he muttered, glancing once or twice at the beetle for reference. "No, my friend, you are not an Oregon Stag Beetle. Not a Japanese beetle, either." He turned the page. "Here. You're," Jack looked more closely, "a Dogbane Beetle." *Dogbane? Could that be right?* He checked again. His eyesight may not be one hundred percent, but he knew his coleopteran. *Yes. And sitting on Pat's damn orchid!*

He read more. *A poisonous insect? Here? A step away from vulnerable residents? Well, that is too much.* Jack put the glass in his mini-sink, making certain the top was secure. He'd figure out what to do with it afterward. *Frank will want to know about this!*

He barely remembered to lock the door. Marching down the hall, he went directly to Pat's office.

"Pat!" He knocked loudly. "Pat!" He tried the knob. Locked.

"Wait a minute." He heard a drawer slam shut.

Pat opened the door halfway. "Why, Mr. Hanson. Such a fuss. Is something wrong?"

"You're damn right there's something wrong. *Ms. Breward.*" Jack moved forward to the threshold. "Do you want to discuss it here in the hall, or in your office?"

Pat stepped back and motioned to an empty folding chair.

"I'll stand," Jack responded.

"Well, what can I do for you?" Pat sat behind her desk and folded her hands on the papers arranged on top.

"There is a dangerous situation here," Jack began. "Dangerous in the sense that we residents have potentially been exposed to poison."

"Poison!" Pat fluttered one hand. "Oh, that sounds dramatic. What are you talking about?"

"I discovered a poisonous insect down the hall. In one of *your* orchids. It's called a dogbane beetle. And the insect and its corresponding plant are both *deadly!*"

"Are you sure? This bug … dog … whatever? I'm sure it's just some little critter that hopped on from somewhere outside. One bug, you say? Oh, dear, Jack. I feel you're overreacting. One little bug! What did you do with it? Flush it down the toilet, I hope." Pat gave a small shudder.

"Pat, I am not overreacting. This thing, and the plant, are all poisonous to animals. And to humans, if they eat it. Even handling the leaves can make you sick. If I found one bug, then the odds are that there are more around. And more dogbane *plants,* too. What if those plants are intermingling with our vegetables out there?" He blew out a breath. "You need to have Frank examine the facility and property well. Maybe call an exterminator. As for the *beetle,* I have it saved in my room. For now." Jack crossed his arms.

"Well, I can see you're quite concerned. I tell you what. After you leave, I'll call Frank and alert him. He can do a thorough search of the building and property if that will reassure you. Do you have a photo of it that I can show him? Or should I go to your room to retrieve it?"

"I'll show it to Frank myself. Pat, this insect is *not* something you want at The Manor."

"Yes, well then, thank you, Jack, for bringing this to my attention. Of course, we'll take care of it. The safety of my residents is of prime importance." Pat stood.

"Oh, and Jack, I was going to let you know that the staff and I listened to you and the others about the food issues. We took notice and we're changing the menu. You can look forward to some past favorites appearing this winter," Pat smiled and walked toward the door. "You might even see a lovely salmon dinner soon."

"Hmmph. I'll talk to Frank," Jack repeated, and he walked out to a late breakfast for which he had no appetite.

Pat waited until she saw Jack round the corner of the dining room. Closing the door securely, she sat down and reached for the phone. She dialed a private number.

"Ricardo. Get in here," she said. Then hung up.

FORTY

At the Bakery – Making Connections

THE EARLY BIRDS ARRIVED AT the bakery before it opened, huddling close to the exterior brick wall as if the coffee and sugars inside could enter their bloodstreams by osmosis. These were the hardy souls determined to go for a holiday hike to the top of nearby Sandstone Mountain, or along the river toward the coast.

Crowds came in surges that morning. After the hikers, other customers rushed in, searching for coffee cakes or Danish to feed their sleepy overnight company. Next and more leisurely, were the ten o'clock folks who, post-turkey coma, gathered for coffee and chit-chat before they wandered around with out-of-town relatives. Long-retired teachers visited with past students, third cousins caught up on the latest family marriages or divorces, and neighbors discussed newspaper headlines and local gossip.

"It's like 'old home week' out there," Robin commented to Jen, as they refilled coffee mugs, and slid plates of scones onto tables.

"What's that?" Jen replied as she passed Robin by the crowded doorway. "Old home what?"

"Never mind." Robin had to raise her voice over the laughter, chatter, and hiss from the latte machines.

Robin was operating on adrenaline and two espressos. *My stomach will pay for that later.* She glanced at her watch. *Maybe I can take a break in an hour.*

After dropping Maisie off the previous evening, and getting her mother settled for the night, she had stayed up late, researching dogbane and its effect on humans. Robin had opened some files, bookmarked others, and set up pages solely for notes. She copied and pasted snippets of articles, and photos of the plant, both with and without its bell-shaped flowers, and of its long leaves. "*Wear gloves when handling,*" warned one author.

She found stunning images of the insect itself. *Javier had been right. That beetle is gorgeous.* Eye-catching.

She learned that indigenous residents had found practical uses for the plant: as ropes, fishing lines, cords, and baskets. And they created safe medicines from it: as a heart stimulant, for rheumatism, a cough medicine, and to treat parasites. *Well, they knew what they were doing.*

Robin read that the plant *and* beetle were both poisonous; much more toxic than milkweed. Dogbane, it said, has cardiac glycosides. *Glycosides, there it is again.*

If ingested, one site told her, *it can slow the heart rate. It can act as a vasoconstrictor. Blood pressure increases. Its root contains cymarin, a potent cardiac stimulant.* Cymarin: researching that path led her on a half-hour journey.

Another page described how dogbane is similar to digitoxin. She dug around further and, in the process, went down some internet rabbit holes. Then, she extricated herself.

Most of the information she found discussed how it impacted animals. Humans, it was thought, wouldn't willingly chomp on a sticky, bitter dogbane leaf. Or on the bug. Robin finally switched off the lights and computer close to midnight. It was a restless sleep. *Toxic, poison, death.*

Robin took her break when the lunchtime crew arrived. When she got to her office, she saw a few missed texts. Nothing urgent. But the one from Yvonne was of note.

I'll swing by around one to get that letter. Make a copy.

Short and to the point. Robin unlocked the drawer. The letter was still there: accusing, goading. Nasty. She made a copy of the envelope, too, and put the original in a folder on the desk for Yvonne to take to the police. *For whatever good that will do. What does it even mean?* What was she supposed to do about that murder?

More pressing to her was the jumble of material about dogbane. Sick animals. Sick people. One common denominator? Or none?

At one-sixteen, there was a knock on her door. "Come in. It's open," Robin called.

"Sorry I'm late. My God, it's a zoo out there." Yvonne entered, carrying a to-go cup. "It took me forever to work my way through."

"Sit," Robin answered. "Can you stay for a little while?"

"I can. Thanks. I don't have a set time to see Angelo." She took off her jacket and sat in a sleek, comfortable chair. "Do *you* want coffee? I can brave the masses and get you one."

"I had my quota. Plus." Robin pushed the folder closer toward Yvonne. "Well, here's the original letter and envelope. I made a copy of both. But I don't understand it. Does someone think that because of my background, I should be working on this?"

Yvonne opened the file folder and gently took the letter out of its envelope. She read for a minute, then placed it back inside. "It's the tone that gets me. Someone who is, or was in authority? An ex-cop?" She took a sip of coffee. "I mean, it *could* be the killer taunting the police through you."

"Wow, great. I hadn't thought of that."

"Sorry. Listen, maybe it's a teenager in their mom's basement playing detective, getting their kicks. Let me, or Angelo, know if you get another one, though. Or any weird phone calls. Okay? I'll keep in touch with the department, too."

"I promise. Can we change the subject to something pleasant for a minute? It was so hectic yesterday, that I never asked how your Thanksgiving went. Is your family okay?"

"They're fine, thanks. Same-same. The kids left early this morning to go home to Mendocino. Madison will miss them. For sure, I'll see them at Christmas, but my daughter and the grands may be back for the tree lighting next week."

"Oh, good. Maybe I'll catch them that night. I'm not working on it, but Jen is going to be Santa's helper and hand out cookies." Robin pulled a colorful flier from a nearby pile of papers and gave it to Yvonne. "Here, this lists all of the activities. You can send it to them."

"And you? Did Charlotte do all right? It must have been a long and busy day for her."

"She was a little tired from it but happy. I swear, she looks so much better since coming home. She's eating more, too."

"No offense, but you look kind of tired, also."

"No argument there. I was up late researching dogbane. Do you know its Latin name 'Apocynum' literally means "away dog" because it's poisonous to animals? What I was trying to find out was how it affects humans. Yvonne, it's a scary plant for people."

"So from what little we saw last night, I'm guessing it causes heart-related issues?"

"Oh, yeah. And fatigue or nausea. It's especially bad if someone *already* has a heart condition. I can send you and Lucia what I found. Let me clean up my notes a little. I can do that later when I get home. I also have to draft and file my complaints about Dr. Tracy and Pat with the county and the Department of Public Health. Those are *whole* other issues." Robin listed them. "The awful and inadequate food, the possibility of residents getting the wrong meds, misdiagnoses, no proper recordkeeping or documentation. No oversight! Do *not* get me started."

"I don't blame you for filing complaints. Someone needs to be a voice for those residents. But know that the county is overworked and understaffed."

"Well, I also shot the Senator a quick email last night. To his private account, giving him an overview. I said I'd send more details later today."

"Mike Chen? Must be nice to have friends in high places," Yvonne laughed.

"Well, he and Patrick *did* go to law school together. And we had that fundraiser in the city for him when he ran for office. Remember?"

"Yup, I do. He's a good guy." Yvonne stood and picked up the folder. "Okay, after I drop this off at the police department, I'll look through the photos from my walkabout with Scott. Maybe I'll spot something. I'll let you and Luce know either way."

Robin stretched. "Time for me to get back out there. No rest for the wicked, as my grandmother used to say." She got up and walked her friend to the door. "You know, after learning about dogbane, I can't shake the feeling that there's a connection between Flossie, those feral animals, and Mom and Maisie. I hope I'm wrong. I dread the idea that my mother somehow accidentally ate dogbane. Could that even be possible?"

"Well, I learned this much from when I was police chief. Anything is possible."

FORTY-ONE

Pat Gets News

"PAT." IT WAS A STATEMENT, not a question.

"What? What do you have?" Pat was walking around the grounds when the call came through on her cell phone. Her only company that morning was some brazen crows by the gazebo, quarreling loudly over a pile of walnuts.

Mrs. Ortega must be feeding those damn birds again.

Pat frowned. "Speak up!"

"Pat," the caller repeated, "I learned that Licensing is planning a surprise visit to your facility this week. Tomorrow. Maybe Wednesday. I don't know the time. Two evaluators."

"Tomorrow? Do you know why?"

"No. Sorry. Get it together there. You know the drill. Residents' rights posters displayed, bleach locked up, kitchen cleaned, records in order."

"I know what to do."

"Well, surprise visits don't just happen. You must have ticked someone off."

"All right. I'll handle it. Anything else?"

"No. Except the funds?"

"I'll send them today. Contact me if you learn anything else."

The caller disconnected. Pat glanced at her phone, making sure it was off. She reached into the pocket of her wool coat, and took out a butterscotch candy, popping it into her mouth. Distracted, she dropped the yellow wrapper on the path.

What in the hell is going on? What triggered social services — or who? A resident — like Jack? She hadn't even dealt with that issue yet. *A family member? God, this town is too nosey, poking into* my *business!*

She headed back to the main building. She would have to go over everything in the facility with a fine eye. Staff would be working late tonight. *Where's Frank? Was Monday his day off? He just had the holiday and Friday off.* She would text him to get here tomorrow at the crack of dawn.

Pat entered the front doors and walked directly to the receptionist's desk.

"Did Dr. Tracy call in today?" She asked the woman, a staff member's niece.

"Nnn-no, Miss Breward. No. I haven't taken any calls from him for a few days. Since he said he would be out sick."

"Let me know immediately if he does call. And clean up this desk. Get rid of the Thanksgiving decorations." Pat turned and walked toward her office. She changed her mind halfway there and went into the kitchen instead.

"Ricardo!" she shouted to the empty room. Her voice echoed against the stainless steel and sharp surfaces. "Ricardo!"

He emerged from a back storeroom. "What?"

"We are to have a 'surprise inspection' this week by social

services. It could be as soon as tomorrow. Make sure the water temperatures are correct. Put any perishable food away. Check storage spaces. Get rid of any old spices. Have your crew clean this place up. I need it to be perfect."

"Pat, this will mean overtime." Ricardo looked around.

"Fine. Just be ready. There's a bonus in it for you. Tell housekeeping that I said to make the dining room and lounge spotless. Laundry room, too."

That administrator-director she hired from Oklahoma wouldn't arrive until January. *If she does show up. Too late for tomorrow. Great. They'll cite us for lack of staffing. That's at least one strike against me.*

She walked from the kitchen, down the hall to Denton's office. Taking a keyring from the coat she was still wearing, Pat unlocked the door.

This disarray she saw made her swear. Files were piled on all horizontal surfaces. The blinds were crooked, and the cramped office smelled sour.

Where are you, Denton, you lazy-ass coward? You're not actually sick, are you? No. Are you on a binge at a casino again?

She raised the blinds and prepared to organize the files. This would take most of the day. Maybe into the night. And what about the hothouse?

What a loser Denton is. Pat removed her coat. *But then, I knew that all along, didn't I?*

FORTY-TWO

Jack and Frank Confer

ON TUESDAY, JACK SKIPPED COFFEE and went hunting for Frank, searching first throughout the facility, and then in the gardens. He had hoped to speak with his friend on Monday about the beetle, but, no luck, and no sign of Frank that day. Jack now made his way to the two low buildings that housed the laundry room and Frank's office. *Eureka!*

Frank was sitting at his well-used desk. Years of motor oil, coffee, and dirt had mottled the original wood color into a brown mosaic. The scent of laundry detergent often overpowered the earthy and mechanical smells in the room. Sometimes, a whiff of lavender fabric softener even wafted in.

"Frank, I found you!" Jack stepped out of the cold and into the office, warmer from the nearby humming dryers. There was no need to knock, the door was open.

"Hey, Jack. I'm here. Trying to avoid Pat." He pointed to a green chair, and Jack sat down. "She texted me yesterday morning and wanted me at work today by six o'clock a.m. sharp. It's still dark at that hour! What can I get done in the dark?" Frank shook his head.

"She's an odd one, I'll give you that," Jack agreed. "But listen. I have some news." He scooted his chair forward, its legs catching on the chipped linoleum floor. Jack unzipped his jacket and removed a brown paper bag. From that, he produced a glass jar.

"Take a gander at this." He placed the jar carefully on the desk.

Frank leaned forward, nose almost to the glass. "What is it that I'm looking at, Jack? All I see is a crumpled paper towel."

"That," Jack exclaimed, "is a dogbane beetle. A *poisonous* beetle. I found it last Friday in my hallway, burrowing in one of Pat's orchids."

"Is it still alive?"

"Alas, no. It succumbed on Sunday. I put hand sanitizer on the towel, to preserve it."

Frank took the jar and rotated it in his hand. "Ah, there it is. Wow, what a beauty. Those colors — like a stained-glass window. Poisonous, you said. How poisonous are we talking about?"

"Deadly for animals. Not pleasant for humans, either. It causes cardiac issues. And the dogbane plant is deadly, as well. I brought this all to Pat's attention right away. This is dangerous, Frank. Because if I found one inside, well ... ."

"Then there are probably more. And there must be some plants around, too," Frank ended Jack's sentence.

"And the beetle lives exclusively on the plant," Jack advised. "Pat said she'd contact you about doing a sweep of the facility and the grounds. Have you seen anything that looks like this?" He gestured to the bug. "I can show you a picture of the plant later. It's in an old reference book of mine."

"No. Pat called me about getting the place spic and span for some inspection or visitors. She didn't say anything about beetles or any infestation. And I can't say I've seen this insect. Until now." Frank placed the jar back on the desk.

"But you know," he continued, "About a month ago my cousin Lucia asked me if I had found any poisoned animals around here. I guess one of the pet sheep at the winery got sick, and there were some rabbits or cats that turned up dead by the feed store. All of them nearby here. Lucia and some of her friends suspected poison. I hadn't come across weird stuff at The Manor, though."

"Maybe you should call her about this."

"Yeah, I will. Have you told anyone else? Besides Pat?"

"No, I wanted to ask you first."

"And you found it on an orchid? Sheesh. How did it get there?"

The men looked at each other and spoke at the same time. "The hothouse."

"Cross-contamination?" Jack speculated.

"Hmmm. I'll look around the area near the hothouse. Pat will think I'm cleaning up there if she checks. I'll be in around lunch and come to your apartment to see that picture of the plant."

"All right." Jack stood up. The air was becoming too faux floral to his liking. "Maybe you can keep this here." He indicated the jar. "I don't trust Pat."

FORTY-THREE

Frank Calls Lucia

WHERE DOES ONE HIDE A deadly (and dead) beetle? Frank took the jar and looked around. He didn't truly think that Pat would search his office. She had rarely entered it, maybe twice, since she took possession of The Manor, preferring instead to text or call him for a command appearance.

Still, he *had* agreed to put the insect in a safe spot and he respected Jack's request.

An oversized, grey metal toolbox was in the corner, sharing space with a few daddy-longlegs spiders.

Well, that would be perfect! Spiders guarding a bug. Frank chuckled.

Reaching into the pocket of his heavy jacket, he pulled out a round ring of assorted keys. Finding a stubby one, he opened the box, repositioned some tools, and settled the jar onto a clean, but rumpled chamois rag.

Locking the box, he had one more personal item to check off before he tackled Pat's long list of projects. He made a quick call but it went to voicemail, so he left a message.

"Hey, cousin. It's me, Frank. Remember when you asked me if I had seen anything strange around here? Relating to poison? Well, something came up. About a beetle. Call me, Luce."

About a half hour later, his phone rang and vibrated. He had been inspecting the locked hothouse and the garden behind it. The sharp ringtone in the silent wintery garden startled him.

Whoa, now I'm *getting jumpy.*

He silenced the ringer, saw the readout, *Lucia R.*, and answered quietly.

"Yeah."

"Frank? Did you call me about a beetle? And poison. What did you find? Why are you whispering?"

"Jack found something Friday. He said it's a poisonous beetle called a dogbane." Frank glanced around, but nobody was lurking nearby.

"Did you say dogbane? Oh, man. Where was it? Did he see a plant, too?"

"He found it on an orchid near his room. It's dead and I have it. Listen, Lucia, I can't talk now."

"Okay, okay. We're short-handed at the winery today. But I can swing by after work and meet with you then. And Jack. Will you still be around, say at five or five-thirty?"

"Oh, yeah, I'll be here. I'm up to my ears in projects and deadlines for Pat. See you later. Come to my office." He hung up without a goodbye.

After poking around, he had found no sign of anything odd or out of the ordinary. It was time to get back to work. Frank trudged over to the flower garden, and pulled out all the dead and rangy plants, making a neat pile in the compost heap.

One job done. A dozen more to go on Pat's list.

It had been a busy couple of days at the winery. Holiday weekends always were, and while Lucia and Robin had texted each other brief missives, *this*, this was different. She called Robin as soon as she hung up with Frank.

"Hi, Robin. I'm on my way to work. But do you have a minute?" Lucia switched the phone to her left hand while she locked the front door.

"Sure. I was going to call you. Everything okay?"

"I'm not sure. No ... I don't think so. It's about dogbane." Lucia was trying to herd Annie into her truck. "Frank called me. Jack found one of those beetles at The Manor on Friday. Inside the facility, near his room."

"What?!"

"I know. Somehow Frank now has it. Dead. The beetle, I mean. Not Frank. Sorry, hold on." Lucia called to her dog. "Annie, come!"

"Lucia, if there are beetles there, inside, then Mom and Maisie *could* have been poisoned. I've been researching the plant. And the insect. This is bad."

"I know. I have to get to the winery now. But I told Frank I'd go over there this evening to talk to Jack and him. And look at this thing firsthand. Can we meet afterward at your place? Maybe ask Yvonne to come over, also?"

"Yes, of course. Come here. Mom is having dinner at Lou's

tonight, so it's perfect. I'll fill you in on what I've learned, too."

"Okay. Later." With that, Lucia started her truck, backing out of the driveway with Annie next to her as the co-pilot.

"What's going on in our little town?" She asked aloud. Annie only shook her head, jangling the silver tags on her red collar.

FORTY-FOUR

Everyone's Plans

FOUR-THIRTY. IT WAS FOUR-thirty on Tuesday afternoon, and no licensing evaluators had come for a "surprise" visit.

Was my informant wrong? Pat mused. *No, she had always been correct before.* Pat tried to recollect their short conversation. *Not necessarily on Tuesday. It* could *be Wednesday.*

Pat decided to regard this as a brief reprieve; an extra day she had been given to set things in order. She had managed to organize Denton's office well enough to find and file the most often requested forms if called upon. Housekeeping had dusted and vacuumed the room.

In her office, she copied the letter from that nurse administrator, proving the woman was coming on board in January. Other, more personal files were safely in her tote bag to bring home. The hothouse had been handled.

Denton was still not returning texts or calls. After lunch, she had driven to his duplex on the east edge of town. His dented, black sedan wasn't in the carport, and nobody answered the door. Pat tried her best to get a response.

She rang the bell, knocked, and called out. "Denton. Denton!" She peeked into the ground-floor windows but saw nothing unusual through the builder-grade curtains.

She decided to check the back of the unit. As she began walking along that concrete path, someone opened the front door of the adjoining duplex. A woman stood at the doorframe, pointed her cane at Pat, and called out.

"Yoo-hoo. Ma'am. Are you looking for the doctor?" she asked.

Pat affixed a smile on her face. "Hello. Did I bother you? I'm so sorry." She walked toward Denton's neighbor. "Yes, I'm his — friend. And I was just concerned about him. I heard that he's been ill."

"Oh, dear. I knew it. He hadn't looked very well lately. I was wondering if something was wrong."

"I don't suppose you've seen him?"

"No. Not since … was it Friday? Maybe Saturday. I guess it could have been earlier last week."

Pat was grinding her back molars, but managed to say, "Thank you, um …"

"Mrs. O'Neill. I'm a widow. But still a missus, right?"

"I'm sorry for your loss, Mrs. O'Neill. And I'm Pat. Would you please call me if you see him? I worry, you know." She reached into her purse and handed the woman a business card.

"Of course. Poor man."

Pat seethed on the way back to The Manor. *Poor man, ha. If I find him,* when *I find him, he'll be a dead man!"*

———

Denton heard Pat, all right. How could he not? Her grating voice had become all too familiar. Of course, she hadn't seen his car. He had been parking it in the alley behind the duplex, away from prying old Mrs. O'Neill, and just in case Pat decided to pay him a visit.

She's not here dropping by for tea. Unless there's a dose of poison in it.

He sat in the short hall between his bathroom and bedroom, waiting for Pat to leave. He had kept any lights to a minimum to avoid attention while planning his next step. He definitely didn't want to encounter Pat before it was accomplished.

Denton sat on the uncomfortable folding chair he had set up in the hallway. And thought.

How had it come to this? To now?

Reno was where he first met Pat, both of them working at a small, cinderblock nursing home not far from the strip. They became buddies, he thought, hitting a casino together once a week.

Nothing romantic. God, no!

Although, it was only in retrospect that Denton realized how little money Pat actually gambled, that she observed more than she played, and always nursed only one drink for the night.

It was after one, stupid, spectacular loss of his that she came to his aid. That night he drunkenly confessed to his "buddy" exactly how much he owed a certain loan shark. And that he had been forging prescriptions to pay off his creditor. But it was no longer enough.

"What a pal," Denton laughed aloud, causing a coughing fit.

Oh, she'd paid off my debts. Had the money, somehow. And she's been blackmailing me ever since. Dragging me around with her like a trained monkey. Embroiling me in her tawdry schemes. Implicating Ricardo, too. But no more. No more, Pat.

He had his plan.

At the end of the day, Pat summoned Frank to recite the litany of chores he had completed. She then conferred with Ricardo and checked the kitchen, halls, and dining room for any out-of-place jars, crumbs, or dust balls.

Pat hated the idea of paying all that overtime. *But it's necessary.*

Posters informing residents of their rights were prominently displayed in the halls, alongside lists of upcoming exciting activities, and the weekly menu — such seasonal delicacies!

A Christmas-red silk poinsettia had replaced the orchid at the reception desk. Soft, 1940s top hits were playing on repeat throughout the lobby area, and the electric fireplace was "blazing."

She would have to tell the officials that Denton was out with a cold and didn't want to expose the residents. That might work.

But Jack Hanson. Jack. What if he tried to corner an evaluator? If he started to rabble-rouse, she could probably play Jack off as one of the dear, eccentric elderly gentlemen whom they humor. Licensing personnel wouldn't have the time or patience to listen to any lengthy, esoteric discourse on insects, and she could steer them away, she was certain. Almost certain.

Pat felt she had accomplished a lot. And a new long-term rehab resident was checking in before dinner. Yes, she had earned the night off.

Tomorrow, though. Tomorrow.

Maybe there *was* one last thing after all. She picked up her phone. "A special menu change, Ricardo."

FORTY-FIVE

A Special Menu

IT HAD BEEN A BUSY day. An exciting day! A far cry from the usual hypnotizing, mundane activities at The Manor.

Yes, today was the first time in a long time that Jack had felt, well, alive. He had begun the morning by presenting the dangerous beetle to Frank. His friend had listened to him and understood. Jack felt relieved, knowing it was now secure — and hidden — with Frank.

At lunchtime, and as promised, Frank came round to Jack's apartment. He only had to knock once.

"Come in, come in," Jack said in a stage whisper. "Did Pat see you?"

"No, I came in the side entrance. I only have a minute, though."

"Sure." Jack led his partner in espionage to the table, where the field guide lay open.

"Here it is. A photo of the insect and the corresponding plant. It's quite a good match to our insect, don't you think?"

Frank leaned over and pulled his phone from a pocket. "I'll

take some pictures and show them to Lucia when she comes later." He adjusted the book, turning it away from the glare of the overhead light, and snapped the photos.

"You got a hold of her? She can come? That's wonderful. We need allies."

"Don't get your hopes up, Jack. I don't know what Lucia can do. And Pat won't budge unless she wants to."

"Yes. But, Frank, this is a danger to the residents. Pat can't just ignore it."

"Hmmph. Sure she can." Frank walked to the door. "Meet me in my office at five o'clock. Lucia should arrive around then. No reason for her to be traipsing the halls around here. It's better for *all* of us if Pat doesn't see her."

Jack agreed wholeheartedly to the rendezvous time and place, and they parted.

It was pushing past the official lunch hour, so Jack heated up some ramen soup in his microwave. He didn't want to run into Pat, either. Frank was right. Better to lie low.

At five-fifteen, Lucia pulled her truck into the back gardens. She rolled the windows down and instructed Annie to stay. Lucia glanced around, but nobody was walking the paths on this darkening November evening. She went straight to Frank's office and found her cousin and Jack waiting for her.

Jack stood when she came in and motioned to the chair he had been occupying. "Lucia. Thank you for coming. Please sit down."

"Such a gentleman. Thanks, Jack. No, I can't stay long. I'm going to Robin's when I leave here." She loosened her wool scarf. "Hey, Frank. Where's this beetle?"

Frank produced the jar, with the intact, deceased insect lying atop the paper towels.

"Wow. It's so colorful." Lucia turned the jar carefully, admiring it from all angles.

"Yes, but poisonous," Jack responded.

"Can you tell me where you found this, Jack?"

Center stage, Jack relayed his story to Lucia, including Pat's response, and then took a breath.

Lucia put the jar on the desk. "Pat hasn't done anything about it? Hasn't gotten back to you?"

Jack shook his head 'no.'

"And she never asked me to do any exterminating," Frank added. "But something is up because she has me and everyone here frantically sprucing up the place. Just not looking for any bugs."

"It's so strange." Lucia shook her head. "I can share this much with you. It's a long story, but those dead animals that were found appear to have ingested dogbane. That's probably what took Flossie down, too. So the plants are nearby, somewhere. Oh, and Frank, Javier told us he found one in a plant behind the fence here late last summer. A dogbane beetle, like this one."

Jack gasped. "Summer! They've been breeding since then?"

Lucia shrugged. "I guess so. One more thing. Charlotte's so-called heart problem cleared up once she left here. Robin is now concerned that her mother might have somehow eaten or drunk something contaminated with dogbane."

"Dear God." Jack slumped in his seat.

"Maybe take the jar with you, Luce." Frank handed it

to her while turning to Jack for approval. Jack nodded his assent. "Safer if it isn't here, I think."

Jack was late for dinner. With his mind reeling, he wished that his dear Margie was still alive so they could discuss what he had learned.

Maybe I can tell Bev.

She had been a good confidante to Charlotte and him in the past. He entered the dining room and noticed that it *was* gleaming. Pots of cinnamon-colored fresh mums were in the middle of each dining table, and on the sideboard.

When he reached the center of the room and his shared table, Jack saw that a stranger in a wheelchair was occupying one of the places.

Pulling out his chair to sit down, he looked quizzically at Bev. She nodded, smiled, and introduced their new tablemate.

"Jack, this is Bob. He just joined us today."

The two men shook hands.

"Bob Cristenson," the man said. "Yup, I arrived this afternoon."

"Jack Hanson. Sorry I was late." Jack noted the man's grey pallor and somewhat bulky frame. "Are you going to be living here full-time?"

"Only here for rehab. I busted my hip helping my cousin clean his gutters. Fell right off his roof, and I had to have surgery. Should have known better at my age." He laughed.

"I moved to a cabin out of town a couple of months ago and don't know many people here yet. Just my first cousin. We're close, more like brothers. Grew up together."

"I think you'll like Miller's Creek," Bev said. "It's a sweet town."

"Yeah, it seems nice. When I can get around again, I'll explore it." Bob tapped the arm of his wheelchair. "I was supposed to check in with some doc here, but I guess he isn't in today."

"Or for a few days, either. I heard that he's out ill," Bev advised.

"No loss," Jack said, barely under his breath.

"Oh, Jack!" Bev scolded.

Before he could respond, kitchen staff brought out the main courses. Ricardo personally delivered the meals to their table.

"See, Mr. Hanson," he said, placing the plates in front of them. "You requested salmon. And here it is!"

"Wow, you folks eat well in this place." Bob eyed the generous portions of pale pink fish, accompanied by mounds of herbed rice, a dinner roll, and string beans dotted with sliced almonds.

Another rarity, a large Caesar salad, had been served before Jack arrived and was placed to his left. Bev and the newcomer had already eaten theirs.

"Jack has been lobbying hard to get us better meals," Bev explained. "Congratulations, Jack. It looks like you succeeded." Never a fish lover, Bev had been given what appeared to be caper-sprinkled chicken piccata, with the same side dishes.

"I … I'm not too hungry tonight," Jack said, picking up his

fork. "And they loaded me up with too much topping." The abundant cream sauce ladled onto his salmon was seeping toward the rice.

"I guess they thought they were treating you." Bev took a bite of her chicken. "Yum! This is delicious."

Bob spoke up. "Want to trade, then? Mine is a little skimpy on the sauce. I never met a meal I didn't like."

"Sure." Jack and Bob switched plates, and Bob dug in with vigor.

"Want my salad, too?" Jack asked.

Bob nodded. "I could get used to this," he said, in between bites.

Jack smiled faintly and rearranged his food. His mind was elsewhere.

FORTY-SIX

At Robin's – Tuesday Evening

ANNIE BOUNDED OUT OF THE truck and arrived at Robin's first. Lucia was close behind, carrying the jar with the infamous beetle.

Robin opened the door before Lucia could knock.

"Hi," Lucia spoke first. "So Annie is with me tonight. I hope that's okay." The dog had already crossed the threshold and went directly toward the kitchen. Annie knew how to herd snacks just as well as she did sheep.

"Oh, sure. Rupert heard you coming and high-tailed it upstairs. Come in and get out of the cold."

"Sorry, Rupert," Lucia called up to the cat, as she took off her coat.

"Yvonne is already here."

"I saw her SUV out front." Lucia followed Robin into the kitchen. "Mm-mmm, smells like pizza."

Yvonne was seated at the oak table, a glass of wine and a small charcuterie plate in front of her. Annie was lying by the chair, correctly anticipating that a slice of Granny Smith apple or a bit of brie cheese would soon fall her way.

"Hi, Yvonne. Sorry to keep everyone waiting. I brought a surprise, though." Lucia placed the jar next to the plate and bottle of wine; the beetle's chartreuse, blue, and gold body shone in the kitchen's light.

"Holy cow, Lucia!" Yvonne reached for the jar. "So this is it — in the flesh, so to speak."

Robin peered at the specimen next. "So much trouble for such a pretty little bug. Jack gave this to you?"

Lucia poured herself a glass of the Italian pinot grigio and sat down. "Yeah, he and Frank wanted it off the premises. Away from Pat and prying eyes, I think."

"I have questions," Yvonne replied. "Why are they worried about Pat?"

"Let's eat first, and then talk. Dinner is ready." With that, Robin brought out two Margherita pizzas, the mozzarella balls on top resembling snow-capped mountains in a San Marzano red lake. "I have news, too."

After the meal, they re-grouped in the living room, the trio settling into stuffed chairs. Coffee and tea were now the beverages of choice.

Annie found a spot in front of the fireplace, her paws on the edge of the emerald-green tiled hearth. Rupert was still in his self-imposed exile.

"When do you have to pick up Charlotte?" Lucia took a sip of Darjeeling.

Robin checked her watch. "Not yet. I have about a half hour. Mom and Lou were going to play cards after dinner."

"Luce," Yvonne said, "why don't you start, since you arrived with *the* conversation piece of the evening?" They had brought the jar with the beetle into the room with them, and it sat nearby on an antique table.

"Frank called me this morning," Lucia began. She explained how she had initially asked him if he had seen anything peculiar there. He hadn't. *Then.* But now Jack had found a dogbane beetle, on an orchid in the hallway near his room.

"On an orchid? Not a dogbane plant?" Yvonne asked.

"An orchid. Pat likes them and has them all over. They said she keeps the orchids locked up in her hothouse and nobody has that combination except her. Anyway, Jack knew this bug was out of place and did some research. When he realized the beetle was poisonous, he alerted Pat. He doesn't think that she took him seriously. Pat said she'd have Frank deal with it. But she never did. Jack preserved it," Lucia pointed to the jar, "and brought it and his concerns to Frank today. The guys suspect it somehow got into the hothouse. They don't trust Pat, so they gave it to me."

"They're smart not to trust her," Robin commented. She had been taking notes, looking up now and then to comment.

"True. I told them about how dogbane caused the death of that rabbit. It probably poisoned Flossie and some feral cats, too. Also, how Charlotte *may* have come into contact with it. Jack is pretty shaken. I think he suspects there is something more malicious going on, rather than random incidents. So that's it. What do you think?"

Yvonne leaned forward. "Okay. Can we connect any dots here? I met briefly with Scott at the feed store yesterday to clarify some of the more pedantic medical terms in the report from his Uncle Rick."

Lucia coughed. "Met with?"

"What? Oh, please. No. Anyway, I'll forward that report to you with our comments. He's posting notices at the store warning his customers to watch out for dogbane. He let Animal Control know, too."

"But right now, it's a cluster of problems only around the store, winery, and The Manor, right?" Robin paused in her writing.

"Yes. Nothing else similar has been reported in the county." Yvonne brought her phone out. "If Jack found an insect inside The Manor, and Javier found one on a plant there last summer, then we have to assume there are more beetles, and more plants reproducing. I went back and looked at those photos I took earlier in the fall with Scott. Here."

She passed her phone to Lucia. "This shot is looking toward the back of The Manor. It's not a great picture, but can you see those clumps beside the bench and the fence? Could be dogbane."

Lucia squinted. "I need readers. But yeah, it could be. Looks like the pictures we've seen of it." She handed the phone to Robin.

"I agree."

"Could a beetle have migrated from those plants into the building?" Lucia asked.

"No," Robin answered, "from what I learned, there have to be some plants closer by."

"The guys told me they haven't seen any. But they did mention that locked hothouse."

"Why would Pat lock up orchids and not give Frank a

key? He does all the grounds maintenance there." Yvonne shrugged. "Unless she has something in there she doesn't want anyone to see."

Annie let out a loud yip just then, startling the group. Still asleep, the dog snorted again, waving her paws as if running after a phantom critter. The women laughed. "Go get 'em, Annie."

"Let me detour here a minute," Robin spoke after the interruption. "I got a call on Sunday evening from my newspaper contact, Lillian. She found out a few things about Pat and Dr. Tracy from an off-the-record, confidential source that she has."

"Spill it," Lucia said.

"First, I think it's odd that Pat has so little online presence, aside from basic information. Lil and I both checked. Not much of a footprint, right? But Lillian's source passed along rumors, mostly things he's heard through the nursing care grapevine. He told Lil that Pat had a reputation for befriending elderly people without family and getting written into their wills. All of it's legal, if unsavory. He said Pat had bounced around from place to place. Some facilities where she worked were considered subpar, without much oversight. He also thinks she spent some time in Mexico. They assume that's where she met Ricardo and that she brought him along to other jobs. This is the first facility she personally owned."

"Really?" Lucia put her mug down.

"And then there's Denton Tracy. Pat seems to have found him when they were both working in the Reno area. The good doctor supposedly has something of a fondness for the blackjack tables and high-stakes poker."

"Whew. And now he's here with her." Yvonne sat back in the chair.

"What an unholy trio." Lucia shook her head.

"I called and spoke with Mike Chen after I learned all this." Robin reported on that conversation, and how the Senator took an immediate interest, and said he'd quietly check it out.

"He's been sponsoring bills on stronger nursing home regulations, and he has connections."

"He's a good friend and resource to have, Robin." Lucia stretched and reached over to turn on another side lamp, for light and comfort.

"That brings me to my mom's heart problem." Robin listed the possibilities: "One, was it real, but mysteriously disappeared? Two, was it nonexistent, and she was misdiagnosed by Tracy? Or three, it was a lie, generated by Tracy."

"But she *was* told by him that something *was* wrong," Lucia added.

"Yes. And it worried her so much that Mom thought she'd be unable to live here at home, that it would be too much of a burden. Don't forget that Maisie got a 'wrong' diagnosis, too. And I never did get Mom's medical records from them."

"So is it? A lie do you think? Does the dogbane even play a part?" Lucia wondered.

"I don't know. Did she — both of them — somehow ingest it unknowingly while there, and it made them temporarily ill? Or?"

"Or they were given dogbane on purpose," Yvonne said aloud what Robin was thinking.

"Yeah," Robin replied. "It makes me furious to think about.

I've been trying to sort it out. What would be the benefit?"

"Follow the money," Yvonne answered. "It's a cliché, but it's often the root of a crime."

Lucia gasped.

"Listen, before I joined the force in Miller's Creek when I was still with the sheriff's department, we helped investigate allegations of infestations, abuse, and misuse of funds at a facility on the coast."

Yvonne recounted how a family member had called them, concerned. The business involved was located in the boonies and was pretty isolated. There was no real supervision.

Yvonne shook her head at the recollection. "Besides really poor conditions there, it turns out the administrators were bilking the county, Medicare, and the patients. They had all kinds of schemes in place before they got shut down. I repeat. Follow the money."

"What would they have to gain by poisoning the residents? What if someone died?" Lucia asked.

"Well, sick rehab patients and residents would have to stay there longer, right? Especially if they are made to feel vulnerable, ill, or have no family to go live with." Yvonne reflected. "Dr. Tracy would ostensibly know the right amount of dogbane to give."

Robin added, "And longer stays means *a lot* more income from private pay residents. Or even from Medicare. They'd charge for additional add-on services, too. Or," she paused, "they are just plain evil."

"Am I hearing correctly? Are you two saying that you think people are being *purposely* poisoned there? Not accidentally?"

"I think we are," Robin replied.

"But how?" Lucia asked.

"The research I did said that both the beetle *and* plant are poisonous to humans. The plant is supposed to be bitter, though, so it would have to be covered up, disguised somehow. In medicine, maybe. Or food and beverages."

"Oh, my God. Poor Jack! Pat now knows he found a beetle there." Lucia looked to her companions.

"Call him in the morning and check in," Yvonne told her. "Talk to him, but be careful. We have no proof of any of this. Only speculations."

"I'm going to have to pick up Mom soon." Robin stood. "Let's talk tomorrow, okay?" The fireplace held faint embers now, and the room had grown cool.

Annie lifted her head, sensing the movement. They could hear the rain falling outside.

"I guess I'll take this home with me." Lucia stood also and picked up the jar. She hugged Robin. "Come on, Annie. Time to go."

FORTY-SEVEN

Mr. Bob's Indigestion

BEFORE SHE OPENED HER EYES, before the phone rang by her bedside, Pat knew the day would go south.

Her plastic bedside clock ticked the time: ten minutes before six. And counting.

Pat picked up her cell phone. "Hello?"

"Ms. Breward? This is Sara at The Manor. I'm sorry to call so early."

Sara? Sara? Ah, that last-minute temp LVN I hired from the staffing agency. Another huge cost.

"I'm up," Pat responded, sliding to the edge of the bed and putting her feet into a pair of grey flannel mules on the floor. She had planned on being awake and moving before now, anyway. The alarm must not have gone off.

"What is it?"

"I'm sorry to call with bad news. One of the residents passed away overnight. A CNA found him this morning when she went to help him dress and get ready for breakfast."

"Oh?" *Was it?* "Oh, dear. How sad."

"Yes, a new resident, as I understand it. Bob Cristenson."

Pat was fully awake now. She stood upright. "Mr. Cristenson? Are you sure? Did you get the name right?"

"Yes, ma'am. Quite sure. Were you, were you expecting it to be someone else?"

"Of course not! But he just arrived. He is — was — here for rehab on his broken hip."

"Yes, ma'am. The CNA reported that to me. She also said that Mr. Cristenson was complaining of indigestion at bedtime. He'd taken some OTC heartburn medication that he brought from the hospital. Would you like me to call his family? A mortuary or the coroner?"

"No! Don't call anyone. I'll be there in half an hour. The calls should come from me."

"Of course."

"Don't say anything to the other residents. It would unduly disturb them."

"I'll alert the staff to be discreet also. I doubt they've had a chance to say anything yet."

It took Pat a hair over 20 minutes to get ready for work. In that time, she had sworn Denton to hell and back 20 times.

He should have been here. Checked that guy in and examined him. Or at least reviewed his medical records. I never had time yesterday. Bob obviously had an underlying condition. What happened?

She threw her purse onto the passenger seat and put the car heater on high against the November frost. Slowly, a film of sweat was emerging on her forehead. Pat switched the heater off and rolled down the driver's side window. The icy blast felt good.

Now I have a corpse on my hands. And I just know those social services evaluators will be arriving today. She cursed Denton again, adding the county, the state, and even Bob to the litany.

Did he have arrangements made at a funeral home to pick him up, in case? Maybe I won't have to call his family. Who is his family? God, will they make a scene?

She pulled into her reserved parking spot and slammed the car door. Luckily, Pat had planned her outfit the night before, so she had dressed quickly and quite appropriately for any county inspectors: a navy-blue pantsuit, cream turtleneck, and low black boots. She wore tiny, faux pearl earrings. Really, it was an outfit that would garner even a nun's approval.

It was too early for the receptionist to be on duty and too early for the evaluators, either. She needed to think, so she went directly to her office.

The first thing to do was to get Bob removed from the premises before the county arrived, or before the residents heard of his death. That meant finding the records he had brought with him. Sara or one of the CNAs had checked him in, seen him to his room, and put his file on her desk. The information should have been forwarded electronically, also, from the hospital. But she had only given a cursory glance at her emails the day before. Maybe it was there.

Pat found and opened Bob's file, thumbed through it to see who was named as his emergency contact and if, in case of death, there was a funeral home listed to collect his remains. A cousin was shown as the contact. But as for where to send Bob if anything unforeseen happened, that box was left blank.

More swearing ensued. *Okay, okay. Call the cousin. Give him the names of local mortuaries. Be sympathetic. Move this along as fast as possible.* She entered the number.

"Yeah?" Pat heard the sound of traffic. A truck's air horn blasted in the background.

"Is this Art Cristenson?"

"Who wants to know?"

Pat could feel the throbbing begin at her left temple.

"Mr. Cristenson, this is Patricia Breward. I'm the owner and director of The Manor in Miller's Creek. I'm afraid that I have some sad news regarding your cousin Bob."

"Bob? What's wrong?"

"Well, when staff went to check on him this morning, they found that he had passed away peacefully in his sleep."

"Passed away? Are you telling me that Bob is dead?!"

"Yes, I'm so sorry. Now we need to know how you'd like us to proceed. You're listed as his contact, and I don't see which funeral home Mr. Cristenson — Bob — had wished to use. Can you tell us what he would have preferred?"

"Dead!" sputtered Art. He was known as A.C. to his friends. However, Pat was not one of his friends at the moment.

"What in God's name happened? He went there from the hospital yesterday. For rehab. He was fine. I saw him. What did you do to him?"

"I can assure you that we are as surprised as you are. Shocked at his sudden passing. Perhaps he had an underlying condition we all were not aware of?"

"Stop! Don't keep saying 'passing.' He's dead. My only cousin is suddenly dead, and I'm holding you responsible.

Bob had a busted hip. Sure, a little ticker issue runs in the family. But, Bob is, was, strong as a horse. They told us you had a doctor at that place. What does he say about this?"

The throbbing had migrated to Pat's forehead.

"The doctor was unable to see him yesterday. It was late when Mr. Cristenson arrived. I *am* sorry for your loss. Now, there are several reputable mortuaries in the area that I can recommend. We can make arrangements immediately for Mr. Cristenson to be respectfully moved to one of them."

"Hell, no! Lady, don't you dare move him. I'm south of Eureka and will be there in about three hours. In the meantime, I'm calling the sheriff. His uncle is a hunting buddy of mine. The only place my poor cousin is going to next is to the coroner, to see what you did to him!"

"I can call the coroner now, Mr. ... ."

But the call ended. Pat was left looking at a blank screen.

She dialed Sara next.

"Yes, Ms. Breward?"

"I'm in my office and just spoke to Bob Cristenson's cousin, the next of kin listed on his forms. The cousin is quite shocked, as we all are, and in a state of grief. We will await his arrival later this morning before we make arrangements for Mr. Cristenson. In the meantime, please keep the staff from entering his room. Again, keep this private."

"Yes, ma'am."

Next, she dialed Ricardo. "Get in here now. We have a situation."

He was there in a minute.

"Close the door. And the blinds."

Ricardo did as she directed and sat down. "Is this about the new guy turning up dead?"

"You already know?"

He shrugged. "Everyone leaks stuff around here."

Pat leaned across her desk. The throbbing had moved to her neck. She felt it loudly in her ears, as well.

"Ricardo. Tell me. *What. The. Hell. Happened?* No one else has been reported sick, I gather. But somehow *Bob Cristenson* is dead? After being here less than 24 hours?"

"I don't know. I swear. It's not my fault! I oversaw and prepared the dinner meals as usual. A really nice menu, like you directed. People were happy. They ate well last night. I only made that one 'extra special' dish. Like you ordered."

The air in the room was close, and Ricardo looked around for a glass of water. There was none.

"Think. There must have been a mix-up."

"No, I served them myself at that table. But … ."

"But what?"

"When the plates came back to the kitchen, I noticed that Mr. Hanson's dinner was barely eaten. More like," he gestured, "more like mushed around. I double-checked the dietary tags. They all matched up."

"What about Bob? Did he eat his dinner?"

"Oh, yeah. Clean plates. For Miss Bev, too."

"Somehow, this is *your* screw-up. It's a disaster! Now, I have to try and fix it."

His face flushed, Ricardo stood and walked to the door. "No. I'm not taking the blame for this. Not for another murder."

FORTY-EIGHT

Wednesday Breakfast Special

THE BATTERY HAD DIED ON Jack's cell phone.

He chided himself, as he plugged it in on that Wednesday morning. *Come on, old man. Keep your wits about you.*

He had been distracted by his discovery of the beetle, and the conversations with Frank and Lucia. But it was unlike him to be forgetful. That, too, upset him. Jack had been awaiting a call from Lucia. Well, it was more like *hoping* to get a call from her. Did he miss it?

When they had parted the prior evening, they exchanged numbers and Lucia told him that she would "keep him posted." *Did she or her friends come up with anything new?*

Maybe I should check in with Frank. See if he learned anything. No. He has enough on his plate dealing with Pat. Jack shook his head. *Pat. That woman was incompetent! Dangerous, even. And up to something.*

Jack finished dressing and went to the dining room for an early breakfast. He was surprised to realize that he was hungry. Well, he had barely touched his food last night. Too nervous.

When he walked into the room, only Bev was seated at their table; the other tables were sparsely occupied. She was buttering a piece of toast.

He poured a cup of decaf coffee from the thermal pot on the sideboard, added a touch of low-fat milk, and sat down. "No Bob this morning?" He asked Bev.

"No, but he may not be familiar with the schedule yet." She waved her slice of browned sourdough. "It's still pretty early."

Jack looked at the paper menu at his place. His finger ran down the list of options. There were so many more items shown today than the scrambled eggs or oatmeal that had been their usual meager choices these past months.

"Smoked Salmon Eggs Benedict? Buttermilk Pancakes?" He looked up at Bev. "Chicken Apple Sausages with Eggs 'any way we want'?"

"See?" Bev said to him. She had added blackberry jelly to her toast. "I'm having the pancakes."

One of the regular kitchen staff approached the table to take their orders.

"Good morning, Ava. Besides my toast, I'll have the pancakes, please. And orange juice." Bev handed the woman her menu. "Thank you."

"Same for me. Thanks," Jack said. "Oh, and Ava, we aren't waiting for our new dining companion, Bob. Looks like he'll be late coming to breakfast."

Ava squirmed a bit and glanced around the near-empty room. She leaned next to Jack's chair and brushed an invisible crumb from the tablecloth.

"Mr. Bob," she whispered, "Mr. Bob is muerto."

Dead? Surely Jack had heard wrong. "Muerto?" he repeated. "The man who was here with us last night?"

"Si."

"But how? When?"

Bev overheard Jack's end of the conversation. Her mouth was open.

Ava shook her head. "No sé. They found him. Today." Looking over to the kitchen doors, she saw Ricardo. Head down, she left hurriedly.

Jack turned to Bev. She was still agape. "Bob is dead? Is that what Ava told you?"

Jack felt his heart racing. "Yes. That's what she said. Bev, can I use your cell phone? Let's go to my apartment and try to figure this out."

———————

Lucia had tried to reach Jack, but it went straight to voicemail. She left a short message, saying she'd call again later. But she didn't know how much she should tell him. That Pat and Denton Tracy are dicey characters? Okay. That they suspected Charlotte and Maisie might have been purposely poisoned? She didn't want to scare him, without enough proof.

She glanced at the jar on her kitchen counter; the gloriously radiant beetle was still reposing in its final resting place. *What a mess.*

Lucia needed to get to the winery. She grabbed a rose-colored wool muffler and matching gloves. The view from her window told her it was overcast and blustery. Their local weather report called for severe, gusty winds for the next two nights. *"Tie down any loose holiday decorations,"* the newspaper advised.

Hopefully, that holds off.

The town's annual tree lighting was scheduled for tomorrow evening. It would go ahead regardless of any but the most severe storms.

Or even an unsolved murder. Lucia had always looked forward to the fuss and excitement of the event; it brought nearly everyone to the center of town. *See and be seen. I suppose it's a good distraction right now.*

The newspaper also reported that one of the mature Douglas fir trees growing in the downtown park had been given the honor this year; the lights had been strung earlier in the week. "Santa" (aka Mayor Joaquin Martin) was due to arrive at five-thirty in a horse-drawn carriage. The Girl Scouts publicized that they would be serving free hot chocolate. With marshmallows. Robin's bakery always had an "elf" passing out sugar cookies, another favorite attraction. Carolers in Victorian garb would be meandering the streets. Not to be outdone, the junior high school band planned to perform a medley of perky, if slightly off-pitch, seasonal favorites.

Lucia had arranged to meet Robin at the bakery first, and then they'd walk the few blocks downtown from there. Charlotte would be waiting (with blankets) for them on a bench near the action. Yvonne said she and her family would look for them all in the crowd.

But now, she had to get to work. Lucia checked the clock on the wall. *Maybe I can swing by and see Jack on my way to*

Jack found Lucia's number jotted on a piece of paper lying on his bureau. Bev was sitting in an armchair by the door, too stunned to speak. He had filled her in about the dogbane beetle as soon as they entered his apartment. But it was a lot to take in. Bob was maybe killed?

Jack called and got Lucia's voicemail. "It's Jack," he said, as soon as it beeped for a message. "There's been a death here. I think the man was poisoned, and I think the poison was meant for me. Please come as soon as you get this. Bev is with me, and I'm using her phone." He paused. "We're okay, for now."

He called Frank next. "Frank. I need you to come over now. I can meet you by the back door."

FORTY-NINE

Lucia to the Rescue

When Lucia arrived at The Manor, she saw two calls had come through while she was driving.

Darn! I must have the ringer off.

One call was from Tom, checking on where they were to meet at the tree lighting the next night. She texted him back:

Look for me at the hot chocolate booth around six.

She couldn't identify the second number, so she didn't even bother to listen. *Spam.*

After signing in at the reception desk, Lucia walked directly to Jack's apartment. In response to her knocking, though, nobody opened the door.

Instead, a voice from inside inquired, "Who is it?"

"Jack? It's Lucia. Is everything okay?"

The door opened. Someone pulled Lucia inside and slammed the door shut behind her.

"Frank? What are you doing here?" Her cousin still had hold of her arm.

"Shhhh."

"What is going on? Bev, you're here, too?"

"Didn't you get my message?" Jack asked. They were all standing in a loose circle. Nobody had invited Lucia to sit down.

"No, what message? Oh, wait, did you call me this morning? There was a number I didn't recognize."

"Yes, I had to use Bev's phone." Jack now pointed to the armchair, indicating Lucia should sit. "If you didn't get my call, then why are you here?"

"Well, I just thought I should check in. Tell you what we found out about Pat and Denton Tracy. They're pretty shady." Lucia looked to Frank and Bev, who had now found places to perch. "Why are you all here?"

"I'd better start," Jack cleared his throat. "Someone is dead. A new resident named Bob. We think Pat poisoned him. And that she meant for it to be me!" With that introduction, Jack related the sequence of events and his suspicions. "We don't feel safe here," he concluded.

Lucia saw they were worried. *Could Jack be right? It sounds outrageous, worse than what Robin, Yvonne, and I imagined, and yet.*

Jack, Bev, and Frank faced her, waiting for a response. *Yes, I believe him. This is so, so bad.*

"We have to call Yvonne and the police," Lucia told them. "And get you out of here. Now."

"Wait, there's more." Frank then added to the story. "Rumor here has it that we're supposed to have the county coming today, checking around. A surprise inspection. They'll find some things, for sure. Like Doc Tracy hasn't been seen for days, and Ricardo is suddenly MIA. If they make Pat unlock the hothouse, we think they'll find some dogbane. Pat is going to blow a fuse."

"Inspectors today? Huh. Robin may have had something to do with that. She called her friend Senator Chen about Pat and this place." Lucia addressed Frank directly. "Can you get to these county people while they're here? Tell them about the poison?"

"I'll try. Pat will be glued to them, but they'll probably shake her. Maybe I can catch them when they go to the gardens or laundry."

"Good. Give them all our numbers." Lucia pulled some paper and a pen from deep inside her hobo-style purse and jotted down her information. She passed it to Jack next, to add his.

"Jack, can you stay at your daughter's house for a few days?"

"Sure. She's always asking me over."

"Bev, do you have any place you can go?"

"Well, my sister-in-law is close by. She has a spare room. I could go there, I suppose."

"Great! Jack, pack up a small bag. Frank, walk Bev to her room and help her get some things together. Then come back here. And everybody, don't forget your meds. I'll drop you off wherever you need to go."

Next, Lucia texted her mother.

Something important came up. Will fill you in later. Pls cover for me at the tasting room. xo

"We can leave by the back doors," Jack told her from the closet, his voice muffled.

"Good idea. I'll call Robin and Yvonne while you're packing."

Dear God. Lucia mentally crossed herself and said a silent prayer. *I can't even process all of this right now. Help me get them away from this monster.*

Frank was already escorting an anxious-looking Bev out the door.

"Don't worry, Bev. It'll be okay." Lucia smiled at her.

But will it?

FIFTY

What Next

LUCIA MADE HER CALLS.

"Let's meet at your house," she told Yvonne. Robin didn't want to alarm Charlotte so they couldn't go there, and Lucia would be driving through town anyway, dropping off Jack and Bev.

"Agreed."

Yvonne got things ready for coffee, a task done by rote, while her mind replayed the brief conversation with Lucia.

Start the hot water. *Someone is dead.*

Grind the Ethiopian beans. *Dogbane poisoning?*

Place three blue mugs on the table. *Was Jack really the target?*

Put the filter onto the pot. *Is he the first?*

She turned the fireplace on. *After this meeting, I'll call Angelo. No, I'll go to the station and talk to him. This is out of hand. Nobody messes like this with my town and people.*

Robin arrived first. "I can't stay long. We're packaging the cookies for the tree lighting, and I'm tying a few hundred bows."

Lucia came shortly afterward, opening the front door without knocking. A gust of wind slammed it behind her.

"Sorry!"

Madison woke up at the sound, sniffed, and gave a short "woof" as a greeting. Since no treats were offered, she laid back down on her plaid bed.

"Here, have some coffee." Yvonne poured Lucia a full cup, with milk.

"Did you get Jack and Bev settled?" Robin asked.

"Thanks. And yes." Lucia took off her coat. "It wasn't easy getting them in and out of my truck, but we managed. Frank will call me later with any news from over there."

"Fill us in."

Lucia related what Jack and Bev had told her: how the new guy had seemed fine last night. How Jack was sure that Bob had been killed in error and that *he* was the real target. They had traded their dinner meals and Jack believed dogbane surely was involved. Finally, Lucia told them Frank had heard rumors that the county was making an "unexpected" visit that day.

"Whew." Robin finished her coffee by the end of the story. "We thought that Pat and Tracy were bad. But this? *This?* It looks like they really might have killed that man."

"Doctor Tracy *may* not have been involved. Jack and Bev said he hasn't been around lately. Your friend the Senator is probably responsible for the county showing up so quickly. I mean, that is warp speed for complaints. Frank will try to talk to any inspectors to tell them what happened. I don't know if he'll get the chance, though. Pat may hover."

"I've been thinking." Yvonne stood up. She brought the coffee pot to the table "You know that weird, anonymous letter you got last week, Robin? What if it's legit? What if the writer is someone on the inside, trying to point you toward Pat as the culprit? That *she* or *someone* there is responsible for Sandy Foster's murder."

"What?" Robin said. "I thought the coroner said Sandy had died of … what was it … blunt force trauma? They thought it was a robbery gone wrong. Did you hear any mention of poison from the police?"

"No, but that third-string coroner who did the autopsy is an idiot. I doubt he was too thorough."

"Dear God, Yvonne." Lucia topped off her mug. "*If,* and that's a big *if,* Pat or someone there was involved in Sandy's murder, what would be the motive?"

"That's a good question. We agreed last night that money could be, probably is, the main motivation for Pat, for all of the crooked dealings we think she's pulling off there, and in her past jobs. So could Sandy have discovered something and confronted Pat and Tracy, jeopardizing their schemes? Or could she have accidentally ingested a lethal dose of dogbane, and then they had to dispose of her?"

"Do you think there's enough of a doubt about the cause of death to convince her family to have the body exhumed and more tests run?" Robin asked. "Or claim malpractice on the part of the coroner?"

Lucia shuddered. "Poor woman."

"I think I should go to see Angelo at the station house. Get him caught up on what we know. And what we suspect," Yvonne told them. "I don't know how much he'll believe, but Pat has to be stopped. The last thing we want is a third murder."

FIFTY-ONE

Coroners, County, and Art Cristenson

THE CORONER'S VAN WAS NONDESCRIPT. Discreet. The driver pulled up to The Manor and parked in a spot away from the main doors. It was a mostly routine run for the two attendants, a man and woman in their twenties, except they had been sent here first, before the other pickups. A slight schedule change, but, no matter. They had their orders.

It was a familiar procedure. They'd remove the deceased from his or her room, using a door farthest from view. Quietly. It was a system designed to not upset elderly residents. Always professional.

They arrived just ahead of two women. The women, one around 30, and the other older, late 50s, wore badges identifying them as social service employees. Inspectors. The evaluators.

The women nodded to the uniformed attendants.

"Please go first. We'll be here a while," the older woman said. Her name tag read *Katherine Jones, Regional Manager*. She smiled pleasantly at them. They were, after all, compatriots in the labyrinth of county and government services.

"Thanks." Smiling back, the man turned and signed in at the desk. "We're here to see Patricia Breward," he told the young receptionist. He lowered his voice and read from his form. "Here to pick up the remains of Robert 'Bob' Cristenson."

The receptionist choked on the word. "Remains?" she repeated. "A ... a body?"

The man nodded.

Overhearing that exchange, the younger evaluator, *Aisha Mehta, Program Manager,* per her name badge, made a notation in the file she carried. Her companion gave a slight nod.

"We also need to see Ms. Breward," Ms. Jones announced.

Viewing four, official-looking people in the small lobby, the wide-eyed receptionist made the call.

"Um, Ms. Breward. There are a lot of people out here who want you." She looked at the assemblage. "It's about a *body,*" she whispered, and then took a big gulp of her macchiato.

Pat hung up. *So they're here. All of them. The coroner didn't waste any time. I guess Bob's cousin has some pull, after all. Social services arrived bright and early, too, I see.*

She applied a touch of dollar store lip gloss and straightened the files and laptop on her desk. She resisted the urge to pop a candy in her mouth. It wouldn't do to be crunching on butterscotch right now. Fully opening her office blinds against the dreary morning, Pat turned on all of the lights, too. *Better.* The orchid on the oak filing cabinet was a creamy, cheery yellow.

She put a faint smile on her face (the lip gloss helped), and walked to the lobby. Extending a hand to the attendants, she said, "I'm the director, Patricia Breward. You must be here for poor Mr. Cristenson. He was *obviously* released from the hospital to our care *way* too soon." She made a 'tisk-tisk' sound. "Let's go into my office first, where it's quiet."

She took one step. Then, Pat turned to look at the inspectors, who had been scanning the lobby walls, looking for emergency signs, fire extinguishers, posters — or violations.

"Oh, my! Are you from … social services?" She squinted at their name tags. "Did you need to see me, also? We weren't expecting you. Was there something scheduled — on the calendar — that I missed?"

"No, Ms. Breward." Katherine Jones presented Pat with her business card. "This is an unannounced inspection. Please finish conducting your appointment with the coroner's staff, and then we can speak. We'll look around on our own, in the meantime."

"Yes, of course. Well, the dining room is over there." Pat pointed. "Fresh coffee. Please make yourselves comfortable, and I'll join you as soon as I can."

"We'll be fine."

Pat led the coroner attendants to her office, signed the necessary paperwork, and provided what little information she had on Bob.

"Such a pity," she said, barely aloud. Directing the next sentence to them, Pat remarked, "The hospital was negligent, in my opinion. They should have recognized that he was in distress."

She got no response to that, no sympathetic murmur, or

tacit agreement. The woman only asked, "Can you direct us to the body, ma'am?"

Pat walked them to Bob's room. The blinds were half drawn, the lights off. His black vinyl overnight case from the hospital was still sitting unpacked on a chair.

"He arrived yesterday?" One attendant asked.

"Yes," Pat replied. "Directly from the hospital."

"Tough luck. Well, our orders are to take him directly in for a criminal autopsy and toxicology. His doctor already advised that the patient was fine when discharged."

"Criminal!" Pat gasped. "I'm sure you'll find it's nothing like that."

The attendant shrugged.

They brought the gurney from the van and went about their work quickly and efficiently. Respectfully.

Pat thought briefly about proclaiming some sort of prayer over Bob. *Would that help my cause?* But she dismissed the idea. It was too much, even for her.

They took Bob out a side door, unnoticed. That was the last Pat saw of her most recent transient resident.

She took his overnight case and went quickly into the bathroom to look for other personal items or any incriminating evidence. A toothbrush, a bottle of heartburn medicine, and a pair of socks were all she found. She put them together on Bob's wheelchair, ready for pick-up by whoever wanted them, and closed the door.

Criminal.

On to her next problem.

Pat found the evaluators, not in the dining room, but in

the adjacent kitchen. She scanned the dining tables quickly as she walked through the room. It was about a third full. No Jack or Bev. No "troublemakers," thankfully.

Pat cleared her throat. "I'm so sorry about that. Poor Mr. Cristenson. Sad, but it happens in this industry. As you know."

The older of the two evaluators, Ms. Jones, glanced at her. The younger woman, Ms. Mehta continued her inspection of the cabinets.

Ms. Jones announced to the air. "I believe we're almost finished in here. We have the menus from the last month. Our initial report will show that the kitchen's hot water is at the incorrect temperature. But we'll also check one of the rooms for that before we go."

Ms. Mehta closed the cabinet and joined her supervisor.

One of the cooks stood in the corner, leaning against the dishwasher. He avoided eye contact with Pat. But Ricardo? He was nowhere to be found.

Where is he?

Ms. Jones turned to Pat. "Shall we meet with your physician and administrator next? Go over some paperwork? We can start with the intake and discharge records of that deceased resident." Katherine Jones flipped a page on her list. "We'll need to see all your med schedules. Your daily and weekly activities calendar. We'll also review the current staff-to-resident ratio, and see if there's sufficient support staff and adequate training. I'm sure you have the CNA and LVN time cards available. Finally, we'll look at one of the rooms and the grounds." Ms. Jones looked squarely at Pat as if she could read her soul.

Pat had seen movies where someone pulled the fire alarm

to evacuate the building. It had always seemed too extreme and fantastical, but now she gave a passing thought to doing just that.

Once more she asked herself, who or what had triggered this? *They were checking everything.*

They walked the short distance to Pat's office. Once ensconced there, she again offered coffee. The women declined. Again. Down to business.

It was excruciating. To start, Pat had to explain that their dear Dr. Tracy had been out ill with a cold and didn't want to infect anyone.

"So perhaps his paperwork is a little behind. In his absence, some intake and discharge forms appear to be missing. Perhaps misfiled?"

Oh, and that nasty cold of Dr. Tracy's? It had been going around, she told them. "So we may have been a little understaffed lately. Nothing to worry about."

More notes. They took *so* many notes.

"A new administrator is coming on board in January. Only weeks away. See? Here's that confirmation." Pat had those emails ready, anyway. "I hired an LVN to assist me in the interim."

The evaluators thumbed through the forms, made notations, and asked for copies. Finally, they requested to see the residents' med schedules.

"Yes, please follow me." They walked to Denton's office. *Marched was more like it,* it seemed to Pat. There, she produced a semblance of some forms to their satisfaction. Others, not so much. Pat reiterated that any disarray was due to the doctor's temporary absence.

If she could have found Denton right now, she would have strangled him on the spot. *And where was Ricardo? Rats jumping from the ship. Both of them.*

Ms. Jones finally spoke. "We'd like to see a resident's room, now. Please lead the way."

Pat had to think quickly. Where could she take them? Not to Jack's or Bev's apartments, of course. *Certainly not to Bob's. Lois? Would Lois's work? Ah, but what if Lois decided to chat too much? No, no.*

Mrs. Ortega. Yes, that would work. She was quite deaf and may not even understand what the evaluators were asking. And she was a stickler for neatness. *Perfect.*

"This way."

They turned the corner and walked until they came to a door with a woven willow wreath hanging in the middle; a red felt cardinal perched on its bottom branches.

"Mrs. Ortega?" Pat rapped loudly. She smiled at Ms. Jones and Ms. Mehta. "Our Mrs. Ortega is a little hard of hearing."

At the third knock, a woman standing barely five feet in height answered the door. "Yes? Pat?"

"Hello, Mrs. Ortega. We have some visitors here who would like to see your room. Can we come in for a minute?"

"What? Visitors!" The woman smiled and opened the door wide. "Come in!"

That, at least went smoothly. The studio apartment was spotless. The water temperature was fine. Mrs. Ortega could hear only enough to comment briefly. Yes, she liked the breakfast she had that morning. But she couldn't remember what she had for dinner the night before.

"It was chicken, I think. Good, though," she told them all. She enjoyed Bingo, the activities, and feeding the birds in the garden.

Further, extended dialogue would be futile.

The next and final stop was to be the grounds. As they went toward the lobby, they heard some shouting.

"I want to see that director. Now!" The gruff voice was becoming louder as they approached.

Oh, God. It must be Bob's cousin. Pat hurried ahead of the evaluators.

The receptionist was in tears. She pointed to Pat. "Her. That's her."

"Sir, can I help you? Would you like to come into my office?"

The florid-faced man was waving his hands. "I will not. I'm Art Cristenson. Are you the woman who called me this morning to tell me my cousin Bob was dead?"

"Yes, I'm afraid he was found deceased by the staff. We are *so* sorry. His remains have already been removed."

"Hell, yes, they have. The sooner the better. I called the coroner's office myself. And lady, I'm here to tell you that I'm talking to the police chief next." He turned to the evaluators. "Who are you?"

Ms. Jones produced a card. "We're with the Department of Social Services. It's our job to investigate any complaints at facilities like this one. Please feel free to call us, Mr.?"

"Cristenson. You bet I will." He grabbed the card. "Bob was fine when he got here yesterday. This is malpractice or something." Art pointed a finger at Pat. "They ... she ... killed him. Investigate *that!*" He stomped out, a whirlwind of grief and anger in his wake.

The evaluators turned as a pair and looked at Pat, who stood in the middle of the terra-cotta tiled lobby. Alone.

"His cousin's death. It's such a shock for that poor man. We can all see that. I'll call him later when he's had a chance to calm down."

"We'll be in touch with our report," was Ms. Jones's response. Then, she and Ms. Mehta left, on the entrails of Art Cristenson's wrath.

It's over. It's over, was the chant in Pat's mind. She needed to sit down. She needed … a drink.

"Well, that was something," Aisha Mehta said, as she buckled her seatbelt. It was her turn to drive.

They had made a quick inspection (alone, they had insisted to Pat) of the grounds. Nothing was out of the ordinary: an older laundry room smelling of bleach, a hothouse, a handyman's office, and the dormant gardens. Next on their agenda was a quick lunch in a nearby coffee shop before returning to the office and filing a report.

"Dramatic finish, wasn't it?" Katherine Jones had seen plenty in her career. Pat and The Manor didn't pass her "smell test." There were too many small to bigger infractions. Too much sleight-of-hand antics from the director. Owner. She wasn't fooled by Pat's dog and pony show. And a suspicious death added to the mix?

She planned to pursue Art Cristenson's accusations and

complaints. She could get his number from the coroner and call him. But Katherine bet Aisha that they would hear from Art personally before the end of the day.

Aisha had pushed the ignition button, checked the rearview mirrors, and was ready to back out. Just then, a figure in khaki and olive green appeared at the passenger window; hunched over, it tapped loudly on the glass. Katherine jumped.

It was a man. His dusty baseball cap shaded his eyes. Katherine was reaching for her pepper spray when he called through the glass.

"Are you with the county?"

"Yes."

"I'm Frank Ricci, the maintenance manager and gardener here." He stood straighter and pointed to his nameplate. "I need to talk with you before you leave."

Katherine had put the pepper spray by her side, still accessible. She rolled the window down halfway. "What do you want, Mr. Ricci?"

Aisha, she noticed, had her hand on the gear shift, ready to go quickly into reverse.

"You need to know; things aren't what they seem here. Folks are scared. It's not safe. We think someone has been poisoned. Now he's dead." Frank hunched over again and passed a folded piece of paper through the window. "Here's my phone number. And others. Call me. Us."

Frank turned and walked away quickly, not even stopping to watch their car pull away.

———————————

Ricardo was avaricious but not stupid. He knew when it was time to cut his losses. He had heard all the yelling today, while safely in his vantage point in the storeroom. He had made himself scarce earlier, but kitchen staff kept him informed of the other comings and goings. They were not unappreciative of his past bonuses.

He sat now in his parked car at the farthest edge of the property and made a call. It rang only once before the other party picked up.

"Pat's going crazy," Ricardo began. No greeting was necessary. "A new guy died. It wasn't my fault. I did exactly what she asked."

He listened for a few seconds and then continued. "Yeah, but it's different this time. The guy's cousin or brother is screaming for her head. And the coroners came to get the body right when those social services women were here. A 'surprise visit.' Her license will be suspended, maybe even revoked. That cousin, or someone else, is going to call the cops. I feel it."

He listened for a few more seconds and then glanced around the parking lot, but it was quiet.

"Well, I'm telling you. It's over. She's going to try and pin all of this on me. The other murder, too. On *both* of us."

FIFTY-TWO

Yvonne Meets with the Chief

YVONNE ENTERED THE FAMILIAR, COMPACT lobby painted in institutional white and blue. A long, metal bench was against one wall. In the back, a phone was ringing.

"Hi, Dee. How're you doing? When's your retirement party?" Yvonne greeted the dispatcher. The older woman smiled from behind the bulletproof window and pushed the speakerphone button.

"Yvonne! Good to see you. It's going to be at the end of January at the Grange Hall. You'll get an invitation. Twenty-four years here. Can you believe it? I was a baby when I started. You here to see the Chief, or to gossip with me?"

"It's more fun to catch up with you, Dee, but is Angelo free? It's important."

Dee knew when to quit joking. "The Chief is in. I'll tell him you're here." She buzzed the connecting door open, and Yvonne entered the office area.

She walked a few steps down the hallway and rapped on the glass window of Angelo's office.

He waved her inside. "What's up?"

"Hi to you, too."

"Please don't start. It's been a morning." A box of antacids was on the desk. "I've got one sergeant on maternity leave, one new officer and the event organizers want to change the carriage ride routes tomorrow."

"I'm sorry to hear that. But I have news. A man over at The Manor just died. He may have been murdered." Yvonne began.

Angelo squinted. "So let me get this straight. You think that a man was poisoned by a plant called dogbane. And this person is now dead. Killed. *And* that the poison was really meant for," Angelo checked his notes, "… an elderly man there named Jack Hanson. Do I have that right?"

"Yes."

"Why? Why try and poison someone, why this plant?"

Yvonne leaned forward and described Jack finding the beetle and Pat's reaction. The locked hothouse. She ticked off the plant's devastating cardiac effects. Motives. She tried to be succinct.

"So this is serious, Angelo."

The Chief looked at his watch.

"Angelo, listen! They switched dinners. Jack is convinced that his own dinner was spiked with dogbane. To make him ill, at the least. I can call and get Jack on speakerphone to talk with you right now. He'll corroborate what I'm saying. It's a grocery list of concerns. Robin dug into Pat Breward and Dr. Tracy's backgrounds. They're shifty. Something is *definitely* off."

"You want me to investigate. I get it. Yvonne, I trust your judgment. But this is pretty strange." The last thing Angelo had expected on this winter's day was a suspicious death. A second murder? He reached for his antacids, popped a pink pill into his mouth, and chewed. *Jeez, Yvonne's relentless once she latches on.*

"If you look at the big picture, it starts to make sense. Remember when those feral animals showed up dead? You said I could look into them. I did, along with Scott Phillips from the feed store." Yvonne then gave him the layman's version of the necropsy results.

"The vet says evidence supports that the other animals probably died of dogbane, too."

"So dead animals, now a dead man. And you think it's all related."

"Yes. The plant must be growing in the hothouse. Maybe it got wild somehow, and away from Pat. There's more. Sandy Foster's murder may be connected to this."

"Yvonne! What are you doing to me? That's a stretch."

"No, no. Sandy worked at The Manor as a CNA. And that anonymous letter Robin received could have been sent by an insider, implicating Pat and the Doctor. You haven't discovered yet who sent it, right?"

"You just dropped it off. It could be a prank. Some kids. We've been busy." Angelo indicated the files on his desk. "The tree lighting, a Hanukkah celebration next week, the holidays, I'm short-staffed."

"Okay, but if you, and the department, felt there *was* a

plausible connection now, and Sandy should be exhumed, you could request a toxicology report. You and I both know that the coroner did a slap-dash job."

"Exhumed. You understand what paperwork and forms it takes to get a body exhumed. Not to mention the family's permission. I can't do it on a hunch you and your friends have."

There was a 'ping' as Yvonne's phone noted an incoming text message. She pulled the cell phone from her pocket and waved her hand at Angelo. "Wait."

"Yvonne, I have to get back to work here."

"Uh-huh. Well." Yvonne paused to read the message and then looked up. "Lucia just heard from Frank. He told her that he heard the dead man's cousin left The Manor after causing a scene. The guy was demanding an autopsy be done. He accused Pat of killing Bob Cristenson! And," Yvonne held the phone's screen out toward Angelo, "that cousin announced to one and all that he's coming to see *you* next, Chief."

Angelo groaned. "Okay, okay. What if I send a detective over there tomorrow to talk to her? To this Pat. An informal interview."

"Good, thanks. Let me know what happens. And lay off the coffee and spicy foods. You look like hell."

A stocky, red-faced man passed Yvonne as she exited the station, nearly bumping into her shoulder in his hurry to enter the lobby. Out of habit, she noted his attire, height, and features.

He looks ready to have a heart attack. Bob's cousin? Well, Angelo is going to get an earful now. Good!

FIFTY-THREE

Pat's Travel Plans

PAT POURED HERSELF A BOURBON and soda. Minus the soda.

She rarely drank. Tonight was an exception. Her apartment was cold, but Pat didn't bother to turn on the heater. She sat on her lumpy sofa nursing her bourbon. One tableside lamp was on, casting a medicinal yellow light into the living room.

She raised her garage sale glass and took a sip. Square ice cubes clunked against the side.

"Here's to you, Denton, you S.O.B. And, to you, Ricardo. Go to hell."

Pat closed her eyes and envisioned sitting on a beach, with stunning aquamarine waves in the distance. She could be enjoying a sweet, tangy Paloma cocktail in Puerto Vallarta. Or maybe a Fernandito in a crystal glass in Argentina. Yes, she could hear how ice would sound against *real* crystal.

It was time.

She knew as soon as those county people had left that she was in big trouble. A phone call from the Miller's Creek Police Chief later in the afternoon only reinforced her precarious position.

———————

"Ms. Breward?" Chief Angelo Belli identified himself. "We received a complaint from a family member regarding a death at your facility. The deceased is a Mr. Robert Cristenson. His relative claims the death is suspicious, and has requested an autopsy. That is being conducted. He has further stated to us that he feels it was direct actions or negligence at The Manor that caused Mr. Cristenson's death."

There was a pause. Pat took a breath. *That was fast. Who didn't that cousin know?*

"Well, Bob — Mr. Cristenson — was obviously too ill to have been released from the hospital into our care. I think his cousin should be taking this up with them. After all, Bob was here less than a day. We are *not* responsible! I'm sorry he passed, of course, but this is insulting and frankly, slanderous!"

"Yes, ma'am. I'm sure you feel that way. He's also filing with the regional social services office and the sheriff. However, given the serious nature of his complaint, I'm sending an officer over tomorrow to speak with you informally. Will you be there?"

"I will."

———————

Pat had hung up and gone directly home. And poured her drink.

She suddenly sat forward.

Lois! Could I take Lois with me wherever I'm going?

It was a passing thought. *No, it's not at all feasible. Maybe if I had more time to arrange it. No.*

She cursed again. Lois's considerable estate would have been the largest bequest Pat had ever received.

Huge! All that old money and investments. And no heirs. It was mine.

Certainly, Pat had quite a tidy sum already tucked away in multiple accounts. She enumerated them in her head: the past inheritances from lonely seniors, funds shaved off from Medicare schemes, and a little blackmail here and there. It was enough for a very comfortable "retirement" in Mexico. Or in a South American country where extradition policies were a bit more forgiving. That legacy from Lois would have put her in a new, rarified category, though.

If only … but even if Lois happened to die, let's say tonight, there still wouldn't be enough time to process everything. I'll have to walk away.

She took another sip. The ice had melted into sharp chips.

This place was where I was supposed to have glided under the radar, added to my nest egg. A final hurrah. But Denton turned into dead weight. And Ricardo screwed up. I should have stayed in Mexico City. Or in Reno. Reno was good to me.

It was no use perseverating. Pat put the sweaty glass down on the side table and walked to her back office, turning on the lights as she went. It was time for practical matters.

She opened a desk drawer and removed the two passports, two driver's licenses, cash, and bank statements from under the false bottom.

Starting up her laptop, she pondered.

Now, where to go first? Cabo or Puerto Vallarta. Then, on to Buenos Aires, perhaps?

An idea occurred to Pat. *Why not Cuba?* Her Mexican passport under the name *Anna Del Bosque* would come in handy for that destination.

She logged on and searched for airfares and flights from the San Francisco airport. Tomorrow or the next day at the latest. She absently took a candy from the bowl on the desk and crunched the butterscotch in two.

I hate this Podunk town. They'll pay.

FIFTY-FOUR

Thursday Tree Lighting

THE ELVES FROM MADAME GEORGETTE'S School of Dance assembled on the west end of the circle. The bells on the youngsters' green tunics jingled as the children slurped hot chocolate, and pelted each other with marshmallows.

A smattering of folks had begun to arrive at the historic mill wheel in the center of town; a few even wore festive Santa hats. Families had bundled toddlers into strollers, while some locals brought their mostly well-behaved dogs. A gaggle of teenagers had extricated themselves from their parents and were practicing their blasé looks.

A block away, the junior high school band was tuning up, an action that caused some of the dogs who were present to tilt their heads. Shop windows and nearby trees twinkled with white lights.

Charlotte was seated on a green wooden bench, a throw blanket over her knees. Joining her on either side were Lou (minus Steve) and Maisie. Neither one opted for a blanket, though those had been proffered.

"Are you going to sit on Santa's lap?" Lou asked her seatmates.

"I don't think so, Lou," Charlotte laughed. "I'm a bit old for that."

"Nonsense! How about you Maisie? Are you game?"

"I'll do it if Char does it. I heard the mayor is Santa this year." Maisie lowered her voice at this last part. Children were nearby, after all.

"Well then, it's almost our civic duty," Lou nodded.

"Oh, all right." Charlotte knew Lou wouldn't give up. "But let the kids go first. I don't want to end up in the police log for elbowing little children out of the way."

"Okay, sure!" Lou had already snagged a cookie from Jen, who had set up the bakery's table by Santa's dais and throne. Lou took a bite and brushed the crumbs onto the ground. "Where's Robin? I haven't seen her yet, but the sweets are here."

"She and Lucia will be here soon." Charlotte looked at her watch. "Robin dropped me off early, so I could get a seat. Oh, there's Yvonne, though." Charlotte waved a mittened hand, but Yvonne didn't see her.

"Yvonne!" Maisie shouted, then put two fingers to her lips and blew. Once more, the dogs did a head tilt. "Over here!"

Yvonne walked toward them. "Hi, ladies." She leaned over and kissed Charlotte on the cheek. "Have you seen Robin or Lucia yet?" Her smile was quick, but passing.

"Hello, dear. No, they'll be here any minute." Charlotte repeated her earlier response. "Why? Is something wrong?" Charlotte gestured for Lou to move over. "Here, sit down."

"No, thanks, I'll stand. Everything is fine. Just wondering."

Lou spoke up. "Is your daughter with you?" As a friend

and long-standing neighbor, Lou knew Yvonne's family well.

"Yeah. Lynne and the kids are around here somewhere. They got in from Mendocino this afternoon."

"Tell them hi, and to stop by if they have time." Lou started to add something else but nudged Charlotte instead. "Oooh," she said in a stage whisper. "Look."

They all turned in the direction Lou pointed. Approaching the group was Scott.

"Oooh," Lou repeated. Charlotte gently elbowed her.

"Happy tree lighting, everyone!" Scott stood next to Yvonne. He wore a heavy Pendleton jacket, jeans, and ubiquitous work boots. His cheeks were a little pink, his chin a little scruffy. He was carrying a paper cup.

"Can I get anyone coffee or chocolate?" he asked after introductions were made.

The women declined.

"Are you ready for all this excitement?" Maisie asked.

"Sure. Small-town stuff like this is one reason I moved here." He turned to Yvonne. "Sorry, I missed your call yesterday. I had to pick up a delivery and didn't get home until late. What's up?"

Damn. "Oh, nothing. I needed some advice about new kibble for Madison."

The three women on the bench followed the conversation as if viewing a tennis match. Heads shifted left, then right.

Yvonne spotted Angelo on the far side of Main Street. "Hey. There's Angelo. Want to go over there with me? We can check if they need any extra help tonight."

They bid their adieus to the curious trio and walked the

diagonal path to the chief's location.

"Kibble?"

"No, that was an excuse. I called to tell you that someone just died at The Manor, and it looks to be a murder by dogbane. *Another* murder. I talked to Angelo yesterday and want to follow up with him now."

"What?!"

Yvonne relayed the key points to Scott, as they made their way across the walkway. "I'll catch you up on all the details later."

"Chief!" Yvonne called out.

"Oh, hey. I was going to text you, but we had another crisis today," Angelo replied. "My p.m. dispatcher got the flu. Dee is covering tonight."

"Any news?"

Angelo looked at Scott and began to shake his head.

"It's okay. This is Scott Phillips from the feed store. He knows what's going on. And his uncle did the necropsy on the rabbit."

"Well," the Chief paused, then continued, "that guy's cousin *did* come in to see me, and man, he was hot. Furious. Convinced of foul play. So I sent a sergeant over there this morning — Ken. Like I said I would."

"Oh, Ken's a good guy. What did he find?"

"Nothing." Angelo waved a squad car and antique fire truck through the barricades. It was getting darker, and Santa was fast approaching.

"That director, Pat, wasn't there. Neither was the doctor. Even the head chef was out."

"Chef? Do you mean the kitchen manager? Ricardo?"

"Yeah, him. The receptionist said *everyone* was out sick.

Ken was able to talk to a temporary nurse who was on duty. But she didn't know anything. Mostly the deceased was a new resident. A recent arrival. They confirmed what the cousin told me, that an autopsy was requested. Also, some county inspectors were on site yesterday. And that they didn't seem too happy when they left."

"No Pat?" Yvonne felt a tightening along her neck.

"Nope. As I said, out sick. Which was fine with the staff. Word is that Pat's not too popular."

"Anything about Sandy Foster?"

"Again, nope. Nobody was there who could answer questions. Ken reported that the housekeeping and kitchen crews were operating on autopilot."

"Pat's gone," Yvonne whispered.

Before she could ask anything more, Angelo's cell phone and two-way radio both went off.

"Yeah, Dee." He answered the phone first. Her message was urgent. *Contact dispatch. Now!* Frowning, he re-dialed on an encrypted line.

His ruddy face began to turn a disturbing light magenta as he listened.

"Son of a … . I'll be right there. Don't let him leave!"

"Angelo?" Yvonne put her hand on his arm. "What is it?"

"That Dr. Tracy just showed up at the station. Said he had information about the murder. *Sandy Foster's* murder. Cover for me," he shouted to the nearest patrol officer.

"I'm coming with you." Yvonne was already beside Angelo, running together against the incoming, jolly crowd.

"I'll meet you there," Scott shouted to their backs.

FIFTY-FIVE

Denton Makes a Move

HIS FEVER WAS BACK. AND he could barely keep food down these days. Sleep sweats were common.

At least I can still drive.

He looked at his face in the rearview mirror. It was close to dusk but still light enough so that what he saw reflected back angered and shocked him: sunken eyes, grey pallor, and a mouth forming a rictus grin.

Denton coughed. His ribs grated. That specialist he saw in San Francisco a month ago only confirmed what he already knew.

I am a doctor, after all.

Things were moving quickly. He had weeks, maybe two months left to live if he was lucky, the specialist had told him.

Lucky! That's a joke.

Denton thought back on those years when everything revolved around his luck. Or the lack of it. Time spent at blackjack and craps tables, inhaling the smell of cigarette smoke, scotch, and fried food from the all-you-can-eat buffets. Following the lure of the next score. It was a heady concoction.

Beeping and clanging slot machines, exclamations by tourists winning thirty-dollar jackpots, and a roulette ball clacking against a mahogany wheel provided his life's background music then.

The race track was where he truly felt most alive, though. Sitting in the grandstands, with horses thundering down the track, and people cheering — or crying — well, that was exhilarating. He went to the Elko County Fair once a year to experience it in person. Otherwise, he sat on a barstool in a Reno casino, wagering on the simulcast races held around the world. *Yeah. The races.*

And then there was Pat. Ha!

His buddy, Pat, slipped up only once during those days in Reno. And Denton had filed it away. They were sitting in one of the smaller casinos, and it was late. Denton was losing, and Pat had decided to play.

"Five, thirteen, and twenty-nine," Pat told him in passing, sitting at the roulette table. "My lucky numbers."

And she *had* won that night. After that, Denton tried playing those same numbers, although with decidedly more mixed results.

But those numbers were lucky enough for me the night I broke into her hothouse. He managed a smirk. No laugh this time. *Oh, yes, I was right. Five, thirteen, twenty-nine. Her 'so-secret' keypad code. She never even missed the two dogbane plants I took.*

He glanced at one of those plants cushioned on the seat next to him. *My insurance.*

Denton pulled into a parking spot under a streetlight, right in front of the Miller's Creek Police Department. The street was mostly deserted, with the locals busy attending the downtown festivities. He could hear some clarinets and drums in the distance as he got out of the car.

He buttoned his wool coat (his fever had become the chills) and reluctantly removed a cane from the passenger seat. It was a humiliating, but now necessary aid. The plant came out next. Closing the car door, he walked to the curb and placed the plant on a bench in front of the police station. He stepped back, evaluating. From the right angle, he could view both the plant and a sign indicating "Police." Pleased, Denton took out his phone and snapped a picture.

He texted a number, attached the photo of the plant and sign, and wrote: *5, 13, 29.* Denton hit the send button.

Satisfied, he picked up the dogbane. Cradling it in one arm, and using the cane, he walked into the station.

He saw two women behind the glass partition.

"I'm Doctor Denton Tracy," he announced. "You're going to want to speak with me. It's about a murder."

FIFTY-SIX

A Busy Police Station

DEE SIPPED HER ENERGY DRINK. She didn't mind taking the extra shift tonight. It should be fairly quiet what with most folks downtown celebrating. She had attended many holiday events over the years, and her attitude was a bit *"been there, done that, bought the T-shirt."*

Anyway, I'm enjoying getting to know Janis. Officer Garcia. Teaching her the ropes around here.

The latest hire, Janis Garcia, was a newly-graduated recruit, brought on to replace an officer who was relocating. She was young and enthusiastic, if a little serious. The two women were on duty and in charge of the station that night. The evening's event had drawn the other officers downtown.

"Let me give you the lay of the land," Dee said, swiveling in her chair to address the young woman standing nearby. "Have a seat."

Dee had just ended a call about a missing cat; a grey tabby who regularly made the rounds in his neighborhood, convincing people he was starving. As a result, he was quite the chonk.

"I'm sure Smokey will be home later tonight, Mrs. Downs. He usually makes it back by eight o'clock, doesn't he? Call us later, if not."

"A regular," Dee advised Officer Garcia when she hung up.

The cat crisis was averted, and Dee proceeded to share her knowledge about Miller's Creek with the newbie. It was a master class in 'who's who,' of the local color and characters, the few citizens who occasionally landed in the one-person jail cell for overindulging, and, finally, more about their boss.

It was at that latter point that Dee saw someone parking under the streetlight. He was lingering outside. She and the cameras noted a tall, angular man, somewhat bent over. His face looked as white as the cold pavement outside the station. Dee leaned forward in her chair and watched closely, alertly, as the man fussed with something on the bench near the glass doors.

Is that a plant? Weird.

Twenty-four years on the job told her this man was going to be a problem.

"Get ready," she told the new officer. "Something is strange here."

Straightening, the man picked up the plant and walked directly into the station.

Dee had not expected, though, that he would announce he was there about a murder.

A murder!

Dee picked up the phone at the same time Officer Garcia used the two-way radio on her belt.

"Chief," Dee said to Angelo, reaching him first. "Contact

dispatch. Now! And you'd better get back here fast."

Angelo flashed the red emergency lights on his squad car, and they raced the few blocks to the station. Yvonne barely had time to send one short text to Robin and another to her daughter.

Robin had locked the bakery doors and was steps away when she got Yvonne's text. As had been pre-arranged, Lucia met Robin at the bakery. They planned to leave their cars there and walk to the tree lighting. Parking any closer would be a hassle, with the streets blocked off. Added to that mix were horses, excited kids, and the encroaching night.

At the message's ping, she read:

Denton just walked into the police station. Says he knows something re a murder – Sandy's?? Can you get there ASAP – I'm on my way w Angelo NOW!

"Oh, my God," she gasped.

"What?" Lucia stopped in her tracks.

"It's from Yvonne. Denton showed up at the police station. Talking to them about a murder! Maybe Sandy's. Yvonne wants me to get right over there."

"Go, go. I'll take care of Charlotte. Call me later." Lucia gave Robin a little shove toward her car. "Go!" she repeated.

With no traffic on the darkened streets, Robin made it in record time and parked next to a late-model sedan. She felt a frisson of energy, the same jolt as when she had been chasing a big story at the newspaper. It was an energy that she had missed. It felt *good*.

"What in God's name is going on?" Robin said as a greeting as she walked in. She waved at Dee but addressed Yvonne.

"All right. You're here," Yvonne responded. "Angelo is in the interview room questioning Denton Tracy about Sandy. An officer put him in there, but I'm not allowed in. Yet." She pointed to a door down the hallway where Angelo, Officer Garcia, and Denton were sequestered. "So I'm cooling my heels out here instead."

"Unclench your jaw. You'll break a tooth." Robin recognized the telltale sign of Yvonne's fuming. "Is he confessing? Did he do it?" The gaunt, brittle man Robin barely knew seemed incapable of murder. *But?*

"Unsure. You're the only one of us who's actually had any interaction with Tracy. Maybe you can help."

"Help? Help how?"

"I don't know. You poked around in his background. Maybe take some notes, or confirm that anything the doctor says about dogbane is true — Dee says he brought one of those plants in with him. Or tell Angelo what you found out about Tracy and his gambling habits." Yvonne turned now to the dispatcher. "Dee, tell Robin what you told me. It's okay." It was the second time that night that Yvonne had vouched for someone close to her.

Robin looked at Dee. Standing up, next to the window, Dee related how Dr. Tracy had entered the station carrying a plant he claimed was poisonous dogbane. Proof somehow, of something. He insisted on speaking only to the Chief and said he had firsthand knowledge of Sandy Foster's murder.

"Holy …," Robin uttered.

"Right!"

"Months after that woman's murder and this guy shows up now? And tonight of all nights," Dee exclaimed. "He looks like death warmed over, himself. Do you think he's crazy or legit?" she asked Yvonne.

"Well, my gut says he's telling the truth. He knows something about how Sandy was killed. At least *he* thinks so."

Robin added, saying to Dee, "Yeah, we *did* speculate there was a connection to The Manor."

They turned as headlights flickered at the front windows. A truck pulled up and parked next to Robin's hybrid.

"Oh, damn. I forgot." Yvonne muttered.

"Scott?" Robin asked.

He entered the brightly lit station, a cold wind following him inside.

"Hey, sorry, you didn't have to follow me," Yvonne said.

"Well, you drove with the Chief. How were you going to get back to your car?"

"Ah. I didn't even think of that. Thanks. But I don't know how long we'll be here."

"It's okay. I can wait. Everything all right?" He sat on the lone bench, crossing his long legs.

"Uh, we don't know," Robin answered. "Probably not."

There was a commotion in the hall, voices, and a door opening and closing. Before she could say more, Angelo came out to the lobby and looked at those assembled.

"Sheesh, what is this? A convention?" He pointed at Yvonne. "Can you come back here with me?"

"Sure. You'll want Robin in this, too."

"No, just you."

"Angelo! She can be a big help right now. She knows Dr. Tracy."

"Okay, okay. *Just* Robin. I'm doing the questioning!" He squinted at Scott. "You. Sit there."

They followed the Chief to the back room.

Dee sat down and looked at Scott. "Want a cup of coffee?" she asked through the two-way speaker. "This might take a while."

FIFTY-SEVEN

Denton Shares

ANGELO SLAMMED THE INTERVIEW ROOM door after they entered. The walls shook.

"All right, Doctor. Tell *her*," he pointed to Yvonne, "what you told me. In detail."

Denton was seated at the end of a long, portable table. There were no handcuffs or shackles around his bony wrists. After all, he wasn't under arrest. His coat was draped on a chair, with a cane leaning against it. The overhead fluorescent lights were unflattering at the best of times, and this evening they accentuated his already chalky skin and the eggplant-purple bags under his eyes.

Officer Garcia was seated at his left elbow, her pen poised above a notebook, with a laptop nearby, and a video recorder propped up logging the conversations. A dogbane plant in a black pot was in the middle of the table, a lone, bizarre centerpiece.

Instead of addressing Yvonne, Denton gave Robin a withering glance.

"If only *you* had acted quickly, Bob Cristenson wouldn't be dead. Some investigative reporter you are. Ignoring my letter. And I gave you such hints. *No coincidence,* I said."

"It was *you* who sent me that letter? Why? Why all that subterfuge?" Robin felt her face flush with anger from the insult and rebuke.

Denton looked at his hands, with their thin fingers, and paused. "At that time, I didn't want to be involved."

"Involved?"

"Robin, stop. We're way beyond that letter, now," Angelo interjected. "Let's get to the heart of this, okay? Doctor, repeat your story."

Denton took a sip from the water bottle in front of him. "This is tedious. But I'll be concise."

He began with how he met Pat in Reno, and how she blackmailed him. "She used my gambling and drinking problems against me. I could have lost my license and been arrested. She took advantage of me. I became her tool."

He told how she dragged him from place to place, finally landing in this godforsaken town. Denton itemized how she made him lie about heart ailments or other illnesses and threatened to expose or implicate him if he didn't follow her orders. He quickly learned to fabricate false Medicare claims and other forms, under Pat's tutelage.

"And the dogbane?" Yvonne finally spoke, ignoring Angelo. "How does it play into this?"

"Ah, that." Denton pointed to the plant on the table. He explained that Pat had learned about dogbane and other poisonous plants in her travels to Mexico and Central

America; and how a little or a lot of it could induce cardiac episodes and other health issues in vulnerable patients. She grew them in the hothouse along with her precious orchids.

"Pat thought dogbane would do well in this climate. After buying The Manor, she had Ricardo plant a few along the creek bed and nearby as a test. When they thrived, she decided to grow them in the hothouse, instead. It made for easier access and more control for her. Less suspicious than Ricardo wandering around, too. Some plants evidently propagated further from the originals. I was able to liberate that one and another from the hothouse." They all looked at the solitary plant on the table.

Denton continued. He recounted that upon Pat's instructions, Ricardo would include the dried or fresh dogbane into a particular resident's food. If the person complained about the bitter taste in their meals, Denton placed the dogbane into capsules instead and administered it that way.

"Is that what you did to my mother?" Robin was reaching across the table now. "You S.O.B!"

"Robin! Let him finish," Angelo barked.

Yvonne laid a hand on Robin's arm.

"Why?" Yvonne asked.

"Pat liked to say it was about 'heads in beds.' A way to keep residents there and the numbers up. More income. As the attending physician, I could also charge back for related services treating the other problems it causes, like gastrointestinal issues and vertigo. Occasionally, it was to control recalcitrant patients. Like your friend, Maisie."

Denton shrugged. "Although, it almost always comes down to money with Pat."

Robin's thoughts were running to mayhem. As she began to speak, Yvonne interrupted.

"What happened to Sandy Foster?" Yvonne asked him the million-dollar question.

Denton shifted in his chair. "I want you to know that I liked Sandy, initially. She was a big help to me. Very capable. I gave her more and more responsibilities. She assisted me with all that vexing paperwork and filing." He waved his hand. "And I, well, often let her dispense medications to the residents. Pat didn't know that. Unfortunately for Sandy, she was a bit too inquisitive. She caught on that there was something off."

"Off?" Yvonne asked.

"Yes. She found some vials of dry dogbane in my office and asked me about it. I lied, of course. But she got suspicious. Then, she started to look at the intake charts and files. She realized that a high percentage of residents developed heart and gastrointestinal issues once they were at The Manor. That Medicare was being overcharged. Things like that. She, incorrectly, thought I was being negligent or corrupt, so she went to Pat to report me."

Denton coughed. "Stupid girl. It was her undoing. Pat couldn't have Sandy exposing her, of course. So she had Ricardo spike Sandy's lunch and dinner with dogbane over a few days. Maybe a week or so. It was easy for him, as the staff kept their lunches in one of the kitchen refrigerators. The goal was to make her sick enough to leave or to scare her away. But."

"But?" Yvonne asked.

"She *did* become increasingly ill. Evidently, late that night, during her shift, she went into the kitchen to get some water and fainted. Ricardo was the only one in there. She hit her head on the counter on her way down. And she fell hard onto the floor." Denton made a face. "Cracked her skull. Ricardo said it was a mess. Blood everywhere. Head wounds do that, you know." Denton looked at Angelo.

"Anyway, Ricardo locked the kitchen door and called Pat. When she arrived, she examined Sandy and told him that the girl was dead. They wore gloves – Pat's idea – and dragged Sandy into the storeroom, in case someone came in. At that hour, it was unlikely. There was hardly any staff. They wrapped her in blankets from the laundry, covering her completely, according to Ricardo. If Sandy hadn't been deceased already, that smothering would have done it. He said they cleaned the kitchen while they decided how to dispose of the body."

Good God. Robin felt sick. She noticed that even Officer Garcia was pale.

"Go on." Yvonne was taking charge of the interrogation.

"Ricardo knows more about the locale around here than Pat does. He suggested a park on the edge of town as a spot they could bring Sandy. It was after midnight, at that point. And this place rolls up the sidewalks by eight o'clock, correct? Who would have seen them?"

"So they took her to the park and left her in a spot near the culvert." Yvonne made a statement; it was not a question.

"Yes, they used the facility's older, used van. It has a wheelchair lift, which made it easier, and it didn't have any identifying logo painted on it."

There was a minute of silence while the group digested this. "What about Bob?" Robin had to ask.

"Oh, cardiac arrest from dogbane, I'm willing to bet. Ricardo told me he wasn't sure what happened, exactly. Dogbane was added to Jack Hanson's meal, per Pat's instruction. His own 'special menu.' I told you that sometimes it was meant for troublemakers. How did Mr. Cristenson get it? Was it switched somehow? We don't know. Ricardo never went rogue when it came to these meals."

Yvonne then asked the next question on their minds. "Why are you confessing all this? Telling us now?"

"Well, as you perhaps might be able to infer, I'm not well. As I told your Chief earlier, I am in fact dying. It was recently confirmed. I have a month, or two. Maybe only weeks. So what can your legal system do to me as any supposed retribution? Also, Ricardo informed me that Pat is planning on blaming the two of us for Sandy *and* Bob Cristenson's deaths. She may be leaving town, as we speak. To Mexico, would be my guess. And really, aren't I just as much a victim of Pat's, as anyone? She's made my later years miserable. So I'm returning the favor to her. She's the one responsible for the murders and I want to see her rot in prison."

He sat back and finally looked at Officer Garcia. "Did you get all that?"

"In my office." Angelo stood and spoke to Yvonne and Robin. "Officer Garcia, you remain with Dr. Tracy. Understand?"

"Surely I am not under arrest?" Denton asked. "I'm ill. I

need to be hospitalized."

"Just … just stay put." Angelo escorted the two women out of the room. The door to the interior core of the station locked behind him. They walked quickly down the secure, short hall to his office.

"You're just leaving him in there?" Robin asked as soon as they entered.

"Well, he doesn't look like he can get too far, now does he?" Angelo snapped.

"Angelo, cut it out." Yvonne admonished him. "This is serious. You have to call the sheriff. Yes, we found Sandy's body in Miller's Creek, but since her murder and Bob's happened outside the city limits, they need to know. This is too big for us to handle here. We … they … have to get a warrant for Pat's arrest. A BOLO. Someone has to find and bring her in. Ricardo, too. Now!"

"I know, I know. Let me get my brain around this."

It was at that moment that all hell broke loose in the form of sirens screaming from the direction of the fire department. Dee's desktop was lit up like the tree at the town center. Alerts were coming in on their cell phones, radios, and to the station's switchboard.

There was a fire at The Manor.

FIFTY-EIGHT

A Fiery Exit

A ONE-WAY, DIRECT FLIGHT from San Francisco to Mexico City, leaving Friday. Tomorrow. *Check.* Pat had purchased the ticket online Thursday morning.

Four hours, once I'm on that plane. Give or take. Four hours and I can be done with this town. Maybe I'll switch to my 'Anna Del Bosque' identity when I get to Mexico. Then, who knows? I could even get a new, different ID when there. I still have my contact. He's pricey, but such an artist. Nobody ever questions his documents.

After booking her flight and making reservations at the Four Seasons hotel in the heart of Mexico City, Pat drove to nearby Santa Rosa. She parked at the large corporate bank with indifferent tellers where she had a safe deposit box. She had opened a small, personal account there when she first arrived in Miller's Creek. It held only a few thousand dollars, enough to qualify for a box. She closed the account and withdrew the money and the box's contents: her original, offshore bank paperwork, more cash, and proof of Denton's gambling indiscretions. While she was at it, she also withdrew most of the funds from The Manor's business account; her role as a signatory came in handy.

Will I need Denton's receipts anymore? He won't even make it here without me. That idiot. Well, you never know. Might as well hang onto them. I've kept them this long. She put the envelopes and cash into her purse. *Ricardo will be on his own now. He's outlived his usefulness, too.*

With her banking completed, Pat stopped at a Latin Fusion restaurant for a late lunch. She ate her spicy Cubano while ignoring the incoming calls and messages from The Manor.

Yes, things were in place. But it wasn't the way Pat had wanted to end her career.

Who had tipped off the county? Who ruined my plans? Where was Denton?

But now that everything was in motion, she would allow herself to feel a little … excited: a new life, tropical weather, and flowers, someplace far away from this piddling and banal community.

Pat had already packed a few clothes and sundries into a carry-on bag. She wouldn't need much, only some items to get her started before her shopping trip in Mexico. She deserved … better.

She'd leave her aging car at an airport parking lot.

I'll be long gone by the time they find it.

She planned on staying at a hotel near the airport tonight, to be ready for her early morning flight.

There was nothing in her apartment she cared about. The furnishings were all cheap or second-hand, creating a low, modest profile befitting a woman whose *whole life* was giving to the elderly; a testament to her self-sacrificing! Pat's rent was paid for the next month. She shrugged off that petty loss. The landlords would have a yard sale, count their dollars, and re-rent the place after she disappeared. She'd only miss her orchids.

Pat sighed. *Lois.* That was the one real fly in the ointment to her plans. On the drive home, her thoughts drifted to the elderly woman. The windshield wipers swished away at the light mist in tune with her musings. *Lois. Lois.* If only she had that money.

*Ah, it was no use. Because somebody or some*bodies *had screwed this up for her. Damn them for it. All those lost assets.* Her better mood from lunchtime evaporated.

Another thought interrupted. Should she leave a note? A farewell kiss saying Denton was the one behind Sandy's murder? And maybe somehow responsible for Bob's, too? Well, he *had* left her in a mess. It *was* his fault in the first place that Sandy died. His and Ricardo's. Denton let that CNA see too much. What else could Pat have done?

She pulled into her carport. The complex was quiet, as usual. Pat had never made an effort to get to know her neighbors, and they, sensing her reticence, had avoided her, as well. No Girl Scouts rang her bell to sell cookies, and the high school Boosters didn't ask for a donation. So if she went missing for a week, a month, or forever, no one would notice and call the landlord. *Good!*

It didn't take long to finish packing her papers, passports, and documents. Everything was ready, sitting at the front door with her laptop.

She was constructing a farewell note in her head. Her final hurrah. She thought it could say: *"Denton and Ricardo are responsible for killing Sandy Foster. Ask THEM about Bob Cristenson."*

She'd mail the missive to the sheriff's department, too. *That would show Police Chief What's-his-name. Embarrass him. The incompetence. Couldn't solve a murder in his own little town. Ha!*

Her phone pinged with another message before she could write it.

The staff again? Or the stupid police department trying to reschedule? Why don't they leave me alone? Why aren't they all at that inane Christmas pageant?

Pat looked at the latest message. From Sara. Again. Then she noticed the one that had come in just before it. *From Denton?*

She opened his. At first, all that she saw was a photo of the Miller's Creek Police Department. Next, she noticed the dogbane plant sitting in front of it. Posed, actually. Finally, she read the text:

5, 13, 29

Pat shrieked a banshee cry and dropped the phone onto the carpet. She swore in two languages and cursed Denton to the farthest regions of hell. Profanities rose and fell around her like bats called up from Hades.

5, 13, 29. How does he know my code? Is he going to the police?

Pat slumped to the sofa. Her head felt like it was going to split open.

"What's he doing?" she said aloud.

Then, like scenes from a movie, Pat saw the events play out.

Denton must have taken the plant from the hothouse. He learned my code, somehow. He's going to expose me. But wait, he'll put himself in jeopardy, too. That's insane! Why would he do that? Does he hate me that much? Unless … unless he really is sick. Maybe too sick to care?

She picked up the phone and looked at the message again. *The time. When did he send it? A few minutes ago. What if he's talking to the police right now? Admitting everything. What we did. That fool!*

Adrenaline made her heart pound. She had to leave. *Now.* Breathe, she told herself. *Get a grip.* Most of the town would be at the tree lighting, right? So maybe they'd be delayed in getting to her apartment. To look for her. And maybe, she could delay them even more. A distraction.

Yes. It's a good idea. An inspiration.

Pat quickly gathered her bags and a box of matches. She locked her apartment door for the last time. Once in her car, Pat drove straight to The Manor. It was dusk, and she saw only a few cars in the lot.

Staffing is sparse tonight. That's perfect.

Pat parked on the road, outside the main entrance and driveway. She walked swiftly to the two buildings that housed Frank's office and the laundry room, and easily found what she wanted inside: a small gas can used for the lawnmower, from Frank's; a stack of sheets, from the laundry. Pat carried the gasoline and the sheets to the hothouse. She bunched most of the sheets up behind the building, leaving one trailing to the fence line. She sprinkled some gasoline on them, nestled the can in the middle, and lit the tail edge of the sheet closest to the fence.

Running past Frank's office, she hesitated. It was an afterthought, but oh-so-perfect. She went back, stopped in the doorway, and eyed the shelves of oils and solutions he used for mechanical repairs. Pat spotted a can of paint thinner. She uncapped it and poured it over the piles of papers he had on his desk. Lighting a few matches, she turned them all into mini bonfires.

When she was certain they had caught fire, she sprinted to her car. Nobody was on the road.

Goodbye, dogbane. I had to sacrifice my poor orchids, though. "So sorry," she mouthed to them, glancing in her rearview mirror.

Pat sped down the rural road toward the highway. South. To freedom.

Dusk. Lois had kept her blinds open all day, to catch whatever winter sun leaked through. Her room overlooked the back gardens and got the afternoon light. Now it was time to close up for the night. Using her walker, she shuffled the few steps and reached for the cord. She might be elderly, and her legs didn't work as well as when she was young. However, Lois prided herself on her eyesight. That was one good thing she had inherited from her mother. Yes, yes, she needed her glasses on, but still — *darn* good eyesight; no macular degeneration, and she had successful cataract surgery in her early eighties.

So when she stood at her window, she saw a remarkable

thing. There was Pat, scurrying around near the hothouse. Pat. Who hadn't been by to visit her lately.

Lois rapped on the window. "Pat," she called out, although she knew her voice wouldn't carry that far. "Pat!" She knocked more firmly.

Pat never heard, never turned in Lois's direction. She just ran down the driveway, her black raincoat flapping behind her like wings.

Like those crows that Mrs. Ortega feeds, Lois thought. *That's curious.*

And then, Lois saw a yellow-orange light, traveling toward the hothouse from the fence.

A fire! Lois scooted to her door. Opening it wide, she shouted into the hallway, "Fire! Everyone, a fire! At the hothouse!"

A few people were walking in the hall on their way to dinner. Sara, the LVN, was with them. She was on the night rotation — taking an extra shift again, in Pat's absence.

"Go to the lobby," Sara shouted, as she ran to the nearest alarm box. She pulled the switch, and the sharp clangs reverberated throughout the facility. Still running and shouting, she took her phone from a pocket and dialed 9-1-1.

Aides and kitchen staff appeared, and they wheeled and directed the frightened residents from their rooms and down the corridors. The clanging continued. Someone was crying.

Lois was swept along, first to the lobby, then outside to the farthest end of the driveway, next to the road. They were all sitting together, huddled under an oversized canvas gazebo, left over from summer.

Two workers had grabbed the kitchen's commercial-grade

fire extinguishers. They were spraying the hothouse and fence, dampening its effects. Further down, smoke was billowing from the empty windows in Frank's office, the glass broken from the heat. The overhead sprinkler system was trying its best in there.

It was becoming darker and damp outside. Two housekeepers had thought to grab blankets from a facility closet and now wrapped them around thin and shivering shoulders. They all heard a siren coming from the direction of town. Others sounded from the opposite direction.

"Pat," Lois said, teeth chattering from nerves and cold. "Sara. It was Pat."

Sara was making the rounds and checking on her charges; everyone was accounted for, thankfully. Staff and residents were turning to her by default. She had tried to reach Pat by phone and text. There was no response.

"You're a hero for alerting us, Lois. You know that?" Sara stood in front of Lois and chafed the elderly woman's hands, now turning blue and verging on chilblain.

"Are you looking for Ms. Breward? Lois, I haven't been able to reach her yet. I'm sure she'll come as soon as she hears what happened. Don't worry. Our guys will have that hothouse fire under control, and there are multiple emergency units on their way. Lots of help. We'll be all right."

"No!" Lois clasped Sara's hands. "I saw Pat outside by the hothouse, just before the fire started. I ... I think she set it."

"You saw Ms. Breward out there? Tonight. By the fire?"

Lois nodded. "I know what I saw."

"I believe you. It will be okay." *Is Lois confused? I mean, this has to be upsetting. Could she actually have seen Ms. Breward? Pat. And, why would Pat set fire to her own facility? It's too crazy. Isn't it?*

The sirens were closer. Sara saw the flashing lights and three fire trucks pull into the driveway. An ambulance, police cruiser, and a few cars were close behind. Air brakes whooshed. Sara hurried to the first truck. She was responsible. As she told Lois, it was going to be okay.

Sara let out a breath.

FIFTY-NINE

Detour

IT WAS CLEARLY THE BIG rig's fault. The road was wet, and the coastal fog had rolled in with its wintery fingers.

The driver was going too fast and wasn't from around the area. He miscalculated, and when the Mini Cooper in front of him stopped suddenly, the truck driver braked, then jackknifed across the highway, blocking lanes, and wreaking havoc. It was a miracle nobody was killed, the newspapers later breathlessly reported.

Nonetheless, there was damage done. Astute drivers heard about or saw the mess and took detours early on. Parallel thoroughfares became congested. Some locals hopped onto other, lesser-known, and more rural roads to make their way home.

By the time Pat reached the slowdown, she realized that staying on the main highway would involve delaying her trip to the airport hotel by hours. Hours she wasn't willing to waste.

Once more she swore. *I hate this place, these idiots.* She tried to calm her breathing. *Perfect sunsets and pampering await me*, she told herself. *Soon. Soon. Just get through this. Just keep heading south.*

Pat followed a small convoy of assorted vehicles off the highway, onto a road that first appeared to run south but then veered west.

What the hell? No, no, no!

Should she follow these fools? West? Then where? She didn't want to end up on the winding Highway 1, weaving down the long, rocky Pacific coastline in the dark. That was unacceptable. *No. There has to be a better way.*

Pat took a left turn at the first opportunity. *South, correct?* She pulled over to check her GPS. *What — no bars?* Oh well, this road would surely lead soon to a bigger juncture. *South,* she repeated.

Her modest sedan was soon cruising at a decent speed along a two-lane road. Oak and madrone trees were the only shadowy companions along the trip. Her headlights caught the occasional insect in their glare along the switchbacks. Yes, it was more zigzagging than she had anticipated, but she was moving along. Moving to her future.

Pat had never taken an interest in exploring the county or surrounding areas. Why? The bucolic nature hadn't appealed to her. She hadn't made any friends to join in wine-tasting adventures. So she wasn't exactly sure where she was at the present moment. Highway markers told her she was still in Sonoma County, but that was all. No street signs or advertising billboards marked the way. She drove over a bridge at one point. Light flickered from a distant farmhouse window around one curve.

Confident, she picked up speed.

Ka-thunk!

Her car jerked up. Scraping and screeching noises emanated from underneath the carriage as it shifted violently toward the hillside and lodged in the adobe mud and tangle of tree roots there.

Pat was yanked to and fro, her seatbelt cutting into her neck. Surprisingly, the airbags didn't deploy.

Stunned and sweating, she tried to back up. Putting the car into reverse, she stepped on the gas. The motor grunted. Then, nothing. No movement, only a final shriek of metal on wood.

This can't be happening. This is a nightmare!

Pat tried again. And again. When it became clear the car wouldn't budge, she hit the steering wheel with her fists and screamed.

Help. She would call someone for help. *But who?* There were no family members or friends to render aid. She certainly couldn't call the sheriff or police. *A tow truck?* Maybe they could give her a lift to someplace where she could rent a car. Yes, that was the only solution that Pat could envision, short of hitchhiking.

She gathered her black purse and the tote bag carrying her financials and laptop and opened the driver's side door. The car was slanted to the right, so Pat had to climb up and out. When on more solid ground, she pulled her phone from the bottom of her purse. Squinting in the dark, she pushed the keypad to unlock it. Clicking the flashlight icon, Pat surveyed what had happened.

She waved the ray of light back and forth to take in the full picture. A sturdy oak branch, with multiple limbs and a few remaining amber-colored leaves, protruded from underneath her car. Smoke was beginning to wisp up from somewhere.

Call the tow truck. She felt that time was laughing at her now, running away. *Call!*

Pat scrolled the phone's search bar, typed in "roadside assistance," and hit enter. A few seconds went by. A few more. No numbers or websites popped up. Pat held the phone close to her face. *"No Service,"* it read. She tried again. But rustic roads and country hillsides were not her allies tonight. No amount of cajoling or threatening would connect her phone to the outside world.

Fine. I'll walk to get help. There was that house I passed further back. They've got to have a landline or service.

She slammed the car door and locked it. The sound ricocheted off the trees, frightening a nocturnal possum family.

Pat hoisted her purse, wearing it crossbody style. She put the tote's strap over her shoulder and aimed the phone's flashlight at the road. It was the only glow. The clouds had masked the waning moon and Orion's starry belt.

She trudged along like this for about 10 minutes, stopping now and then to listen for a car or sounds of civilization. Wet leaves and forest detritus stuck to the soles of her shoes, making them slippery. The night's dampness was seeping into her coat. With no gloves or hat, her extremities began to chill.

Hurry, hurry, she chanted as she walked. *Hurry.*

A barn owl swooped low to investigate the intrusion to his hunt, his white face appearing suddenly, like a ghost against the blackness.

Pat yelled and stumbled. Still clutching her phone, she fell into a ditch, hitting a long-forgotten, cracked concrete pipe.

She knew. As a nurse, she knew within seconds that her leg was broken. Maybe even a compound fracture. She groaned as she tried to move it.

"Help!" Pat cried into the night. "Somebody help me."

The owl flew off. The human was not his prey.

SIXTY

The Hunt

THE MANOR!

"Chief," Dee shouted to them. "Tim called in and said he's trying to go to the fire but there's a traffic jam downtown. He's radioed ahead for two trucks and an ambulance. He asked for the county to respond, too. He said he'll meet you there."

Tim Miller, the Fire Chief, was not the only one attempting to leave. When over half a town owns scanners and pagers, are volunteer emergency technicians, or firefighters (or are related to them), word of a disaster spreads quickly.

The Chamber of Commerce President, Tania, had just gotten the information from Tim. Seeing the early panic from the crowd, she stepped onto the event stage, quickly shut off the holiday music, and took the microphone. Murmurs had become loud chatter. People were headed to their cars.

Tapping the mic first, she called out. "Everyone. Your attention, please. Quiet!"

Heads turned in her direction.

"We have been notified of a localized fire at The Manor.

Emergency vehicles are on their way, and we have requested additional assistance from the county. We have confirmation that the residents are safely sheltering in place, and are not in any danger. No other areas are affected. Our fire department will have this under control ASAP. In the meantime, please do not block any emergency personnel or vehicles leaving this area. Let them do their jobs. Do not drive over there, as we need to keep all the roads clear. This will be resolved quickly." She paused for a breath and then added, "Santa is staying right here, kids. So please come on up! Thank you." *Jingle Bells* commenced playing.

Lucia was sitting on a bench with Charlotte, Lou, Maisie — and Tom. She had received a text from Robin about one minute before Tania made her announcement. It read:

Going to The Manor now. A fire! Tracy says Pat's responsible for Sandy & Bob's deaths. God, it's a mess. Pls. take Mom home. Will text/call you.

Lucia had lied to them when she first arrived.

"Robin's delayed at the bakery," she said. If Charlotte was suspicious of anything, she didn't express it. But these women were smart. She couldn't hold them off for too long.

She had called Tom on her initial brisk walk over to the center of town. When she got his voicemail, she left a message:

Hey, change of plans. Look for me near the stage. I'll be with Robin's mom. Can explain later.

So, when Tom Kikugawa walked over and found them, he

got a hug and a shrug from Lucia. He was now sandwiched next to Lou on the too-short bench.

Charlotte turned to Lucia at Tania's message. "My friends are over there, Lucia! What could have happened? Oh, I hope they'll be all right." Then, as an afterthought, "Where's Robin?"

Lucia leaned forward, speaking to them all. "You know, I trust our fire crew. Tania said the residents were okay. It's under control, probably a little vegetation fire. It's so wet outside, that I'm sure it won't be a big problem. I can take you ladies home now if you want to leave."

The women looked at each other. Nobody budged.

"Or," Lucia added, "I can bring you all over to my place. We can wait there together instead."

They stood as a unit. "Your place," Lou declared for them.

Lucia looked at Tom. "I'm going, too," he said.

———————————

"Deputize?" Angelo sputtered, amidst the cacophony of cell phones and alarms at the station.

"Yes! Come on, Ang," Yvonne said.

"No."

"Then, let me talk to Tracy, again."

"Go, I have other problems right now." Angelo hurried out to the lobby. "Dee, call the sheriff's department. Tell them to send a detective here for the doctor. Maybe an ambulance. Explain what we've got." He was halfway out of the front doors now. "And tell Garcia to keep Dr. Tracy here until they do come. You hear?" He shouted behind him.

Robin and Yvonne looked at each other. "I'm following Angelo," Robin said.

"I'm going after Pat." Yvonne was already headed back to the interview room.

"Good luck," they said at the same time.

Yvonne entered the room. Officer Garcia sat at stiff attention. Denton was slumping a bit, but his grey eyes hit on Yvonne as she entered.

"Not satisfied, yet?" he asked.

"Not quite. What do you mean she might be on her way to Mexico right now?"

"Well," Denton shifted in his chair. "She mentioned once or twice that would be her ideal retirement spot. Mexico. Mexico City. I may have hastened the process."

"Go on."

"I texted her tonight when I arrived here, showing her that I won. I won!" He preened. "I sent a photo of the dogbane plant, and intimated that I was telling all of her dirty little secrets to the police." He cleared his throat. "So I would guess that I might have scared her into running 'to the border,' so to speak." Denton laughed.

"You're a bastard," Yvonne muttered.

"I am a *physician*!" Denton replied. "Show respect."

"Give me the make and model of Pat's car. Now."

Denton complied, sullenly.

Yvonne left the room. She passed Dee, who had calls coming and going. Yvonne had forgotten again about Scott waiting in the lobby.

"Oh," she said. "Sorry. I need to find Pat."

"Okay. Pat. And where are we going next?"

"We?"

"I'll drive."

"Fine, take me to my car. I'm going over to Pat's apartment. Although I doubt she's there. I also have to find the next flights from SFO to Mexico City." Yvonne was already online searching airlines as they went through the doors into the night.

On the drive to her SUV, she left a quick voicemail for her daughter (*"I'm OK, emergency, catch you up at home later"*). Then Yvonne filled Scott in on Denton Tracy and Pat, listing their sordid crimes, and telling him what she felt he should know, for now.

"Damn."

"Yeah."

Yvonne kept scanning her phone while he drove. No flights were scheduled for tonight. There were a few leaving tomorrow.

"Thanks," she said, as she began to step out of his truck.

"I'm going with you," Scott told her.

"No."

"Yes."

"I don't have time for this. For civilians."

"The hell you don't," he responded, taking a handgun from a locked case.

"Oh, Lord, okay. Just don't do anything stupid."

They got into her car and drove straight to Pat's apartment.

"Are you sure this is where she lives? Do you even know what she looks like?" Scott asked Yvonne.

"Yeah. Yesterday I had her driver's license and photo texted to me by an old sheriff buddy. She's pretty unassuming in appearance. For a murderer."

Scott looked at her.

"Oh, come on, just because I'm retired doesn't mean I don't still have friends on the force."

They parked and walked upstairs in the dark to the third floor. Yvonne had her gun with her, close by. She knocked on the door once, twice. She tried the handle. It was locked. No lights were on inside Pat's place that they could see. As Yvonne expected, nobody answered.

"Now what?" Scott asked.

"I don't know. I guess we head toward SFO and look for her there. By now Dee's contacted the sheriff's department. Maybe they've put out an APB or BOLO. Or Angelo had a sergeant do it."

They walked toward the staircase. A woman carrying a laundry basket passed them and then paused.

"Are you looking for Ms. Breward?" she asked.

"Why, yes," Yvonne smiled. "There's an emergency where she works. It's urgent that we find her. Do you know where she is?"

"Gee, no. I'm sorry. An emergency? I think I saw her drive off less than an hour ago. I hope everything is okay."

"Thank you. I'm sure it will be."

"Airport," Yvonne said to Scott. He nodded.

By now, the congestion from the jackknifed truck was a misery. Scott was the navigator and plugged the quickest routes to SFO into the GPS. It directed them off the main highway, onto secondary roads.

"If Pat was headed this way, she must have gotten caught up in the traffic," Yvonne said. "Forget GPS, I know a detour, a country road that will get us connected to the highway faster, past this chaos."

"I'm along for the ride," Scott answered. "So what do you intend to do if we find her?"

"Detain her. Have her arrested for murder."

"Huh. Okay."

Yvonne's phone pinged with a message. *"Robin,"* it blinked.

"Look, I can't read this right now. Can you …?"

Scott picked up the phone from the cup holder, and per Yvonne's instructions, hit the keys to unlock it.

"It's from Robin. Says she's there at The Manor. Residents are cold and frightened but safe. And someone named Lois swears she saw Pat start the fire."

"What?!"

"That's what she says."

"Okay. Go on."

Scott read the rest of the message. "Well. Pat seems to have started at least *two* fires. At the hothouse, and evidently at Frank's office. The hothouse is melted. Fence damaged. Frank's office is soaked and ruined. Laundry building might be all right and the main building seems untouched. The fires are under control and the fire department's staying on site tonight. Nobody knows where Pat is. Lucia has Charlotte, Maisie, and Lou at her place. They're all fine." He scrolled down further. "She says she's going to get her mom soon. To keep in touch."

"Thank God nobody was hurt."

"Yeah. It could have been so much worse. Arson, too? What was Pat doing, setting fires?" Scott remarked.

"Who knows? A diversion or revenge? Just plain crazy?"

They drove in silence for a bit. Then, Yvonne took a turnoff, and before long they were on a stretch of mostly deserted county road.

"Ever been out this way?" she asked Scott after they had traveled on for a while.

"Can't say that I have." He turned his phone toward the passenger window this way and that, but no Wi-Fi or connection showed up.

"A country boy like you? Hmmph. What have you been doing?" Yvonne took the next sharp turn expertly, with the confidence of a horse returning to its barn.

"Well, working."

"Right."

They passed a single light from a farmhouse, and Yvonne braked when a deer decided to cross their path.

"Their roads, too," she said, going more slowly around the next curve. "You don't get carsick, do you?"

"Nope." He maneuvered the phone back and forth again. Still nothing.

It appeared suddenly. An intrusion on the pastoral landscape. Their headlights caught a lone car, tilted at an awkward angle, nose first into the hillside. Yvonne swerved around it. She stopped, then put her SUV into reverse and parked as close off the road as she could. She clicked on her car's hazard lights.

"What do you think? I mean that might be Pat's car," Scott said as he started to get out.

"Offhand, it matches the description that the doctor gave me." Yvonne pulled a heavy, utility flashlight from her glove compartment. She took another few seconds to check that her revolver was on her side.

"Be careful," she told Scott.

"I am," he responded.

Their footsteps crackled on the layer of twigs and leaves, echoing slightly in the night. Yvonne waved her flashlight into the car's interior. Her gun was in her right hand. Scott, she noticed, had carried his handgun out with him, too, and had it ready. There was nothing to be seen inside the vehicle. They looked under and around it. They saw the damage to the car, but no Pat.

"It has to be her car," Yvonne remarked. "And she got into some trouble here. Wrecked it pretty badly. If she is on the lam, as we suspect, then she must have tried to get help after this. She might be hurt, too."

"Well, good luck trying for cell service. We haven't had any for miles."

"Then, she couldn't have had any either. No way to call someone, or for a tow."

"Do you think she would have walked out of here? It would be a hike."

"Maybe. Let's drive back toward that house we saw. Knock on their door. If nobody has seen her, we can turn around and follow this road south."

Yvonne flashed her light up and down the road but saw no figures, human or otherwise. Even the deer was long gone.

"Let's go," she said.

SIXTY-ONE

Dreaming of Argentina

IF SHE DIDN'T MOVE AND barely breathed, the pain stayed right at the edge of hell.

At first, Pat had tried to pull herself out of the ditch. It was a mistake. She couldn't get any purchase in the slick dirt, and the movement jarred her broken bones, making rational thoughts impossible.

So she lay there, the dampness from the clay earth creeping into her coat. Her chilled hands still held her cell phone. Not that she could make a call. No, any calls seemed hopeless here. But her flashlight still worked and could be a beacon. Surely someone would drive by soon — a trucker, a lost tourist, or a local on their way home from work.

Yes, surely, she told herself, someone would see her wrecked car and investigate.

Of course! Somebody will see it, and find me.

Pat waved her flashlight up and to the right, toward the road.

"Help!" she called again. It was a plea, not a prayer. Pat hadn't prayed since her grandparents had dragged her as a child to the tent revivals in Nebraska. Even then, she hadn't seen the necessity. Rather, she had taken her religious dictum from her grandmother's sampler: *God helps those who help themselves.*

There was rustling nearby.

Were there wolves out here? Coyotes? Mountain lions? Are you supposed to keep quiet or make noise?

Pat couldn't remember.

She felt nauseated, and the redwood branches overhead spun if she tried to stare beyond them to the winter sky.

Shock. Am I going into shock? She had no idea if the dampness she felt on her left side was blood or from the wet ground surrounding her.

Concentrate. Don't go into shock here or you'll die. Think about Argentina and its long white beaches. And Cuba. Yes. Almost there.

Picture it, she told herself. *All I need to do is get to urgent care somewhere. Maybe to an emergency room. They can cast my leg. I'll miss my flight tomorrow, but I can re-schedule. I can still get on a plane in a couple of days. I'll use my other ID. Recover for a little bit in a nice San Francisco hotel. The Mark Hopkins or Fairmont. Yes. All of the airlines have wheelchairs now. I can still fly. This will work out. It has to.*

This will work out. Pat closed her eyes.

"I might know the people here," Yvonne told Scott as they drove into the farmhouse's circular, gravel driveway, and parked next to a late-model Jeep. A dog barked from inside the house.

"What — do you know everybody in this county?"

Yvonne gave him the side-eye.

"Rude. The owner was a judge in Superior Court, and he and my dad were friends."

The barking grew louder as they stepped onto the wide porch. Yvonne knocked and took a step back. The front light went on, illuminating wicker chairs and decorative planters.

A man in his forties opened the front door but left the screen in place. He was holding the collar of a white boxer.

"Can I help you?"

"I'm so sorry to bother you," Yvonne spoke. "Does the Ellis family still live here? My name is Yvonne Rousseau and my dad, Nick, knew Judge Ellis from the courts." She pointed. "This is my friend, Scott, and we're trying to locate someone who we think is lost around this area, and might be hurt."

The man opened the door wider and told the dog to sit. It obeyed.

"Nicholas Rousseau? Sure, I remember him. My dad and he played pinochle together. You're his daughter? The cop?"

"Yes. And you must be … ? "

"Dan. Stay, Betsy," he told the dog, before walking onto the porch to join them. "My folks retired to Washington last summer. I'm living here now. Someone is missing you said?"

"Yes, and we saw their car, jammed against the hillside along the road. Did you see or hear anything?"

"Wow, no, I didn't. I had my earbuds in and was on the computer. Betsy barked a while ago, but I didn't think anything of it. She didn't carry on like someone was nearby."

"Thanks, Dan. I just took a chance." She pulled a card from her pocket. "Here's my number. If you do see anything, please call. We're looking for a woman in her sixties. She could be injured."

"Sure. Will do. Tell your dad I said hi. He might remember me. I hung around sometimes while they played cards."

Yvonne and Scott walked down the driveway and stood next to her SUV.

"Well, it was worth a try," Scott told her.

"Yes, but no luck. I don't think Pat could have gotten far unless she hitchhiked out of here. Let's drive along the road again. Slowly. Maybe we'll spot something."

The canopy of trees and overcast night gave the feeling of being in a misty, primordial cave. They were about halfway between the house and Pat's car, when Scott said, "Wait. Did you see that?"

"What? See what?"

"I thought there was a light. A glint of light anyway. On my side of the road."

"Are you sure it wasn't a reflection of our headlights off a stray hubcap or something?"

"Maybe. It seemed fainter."

"Okay then. Let's take a walk."

Yvonne parked the SUV and once more patted her side, feeling for her gun. She removed two orange, reflective signs from the trunk and put one each in front and back of her car.

"No use getting hit by someone rounding the bend," she told Scott. "Now, where did you see it?"

"Up about 200 feet."

They began walking single file.

One hundred feet, one hundred fifty feet. Nothing. Yvonne swung her flashlight in a circular motion.

Then. "There! Did you catch it?"

"I did." It was a faint beam, flickering in the overhead brush. And more, Yvonne heard something. A groan. An animal in pain? But an animal wouldn't have a light.

Yvonne took the lead. She saw they were now next to a low ditch and culvert, probably abandoned years ago, and only recently revealed after rains had washed away layers of soil.

"Help! Is someone there? Help me!"

They hurried to the sound, leaning carefully over the side of the trench. Yvonne turned her light downwards and saw the pale, scratched face of a woman: disheveled, wet, one shoe off. But she knew who it was. They had found Pat.

Yvonne felt a trill of … excitement? Satisfaction.

"I need help *now*," Pat exclaimed. "You have to get me out of here. I think I've broken my leg."

Yvonne quickly assessed the situation. From her law enforcement experience, it looked bad. Pat was scraped and filthy, shaking. Her left leg was oddly twisted. There was no way they could safely extricate her themselves.

"We have to call for some help," she told Pat. "We'll get you out of there as soon as possible."

"No, now! Who are you? Are you EMTs? Why can't you get me out now?"

Who are we? Of course. Pat knew Robin and had even seen Lucia. But she has no idea who we are! Well, well.

"We don't want to risk further injury. I'm sorry," she told Pat.

"There's a silver emergency blanket in my car. In the back. Get it," she instructed Scott. "And there's a pager in my console. Bring that, too. It might work out here. Otherwise, you'll have to go to Dan's place and call for an ambulance."

"On it." He was already running to the SUV.

"What's your name?" Yvonne asked her. "Is that your car on the road? Did you have an accident?"

The woman whimpered. "Pa … I mean Anna. My name is Anna. Yes. My car. I hit something. A branch, maybe. Then I was going for help and I fell. *Ohhh.* Lift me up. Lift me up!" Pat raised her arms toward Yvonne.

"I can't. It's not safe. I promise we're calling for an ambulance." She hesitated. "Pat."

The woman's eyes, which had been shut tightly, opened. "What did you say?"

"I said help is on the way. Pat."

"No. No! I'm … Anna."

Scott returned. He handed the pager to Yvonne. Then, he unfolded and carefully dropped the blanket over Pat. Its shimmery foil exterior reflected the flashlight.

"Holding out on me about the pager?"

"I didn't know we'd need it." Yvonne tried to connect. Nothing. "Go on back to Dan's."

"Yeah." Scott was steps away.

"Wait, wait. When you call 9-1-1, tell them that her leg looks to be at an unnatural angle. Possible shock. Facial contusions. And besides the ambulance, they'll need to contact the sheriff's department and send a detective. And a tow truck. Tell them — tell them that we have the suspect responsible for the Miller's Creek murder. Murders. And arson. Angelo needs to know, too."

Scott took off for the farmhouse. Running again.

Yvonne shivered from the cold and adrenaline. She holstered her revolver and zipped up her jacket. She found a pair of gloves in the pocket. There would be a wait now. She decided to shift to more stable ground on the roadside. She heard some creatures rustling around in the quiet night, seeking their dinners. A fox shrieked in the distance.

Before she moved, Yvonne leaned over to check again on the injured woman. Pat's color and breathing were poor.

The whole situation was so sad.

"Is this how it ends for you, Pat? Ruining lives, poisoning *my* town. Was it worth it? Was it all worth it?"

Pat moaned.

SIXTY-TWO

Reinforcements

"SAFE. SAFE." ROBIN KEPT REPEATING aloud the words as she finally drove down the lane to Lucia's house. *The residents are all safe.*

When she first arrived at The Manor, following behind Angelo, all she saw was chaos. The elderly residents were gathered by the entrance. Covered in multi-colored blankets, most were sitting, with staff surrounding them, acting as a shield against the cold, and ready to take action if they were told to relocate. EMTs were already weaving through the chairs, asking questions, and checking vitals. Someone had parked the facility's vans up the road, to transport people if necessary.

Robin kept to the edge of it all, at first. She saw familiar faces, friends of her mother's. Her reporter's mind was taking it all in, making mental notes.

Thank God Mom is with Lucia. And Bev and Jack are far away from this, too.

Lucia had texted Robin that everyone in her charge was fine and at her place.

Don't worry. It read. **Everybody is safe.**

Robin wondered briefly who *everybody* meant. *But Mom is okay, anyway.*

Evaluating, she carefully ventured forward to where staff and residents were grouped. Robin asked questions until she found out who was in charge. They pointed to Sara.

She tapped Sara on the shoulder. The young woman turned around. Her brow was furrowed, and her eyes darted from the residents to the heart of the damage.

"Hello. Sara? I'm Robin Hill O'Connor. How can I help? My mother used to live here. She knew most of these people. Are you all right? What do you need?"

It was loud. She had to shout. Lights were flashing and firefighters were calling to each other. Radio transmissions squawked intermittently. Smoke and an acrid smell loomed in the night air. Foam was being sprayed on the buildings that had housed Frank's office and the laundry.

"Hi. Thanks," Sara responded, shouting also. "We're waiting to see if we need to move out, and if so, to where. I can't seem to reach the director. You must know her if your mother was here. Maybe you can help locate her — Patricia Breward? Lois, one of our residents, told me she saw Pat here earlier. Around the time the fires broke out."

"Pat? She saw Pat?"

"Yes. But she may be confused."

"I'm going to get the police chief. You ... and Lois need to talk to him."

Robin got as close as she safely dared to the edge of the commotion. She looked around but couldn't see Angelo. Too many moving parts and people. Turning for a better vantage point, she spotted someone she recognized as a regular from the bakery, a reporter from the newspaper.

"Kate!" she called, moving closer to the woman taking photos. "Hey, Kate!"

The reporter swung her camera down. "Robin. What are you doing here?"

"Long, long story."

"Yeah? Anything to do with this?" Kate gestured toward the near-smoldering mess.

"I'm afraid so."

"Hmmm, well, call me later and we can talk."

"Sure. Right now, I need to find Angelo. It's urgent. Have you seen him? I know he's here somewhere."

"I just saw him with Tim. I took a photo of them. Hold on. He's over there." She pointed to the periphery of the crowd.

"Thanks." Robin made her way to where Kate indicated.

"Angelo," she called twice, getting his attention. "Come quickly. It's about Pat."

Angelo was surprisingly gentle in questioning Lois. Robin stayed by her side, in case. Lois repeated what she had seen, in detail, and how her eyesight was fine, thank you. She relayed how Pat had been so kind to her, how she was even going to use Lois's new trust for the needy residents here. So it was all bewildering, you understand, to see Pat set fire to the hothouse.

"Her orchids were in there. Pat loved those orchids. Do you think she had a little breakdown or collapse?"

Robin met Angelo's eyes. "Probably something like that,

Lois," she told her.

"Lois is a hero. She alerted us to the fire," Sara interjected.

"Yes, you are," Robin concurred. "Thank you."

"For now, though," Angelo said, "don't tell anyone else about seeing Pat. I'll convey what you said to the fire chief. And don't talk to the press." He looked at Sara.

"Hush, hush," said Lois, making a zipping motion across her lips.

"Right," Angelo replied.

He took Robin's elbow and walked her across the parking lot. "Murder *and* arson?" He swore. "She could have killed these old people!"

"I know. Have you heard anything from Yvonne yet?"

"No. You know Yvonne. She's like a dog with a bone. Who knows where she went off to."

"She might have Scott with her, too."

"Whatever. Now, I've got to let Tim know we have an arsonist on the loose." He shook his head. "At least the fires are under control. Tim told me they'll be keeping a crew here to monitor things. The fire marshal is going to inspect the main facility soon. She doesn't expect any problems to be there, so the residents and staff can probably go back inside later tonight."

"Good. They'll be exhausted. What are they going to do in the meantime? It's cold out."

"We're working on it."

"I can make some calls."

Angelo waved his hand. "Fine. I gotta go."

"Wait, one more thing. Pat's accomplice. What about

Ricardo? Has anyone checked on him? Maybe he knows where Pat is. Or maybe he had a hand in this, too."

"No luck there. He's MIA, also. My guy, Ken, got some info about him yesterday from the staff. They liked him well enough, I guess. He was their buffer against the boss. And he handed out bonuses to them from time to time. Payback he got from Pat, maybe?" Angelo coughed. "Damn smoke. I sent Ken to Ricardo's apartment tonight. No sign of him. His neighbors weren't any help, either."

"Can you send an APB or county lookout?"

"Done. I contacted the sheriff's department and they posted a BOLO. For both of them." With that, Angelo left.

Robin stepped away to call Yvonne, but it didn't go through. She tried Lucia next.

"What's going on?" was Lucia's greeting.

"Luce, don't gasp or say anything yet to Mom. But Pat set the fire — fires, plural. I'll tell you all about it when I get to your place. I'll be leaving in a minute. Things seem in hand here. The residents are frightened, but hanging in there. Nobody is injured. Angelo says they can probably get back into the facility tonight. It's not damaged, only some of the outbuildings are burnt."

"Pat. Got it. Listen, my parents have already talked to Tim. So let the staff and residents know they aren't stranded. Reinforcements are coming."

"What?"

Lucia explained. She ticked off what had been happening behind the scenes. Calls had been made. Her father was opening the winery next door as a temporary rescue site. In addition, her mother was bringing urns of coffee, and hot water for tea. The taqueria was delivering trays of food. Her winery crew was already setting up outdoor heaters. Father Art was heading over also, to check on his "peeps" and be available to listen.

In addition, the bed and breakfast had offered to house any displaced people overnight, gratis. And the manager of The Grange said they could use that building, too.

"Oh, Jen and Thad said they could bring some pastries if you approved."

"Oh, sure. Tell them I said yes. Everyone else is okay with this?"

"Well, it's the fire chief and Angelo's call. But Daddy said Tim agreed they could go to the winery, and that the facility vans are available to take them. Frank can go there now and drive one. He has before. Staff can bring over some people, too. Tim said nobody seems to need hospitalization, but an EMT will go along, in case. The residents will be warm and fed until they can return to their apartments."

"Amazing."

"Think of it like a late-night field trip. It gives staff a chance to regroup, too, until the county or someone figures out who's in charge. Any word from Yvonne?"

"No. I tried reaching her. It went to voicemail. I'll call again. Or text."

"Another thing, be prepared. Besides your mom, I have Lou and Maisie here. And Tom."

"Well. Okay. Thanks for the heads-up. See you soon."

Robin hung up with Lucia and tried to reach Yvonne. She

got voicemail once more and texted Yvonne instead with the latest news. Then, Robin found Sara and told her what to expect in the way of incoming help and temporary refuge.

"Check with the fire chief or Angelo for details," she told the grateful young woman.

Robin left and walked down the road to her car.

Off-duty fire and police from around the area had arrived by now and set up barricades and cones. Someone was directing traffic.

Miller's Creek took care of its own.

SIXTY-THREE

Luck

THE QUIET COUNTRY ROAD DENIZENS had never seen such commotion. An approaching ambulance, squad cars, and one noisy tow truck disrupted the usually serene locale. All four-legged and winged creatures had scattered, eyeing the intrusion disapprovingly, and from afar.

Dan, the farmhouse owner, had turned his property's floodlights on, and stood at the road with an LED camping lantern, ready to direct the caravan to the right spot.

Scott rejoined Yvonne after placing the emergency calls. As they heard the distant sirens, he poked his head over the ditch to check on the injured Pat. She was mostly silent now.

"I hope she makes it," he told Yvonne, as they stood watch together. "I'd like to see her pay for what she's done."

"Me, too."

"It was a smart move on your part, to take this side road," he added. "She could have gotten away. Or be dead right now."

"Luck," Yvonne responded.

He shifted his footing. "What happens next?"

"When the detectives come, they'll place Pat in custody, and read her Miranda rights. Someone from the sheriff's department will probably ride in the ambulance with her, too."

"To the hospital? Why?"

"They'll be interested in getting some kind of statement from her." Yvonne lowered her voice, "If she expires, a dying declaration would hold up in court."

"It would be admissible even if she's medicated or drugged?"

"Uh-huh. And they'll assign an officer to her hospital room at County General until she's well enough to go to jail."

"If she survives."

There was a pause in the conversation. The sirens were growing louder, echoing off the redwoods.

"Do you miss it?" he asked.

"What? Miss what?"

"Being a cop."

"Oh. I guess maybe I do. Sometimes. Like now, when we get the bad guys."

"Well, thanks for bringing me along. This turned into a surprising evening. I'd guess most tree lightings don't end like this."

"No kidding. Scott, you ... you've been a big help tonight. And before, too, getting the necropsy, and all. Thank you." *It had been an intense, wild time.* Not that Yvonne had felt any fear, but still.

"Sure."

"Really. It was good to have you here for all of this, and not be going solo." She added, "Sorry. You didn't sign up for it."

"No problem."

The ambulance was the first to roll up, with the sheriff's department next, followed by the tow truck. Angelo and his sergeant were last.

As she led them to Pat, Yvonne described the situation to the EMTs. The two detectives who exited the squad car were unfamiliar to her. She introduced herself and filled them in. Scott responded to their further questions.

"Did she say anything to you?" the older officer asked.

"No. Mostly mumbled," Yvonne told him. "She tried to claim her name was Anna. But this is Patricia Breward."

"Besides murder, I heard that she's an arson suspect, too."

"Yeah. That was her latest exploit. Tonight at an assisted living home."

"Jeez."

The tow truck eased past them toward Pat's damaged car. The air brakes, beeps, and various radio blips were interrupted by a scream from Pat as the EMTs lifted her out of the ditch.

The detective didn't flinch at the sound. "Well, thanks," he said, "we'll be in touch." And he walked toward the ambulance.

Adding Angelo to the mix was another layer of craziness for the night. He exited his car quickly, signaled to Yvonne and Scott, and then waylaid the second sheriff's detective. The ambulance was already pulling out.

"So do we leave soon?" Scott asked Yvonne, as the bizarre spectacle unfolded.

"In a minute. We'll need to talk to Angelo first." It was

getting colder, and the earlier mist had become a bleak drizzle. Yvonne raised her jacket hood.

Angelo finally made his way over to them. "Whew, what a night! Good job, Yvonne. You, too," he added, finally acknowledging Scott.

"Luck," Yvonne repeated.

"Okay, let's talk. I want to sit in the squad car, though." Overhead branches were beginning to drip on them.

"What about Tracy? Is he in custody?" Yvonne asked as they walked the muddy roadway to the car.

"Ah. After we left, he told Officer Garcia that he felt sick. Then he fainted or something when the sheriff's guy came in. So Denton Tracy's on his way to the hospital, too, last I heard."

"He and Pat will be in the same hospital, at the same time?" Scott asked.

"Good riddance, right?" Angelo said.

"What about Ricardo?" Yvonne asked him.

"Still not accounted for."

"Are the residents all okay?"

"Yeah, they're fine. No injuries. Everyone was transported to the Ricci winery. A sort of 'pop-up' shelter. I guess they'll be there for a few more hours until we get the all clear to enter the facility again. It doesn't seem to be damaged by the fires, although part of the grounds are a mess."

"Do *they* know about Pat? And Denton?"

"Not yet. Only rumors."

The trio entered the car; the heater was on and the motor was running. A sergeant sat in the driver's seat and said hello to Yvonne, but glanced at Scott.

"You know," Angelo said, "it's already late. Just give me the main details. Both of you can come in tomorrow for more formal reports. Okay with you? I've got to get back to the station soon. It will be an all-nighter for me. You know the drill." Angelo shook his head.

Their conversation with Angelo was brief. On the way back to Miller's Creek, Yvonne called her daughter, Lynne, as soon as they had cell service. She reassured her, "I'll be home later, kiddo, and fill you in. I'm fine. Kiss the grands for me."

She also called Robin. "We got her," she said to her worried friend. "Yes, yes. I'll meet you at Lucia's and explain it all."

———————

It was dark when they finally drove into the now-quiet town. Beams from streetlights reflected on the wet sidewalks. Yvonne dropped Scott off at his truck.

He stepped out of the dirt-spattered SUV. "I'm sure your friends are anxious to hear the news." He cleared his throat. "Hey, how about we go together to the police department tomorrow?" Scott checked his watch. "Or is it later today?"

"Oh, that's not … ," Yvonne began to decline. Then, she said instead, "Okay, sure. Pick me up at ten o'clock, I'll text you my address. Thanks."

———————

The road to Lucia's was deserted. When Yvonne pulled into the driveway, the house lights, though, were ablaze.

Robin opened the kitchen door and tugged Yvonne inside. "Thank God you're all right!"

The domestic sight was a world away from the country road and a murderer and arsonist. Empty mugs filled the sink. A plate half filled with snickerdoodle cookies was on the counter, next to a single, flickering pillar candle. The scent of warm spices filled the house. Beyond the kitchen, Yvonne could see Charlotte dozing on the sofa, by the fireplace. Annie was lying next to her, with one doggie eye open.

Lucia was on her phone, speaking low. She looked up and waved to Yvonne.

"Thanks, Daddy. Uh-huh. I told everyone. And I can come and relieve you and Mama, you know. Or Sal could. Okay, Okay. Phone me when you get home, then." She ended the call and turned to her latest guest. "I'm *so* glad to see you."

She pointed to a kitchen chair. "Now, take off your coat and sit here. That was my dad. He says they'll keep the winery open until the fire marshal gives the approval to let people back in. Lots of volunteers showed up, and Mama reported that folks are coping. They're playing cards, chatting, or resting. And they're all well-fed. How about you? Want some wine or coffee? A shot of brandy?"

"Water, thanks," Yvonne answered, sliding onto the chair. "I thought you had Maisie and Lou here, too."

"Tom took them home once we knew everyone was settled," Robin told her. "You just missed them. My mom wanted to wait it out here."

Now that it was over, really over, Yvonne felt the adrenaline leach from her body. She gulped her water. Her friends sat and waited while she gathered her bearings.

"We got Pat," she repeated. "We got her." Once more that night, Yvonne told the story.

EPILOGUE

One Week Later

THEY ALL AGREED IT WAS a magnificent tree. The Douglas fir filled the casement window in the living room, its branches gently unfolding from the warmth of the house. The lights and ornaments glittered and created a colorful mosaic on the floor.

Robin hadn't been in the mood to decorate for the holidays the last few years. This season was different. With her mother home again and the troubles in town resolved, she was feeling actually merry.

The townspeople had breathed a collective sigh of relief, as well, and the chatter at the bakery and shops seemed lighter.

Robin sat now with her mother and best friends, close enough to their tree to sense a whiff of the forest still lingering on its branches. The evening's beverages were a choice of sparkling wine or hot cider. Thad's latest creation, Gouda mini quiches, sat warmed on a tray, alongside a savory charcuterie platter. A plate of the bakery's iced shortbread cookies was also nearby. The dogs were at their respective homes, so Rupert had all the attention, as was befitting.

When Lucia first arrived, she handed a bag to Yvonne. It contained the dogbane beetle that Jack had found, still in its final repose in the glass jar. "For you," she said, "to give to the police."

"Gee, thanks."

After the toasts were made, and sips taken, Charlotte asked Yvonne directly, "So what can you tell us? I've only heard snippets in town, so I need an update."

"Well, you probably know most of it by now." Yvonne munched on a quiche. "I did learn a little more from Angelo, yesterday."

The group leaned forward expectantly.

"How Pat even made it through that night is amazing. The doctors told Angelo it was touch and go at first. She was in shock and *did* have a compound fracture. They performed surgery, and she's held together with metal rods and a plate. They posted a guard outside her hospital room for now, until she's well enough to be transferred to jail. She's been formally arrested."

"Evil woman," Robin muttered.

"The sheriff's department has all of the documents Pat was carrying when Scott and I found her. It included a wad of cash in her purse, a fake driver's license and matching passport, and confirmation of a one-way airline ticket to Mexico City. That was in addition to the bank statements from multiple offshore accounts."

Charlotte gasped.

"And," Yvonne continued, "Pat had evidence of Tracy's indiscretions and outright crimes. We think she was holding on to that information to continue to blackmail him."

"What about all the Medicare fraud he mentioned that night at the station?" Robin asked.

"The federal government doesn't take too kindly to that, either," Yvonne answered. "Our local cops have notified the FBI office in San Francisco. They'll be paying Pat a visit."

"Did she confess?" Charlotte asked. "Like on TV?"

Yvonne shook her head. "No, not officially. But she said enough when they were transporting her in the ambulance, and the district attorney can use that. Plus, they have her paper trail."

"And Tracy?" Lucia spoke up. The cat had settled on her lap.

"On hospice, at the same hospital," Yvonne answered. "He, um, won't be leaving from there."

Lucia petted the purring Rupert. "Is it true their paths crossed in the ER that night — Pat and Dr. Tracy?"

"That's what I heard from a cop who was on duty. I would *love* to have been a fly on the wall for that exchange."

Robin turned to her mother. "Mom, have you heard anything about the residents? Where they'll go now?"

"Oh, oh, I know," Lucia responded instead. The women looked at her.

"What? I can't have a network, too? I bonded with Bev and Jack, you know, during all this. Jack called me this morning. *And* I talked with Frank. They said everyone there got a notice that the old owners are temporarily coming out of retirement to run the place."

"Really? That's wonderful news," Charlotte smiled. "Alicia and Anson are such nice people. We missed them."

Lucia explained further. "It seems that they were holding a second mortgage on The Manor. When Pat's main investors, a couple of wealthy guys, I think, found out about her arrest and the whole mess, they threatened to foreclose. So the former owners," Lucia nodded to Charlotte, "joined forces with them to save it until a new buyer can be found. Alicia and Anson had retained their licenses and will work with the county to fix any violations. And they hired that LVN, Sara, full-time."

"Well, aren't you a font of information!" Robin laughed.

"Thank you. And I decided to host a monthly happy hour at the winery for the residents. I have a great Valentine's Day theme planned already. Frank volunteered to shuttle them over. You come, too, Charlotte."

"I don't suppose anyone has seen Ricardo?" Robin asked, in general.

"He's in the wind," Yvonne said. "And probably long gone. I hate loose ends."

"How's Angelo taking it? He's not one to let things go, either." Robin reached over and topped off their glasses.

"Well, in other news, he's decided to retire at the end of January. His ulcer and Rosalie helped him to make *that* decision. The city council has asked me to come on as the interim chief until they hire someone else."

"Way to bury the lede," Robin exclaimed. "Congratulations! Are you sure it's short term?"

"Yes, I am. But it will be good to get back in the game again. For a while."

"I may have a new part-time job, too. Don't worry," Robin winked at her mother. "Mom already knows that I'm not leaving the bakery. After the fire and ... everything, Kate interviewed a few of us, you know, for that article in the newspaper. Anyway, she and I got talking and she offered me a byline, writing a column on the comings and goings at city hall. I get to wear my reporter's hat again. Huh, maybe I can even cover Pat's trial."

"This calls for a toast, ladies." Lucia raised her glass. "It will be a good year ahead. By the way, I'm hosting a small New Year's Eve dinner at my place. You're all invited, of course. It will be casual, and an early night. I promise. I've already asked Jack and Bev, and they're coming. I'll call Lou and Maisie tomorrow. My parents will be there. And Tom." Lucia addressed Yvonne directly. "You should bring Scott."

"That sounds great, Luce, but I have to decline. I sort of have plans for that night already."

At the stares, Yvonne continued, "With Scott. He, uh, asked me to go to dinner at some seafood place he likes over on the coast." She looked around. "Oh, please. It's nothing big. Honestly."

"Good for you," Charlotte said. "Have some fun."

"I love *good* surprises, like these," Lucia said. "Well, here's to all of us."

"And to Miller's Creek," Charlotte added, as they clinked glasses.

www.ingramcontent.com/pod-product-compliance
Lightning Source LLC
Chambersburg PA
CBHW030516120726
47904CB00005B/1496